TO SLAY A GOD

TO SLAY A GOD

AN ORIGINAL NOVEL FROM THE BLACK BALLAD

BRIAN FITZPATRICK

DEDICATION

To my wife. You are my partner in crime, my ride or die. Our adventures together rival even the greatest sword & sorcery stories. And the fun's not over yet!

To my Friday night D&D crew from high school and college. Our many adventures together laid the groundwork for this new epic tale.

TABLE OF CONTENTS

TO SLAY A GOD

EPILOGUE 276
BOOK CLUB QUESTIONS 279
AUTHOR BIO 281

CHAPTER 1

When slaying a god, preparation is key. It takes strategy, courage, powerful allies, and a dash of insanity. Poke power and power pokes back, and woe to those mortals who attempt such a feat and fall short, for aggrieved gods are not known for their compassion.

All these thoughts raced through the mind of Severina Stormbringer, champion of Tormelund. The daughter of a human father and elvish mother had given her advantages both internal and external. Despite her forty-three years of life, she appeared only half that age. Her prowess on the battlefield, both with blade and magic, was legendary. Many of these talents could be attributed to her elven heritage. But her stubbornness? Her grit? Her unrelenting determination? That was all her human half.

Severina sat quietly in a field of dead grass. She closed her piercing dark eyes and breathed calmly, focusing on the task set before her: lead an army to kill a deity. Even the thought of it sent her mind reeling, and she had to battle herself just to keep from fleeing this place. This responsibility was too much. How could she possibly accomplish this quest? How could she recruit an army knowing most, if not all, would surely perish? But then, how could she refuse when the threat was so dire?

Her burden weighed heavy upon her as she sat in the barren field. Her cascading black hair was in a ponytail to keep it from tangling from the breeze that crossed the plain. A soft blue glow danced over her cheeks and forehead, a reflection of something before her, and a soft hum carried over the breeze.

Severina opened her eyes and stared long at the abomination some fifty feet ahead. A thick, unnatural line jutted upward from the earth into the sky, stretching beyond sight. Jagged and bent, the otherworldly seam appeared like a massive lightning bolt frozen in time. The Void, as it had become known, bore the thickness of a broadsword, and emitted a bright blue light that cast a soft hue over the land.

But what cast fear in the civilians was the nature of the crack. It stood as a singular beam from the ground to the sky. However, within the light, people saw an unnerving depth. The kingdom had become convinced this was a portal to some fell dimension.

Given the misfortunes Tormelund had suffered over the past decade, everyone believed this latest development was part of it all. The once lush and beautiful realm had fallen into despair as the land had slowly begun to decay and dry. Over the past ten years, crops mysteriously rotted, the soil became tainted and unable to grow anything, and livestock fell to illness and putrid death. No one had any explanation for the change. Superstition took hold and belief in curses grew.

Now, Severina gazed over this desolate land that had once teemed with life and understood her role. King Ulren Grizzletooth knew exactly what he was doing when he chose her to gather a massive force to combat whatever was destined to push through the portal. The dwarven king exploited her fame, and she was fine with that. Tormelund would soon face an unnamed threat from something coming through the Void, and they all had to be ready.

She stood and began walking back to her waiting horse. The capital city, Durren, was a two-hour ride away, and currently, the king's castle was her home, an invitation extended from Ulren himself.

As she reached her black steed, the ground rumbled and shook. The blue light of the Void burst brighter momentarily, lighting the area in pale blue. Severina spun around to see the portal had tripled its thickness, the crack having expanded in the briefest of moments.

"Shit," she whispered, urgently mounting her horse and racing toward Durren.

Karas stood outside a wooden door set deep within the castle, the entirety laden with intricate runic patterns. Dressed in full regalia—gleaming plate armor, flowing green cloak, and a deadly bastard sword sheathed at his hip—he was ready to meet his king.

Karas, the right hand to King Ulren Grizzletooth, was a gruff but fair dwarf, and he never doubted the king's rulings. His love for Tormelund never wavered. Still, when the king put Severina in charge of gathering the forces from the citizenry to bolster the royal army, Karas couldn't help feeling confused and disappointed.

He had led the military in countless battles and skirmishes over the years. Sure, he had retired from battle, but he felt he remained as sharp and courageous as ever.

Standing outside the king's quarters, he paced the hall, his large build taking up much of the space. With his hair remaining thick and only graying despite the years, he took to stroking his beard as he pondered his king's choice. His green eyes still held plenty of fire within them, and he felt nearly as virile as he did in his youth. He still had value as more than a king's right hand.

Not to say he did not value his position. The Right Hand acted as both elite bodyguard and most trusted advisor. He was needed and played a vital role. It just stung him when a new military crisis emerged that he was not a part of.

He did not begrudge Severina, quite the contrary. Karas held her in respect and even admiration. Her exploits over the years were the stuff of legend. With her magic blade and courage that bordered on insanity, everything showed in her antics.

Circumstance had put them together, and a deep friendship had developed over the years. He truly missed her when she was away... And yet, he felt he would have been the appropriate choice to walk among the people and ask for volunteers to join the royal forces.

"Do stop pacing and come in," came a deep voice from beyond the door.

Karas took a deep breath and entered King Ulren's quarters. The suite, though large, was devoid of the luxuries one would expect of a royal. King Ulren could not shake his dwarven upbringing, despite decades of residing on the throne in this mostly human-inhabited land.

The walls held decorations and armor of his beloved Grizzletooth clan—gray and red, with images of bears wherever possible.

The king sat on the edge of his bed, which, like all the furniture in the room, had been adjusted to suit the dwarf's height. At just under five feet, the king looked to be a child next to his Right Hand. His red beard rested on his stout belly, and his crown leaned to the left unevenly. He pulled on his second boot and stood to face Karas.

"What news?" he asked, never one for small talk.

"Five more families have had to burn crops to slow the disease. Some have been able to salvage half or more of their harvest. Livestock deaths have increased. We're seeing a fifteen percent loss this year so far. And the report this morning from Seafare revealed a thirty percent drop in fish yield from the nets over last month's haul. The ocean's surface is covered in dead fish."

"How long before our people begin starving?"

"Eight months at best."

Ulren's demeanor demonstrated his obsessive worry. His shoulders slouched and his brow was ever grim.

"And what of the portal? Any update from Rennard and his team?"

"Not much new, I'm afraid. The wizards and clerics are harnessing what magic they can to discern the nature of the crack and ways to stop its growth. It's clear to everyone that the plagues sweeping the nation and the arrival of the portal are connected."

"But who, or what, is causing all this?"

"Rennard's team is still convinced a deity is involved."

"Which one? And how can we get it to stop? Our people grow more desperate every day. Rennard the Wise needs to start living up to his name, and soon."

Karas hesitated, but then asked, "What of Severina? Her recruitment?"

"I have not seen her in days. Nor have I received any new reports."

"Perhaps if I—"

"No," barked Ulren, cutting off the former general. "I know you've had misgivings about Severina heading up this project."

"I have, sire."

"And you wish I had appointed this task to you."

"I do."

"I must ask that you put your trust in me on this. Like you always do."

"I do, Ulren."

"I know you feel you are more suited to this work. And under other circumstances, I would agree. But this is a different threat that requires a different recruiter."

"Knowing Sevi, she'll just intimidate them into joining the army."

"That's what I'm counting on," Ulren replied with a grin. "This task requires a bit of showboating."

Karas couldn't help but agree despite his desire to connect with the people. Severina had the celebrity and adoration of the populace. He was respected, but she was loved.

Severina rode hard into the late afternoon. With the change in the crack occurring, urgency spurred her onward to get word to Ulren and the court. She felt they had even less time to prepare than they had anticipated, and so prayed to her goddess, Menavaria for a guiding hand.

She felt a deep connection to this deity, being that she was the goddess of instinct and war. She had even felt her presence in certain times of desperation—usually right before turning the tables on a foe and burying her sword in their flesh.

Severina envisioned Menavaria as a physically imposing woman wielding a sword in one hand and an owl on the forearm of the other. Her wild mane of long hair reached down past her knees and her armor gleamed of silver. She could not be certain this was the true form of her goddess, but this is how she came to her in times of need.

Menavaria guided her soul, but it was another otherworldly thing that helped guide her mind: her sentient black onyx sword, Wrath. Imbued with self-awareness, this cunning blade helped Severina discern complex decisions and complicated situations. Though the blade didn't speak aloud or whisper telepathically, she still felt the connection and communication through various physical signs. An unnatural tingling in her torso, or pinpricks down her arm, were a few of the physiological changes employed by Wrath whenever it had something to say.

And at this moment, as she rode toward her king, Wrath made her aware of its worry at the turn of events.

I know, old friend. I'm afraid as well.

They had been on countless adventures together and had slain thousands of foes, yet this was the first time her sentient blade had ever expressed any trepidation. This realization gnawed at her thoughts. Could she and her companions lead an army against this unknown threat? Could anyone?

She quelled the fears and doubts as the castle came into view, spurring her horse to hasten.

The castle rested at the edge of the capital city, Durren. Its high walls, arches, and buttresses made an awe-inspiring jewel in the crown of the city. With a mountain range behind it, and expansive plains surrounding it, Durren stood in a strategic position against any enemy who dared launch an attack. But given that Tormelund had built its reputation on diplomacy and trade, surrounding nations embraced them with brotherhood and commerce.

Tormelund had not been under threat of war in nearly a century, but maintained a powerful and innovative military. Kings of the land had ruled with compassion and contained might throughout history, and Ulren Grizzletooth carried on that tradition.

Severina never doubted her king's intentions. Never questioned his decisions. Even this new charge of her recruiting a citizen army, thought highly unorthodox, had a certain logic to it.

She wondered how her news of the portal would change things.

Severina navigated the bustling streets of Durren, bypassing the market district—which she knew would be a nightmare to get through on horseback—and dismounted inside the castle walls. She raced on foot into the courtyard, past the guards, and into the king's court.

The massive stone chamber held the royal throne, rows and rows of pews, and garish displays of Tormelund heraldry. King Ulren Grizzletooth sat sternly upon the throne at the opposite end of the chamber from where Severina entered.

As she approached, she spotted Karas, the Right Hand, Heliosa, the king's cleric and advisor, Rennard the Wise, the king's battle mage, and a multitude of sycophants and naysayers.

Ulren spotted Severina rushing in his direction and perked up. "Make way! Make way!" he ordered, rising to his feet.

The crowd glanced around and, spotting the charging warrior, parted to give her access.

Before she could arrive at the dais, Ulren launched into a speech, sternness lacing his words. "Where have you been, Severina? We've needed updates, and we have gotten nothing from you for days on end. What do you have to say for yourself?"

Severina reached the base of the dais and made a brief, sarcastic curtsy.

"Enough, girl. Speak!"

"The portal has grown."

Gasps from the crowd flowed through the room.

"Are you sure?" asked Rennard. The elder statesman carried himself with an air of respectability, and he'd earned it through years of magic innovation, wisdom for the crown, and unshakeable integrity in everything he did. His words were his bond.

"I saw it expand myself."

Murmurs, edged with worry, began to swell, never rising above a hushed volume.

Rennard stroked his long gray beard in thoughtful contemplation.

Ulren looked at his advisor and asked, "Can the damn thing be sealed? What has your team determined?"

"We need more time, sire."

"Time is something we don't have," interjected Karas.

Heliosa stepped forward. A waif-thin woman dressed in flowing robes and talismans of her deity, her bald head was covered in a form-fitting leather cap, painted over in the colors of her god—green and gold. Her frail frame disguised an inner strength that came through in her words and actions.

"Sire, a word."

Everyone turned to her, and Ulren's gaze carried the weight of someone hopeful for good news.

"We are close to knowing who it is that is attempting invasion. Quellon is investigating and assures me an answer is near."

Quellon, the god of agriculture and luck, had delivered for his loyal servant countless times over decades of Heliosa's service. In return, she had served him in worship, communion, and proper gifts of fruit and coin.

"I hope you are right," stated Ulren flatly.

"It may help if you were to have faith," she replied, reading his skepticism.

"Faith is a tough thing to come by these days," he grunted.

CHAPTER 2

Severina spent the next three days visiting the citizens of Tormelund. From the rural farming community to thriving towns, she was welcomed as a friend and hero. Spreading the word for recruitment into the royal army took almost no effort, for her name and mission preceded her everywhere she went. Reactions to the call were mixed, however. Many men of age took pride in defending Tormelund against her enemies, while others, mostly those with families, hesitated. What should become of loved ones and businesses if they were to perish?

Severina had answers ready for all queries and possessed a gift for swaying people to her way of thinking—be it through words or fists. And in this mission, she would not fail. Everyone in Tormelund had felt the sting of this plague of pestilence. Everyone had a stake in this fight.

She rode into the port city of Seafare, just an hour's ride from Durren, and gathered folks to the town square. She'd visited a few times already, planting the seeds of fear, courage, and loyalty. Today's visit held something new.

After she had a sufficient crowd, she began her plea.

"Friends, gather up," she called out. Along the docks behind her, and the merchant streets before her, the attention of those present locked onto her, dedicated to hearing her next words.

"The horror is upon us, and the time is now. Muster your courage, kiss your loved ones goodbye, and join me in Durren! The greatest military in the world is waiting for you. Become one of us and stand up for Tormelund. Stand up for your homes! Your lives! The lives of your families, friends, and children!"

The crowd reacted with a mixture of cheers and worry. She would not let them waver.

"Depart post haste and reach the castle as soon as you can. We are running out of time. I will see you there! I will fight alongside you in this upcoming challenge!" She drew her sword, and with determination steeled on her face, held the magical blade high above her head for all to see.

The cheers increased. She had them.

"For Seafare! For Tormelund!"

The crowd exploded, fire in their eyes. *Mission accomplished.*

She kept her legendary blade above her head as she rode away from the town square. Leaving the bustling crowd behind, she navigated the streets and found herself in front of the Seagull Shanty, the tavern she once called home.

She noted the familiar sign and door she had entered a hundred times. She stared a moment longer as the desire to charge in and embrace the old woman inside tugged at her heart. She desperately wanted to tell her how much her kindness had meant over the years.

There were still many towns to visit, and time was running out. Holding back tears, she instead rode on, for she knew in her heart if she allowed that vulnerability, she would not be able to face what was ahead. She had to remain hard, steeling herself for the upcoming fight.

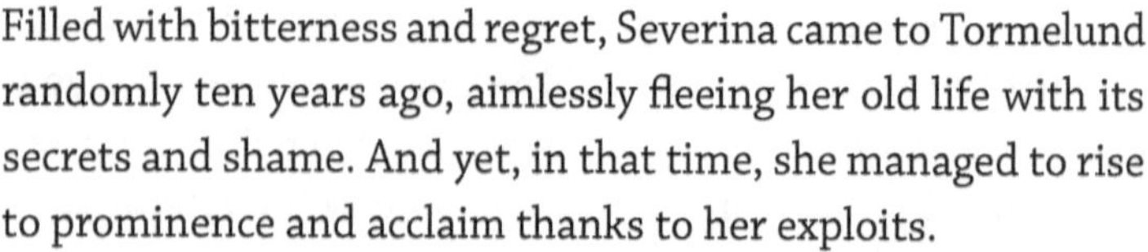

Filled with bitterness and regret, Severina came to Tormelund randomly ten years ago, aimlessly fleeing her old life with its secrets and shame. And yet, in that time, she managed to rise to prominence and acclaim thanks to her exploits.

No one knew her here. No one knew what she was or what she had done. This was a fresh start where she could bury her past forever.

She had quickly found mercenary work, as one does in larger towns. The unexpected deadliness contained in her small frame made her a most effective merc, with most targets never seeing her coming. Until her fame built a reputation and ruined the surprise that she worked to maintain. While benefits came with fame, so did setbacks, including everyone becoming aware of her and her prowess, and so her mercenary days ended. She had put herself out of a job.

She pivoted to legitimate bodyguard work for wealthy merchants and even lower-tier royalty. Her name slowly became synonymous with loyalty and trust, traits she displayed during her time working.

But what carved her name into the hearts and minds of every citizen of Tormelund was the day she fought and took down an invading blue dragon. The blues were known for three things: their rage, their greed, and their breath of a dozen lightning bolts.

And on that dark day, some five years ago, Severina single-handedly slew the dragon.

The moment became a catalyst for change in her. For the first time, the citizenry witnessed her displays of spellcasting, and they cheered her on.

She had felt a joy rise within her that she had not felt since childhood. She knew right then that she had found her home in Tormelund.

Karas knocked Severina out of her memories with a friendly clap on the back. She had returned to Durren after another week of recruitment. In that time, able-bodied men and women began arriving, ready to do their part in the fight to come.

"I gotta hand it to you, Sevi," he began cheerfully. "You did it. You convinced them to come. You're truly living up to your namesake, Stormbringer."

"I simply laid out the facts."

"There's that charm that won 'em over," he teased.

They stood on the balcony attached to the ballroom of the castle, granting them a view of the massive encampment just outside the castle walls. Endless rows of tents had been erected as the royal army was called up and the citizen forces began arriving.

After a long silence, she said, "I know you would rather it had been you riding from place to place, putting out the call to arms."

"Indeed."

"I was only following orders."

"Aye. I bear you no ill will, my friend. I just want to be a part of this."

"I understand, and you are, Karas. You're leading the whole damn army."

"And for that, I'm grateful to Ulren. One last war to wage."

"Last? You aren't that old, old man."

"Old enough to know when it's time to retire, yet still young enough to feel that fire in my belly for the fight."

"I suspect you won't be able to resist carrying your blade to the battlefield even long after this mysterious enemy is slain."

"I have to confess, I do miss the command and am anxious to get out there."

She noted his eyes drift to memories of battles long past.

"And we don't even know what we're up against," Severina commented, staring down at the soldiers ready to fight and possibly die for this cause.

"That's the twist of it all. Knowing your foe, you can prepare and plan. This nightmare is something else entirely."

"Are you frightened?" she asked.

"Only a damn fool wouldn't be."

"Good. No delusion. No bravado. Just pure fight."

"I hope it's enough."

Severina returned to her chamber in the castle. After slaying the dragon, King Ulren insisted she move into the keep and work for him. She looked about the luxurious bedroom, and even five years in, she couldn't get used to such opulence.

In the silence, she felt overwhelmed by thoughts of her past. Loneliness. Pain. Guilt. Abandonment. She shook her head clear, taking a slow and deep breath, refusing to let her mind wander back down that dark path. Tormelund and its people had saved her from herself, had unknowingly pulled her out of her rage-fueled bitterness, and shown her what life could be. For that, she owed them everything.

She wandered to the window and gazed out over the sleeping city. Would they be ready for what was coming? Would she be able to protect them?

She sighed and lay on the bed, staring at the ceiling. Her thoughts spiraled back to her memories, despite her best efforts to run from them. Visions of her adoptive parents were pushed to the forefront of her mind, the disappointment on their faces permanently etched into her soul.

Her father's words rang loud, "You are no daughter of mine!"

She tried to shut out the memories, but they invaded her thoughts regardless of her efforts. A single tear rolled down her cheek. She choked back emotion and tried in vain to fall asleep.

CHAPTER 3

"**W**e have it!" Heliosa yelled as she charged into the king's court. She bolted to the throne where Ulren, Karas, Rennard, and Severina waited anxiously.

"Quellon has revealed the source."

All eyes focused on the cleric as she came to a stop, panting.

"It is a god. The plague is definitively from a deity," she blurted out once she had regained her breath.

"Which one?" asked Ulren, desperately.

"Quellon doesn't know. This being's origin is unknown in his circle."

Everyone let out frustrated groans and grunts. The king waved everyone down and continued.

"What can you tell us? Did Quellon offer any information?" inquired the king urgently.

"This god deals in pestilence, as we've seen. But there's more. He feeds on decay, spiritually gaining power from the rot. He infests and devours until there's nothing left. He is a world destroyer."

"And Tormelund is next," whispered Karas.

"Not just us," added Rennard. "Our entire planet. All nations. All lands."

Everyone stood silent, letting the revelation sink in.

Severina broke the silence with the question on everyone's mind. "How long do we have?"

"Quellon advises it's a matter of days before this deity can punch its way into our world."

Ulren stood and declared, "We march immediately! We will not let this scourge conquer our home."

And from that moment on, the invader became known as Scourge to all.

Two days later, the royal army, bolstered by thousands of armed citizens, arrived at the portal. The dead grass fields bore the weight of their armaments and supplies. Above the pending battlefield, the sky grew dark, with storm clouds approaching—a fitting arena for what was to come.

The crack had widened to a full six feet at the base, tapering as it rose higher into the air. The blue light and low hum had increased in intensity since Severina's last visit. The time drew near.

Further details from Quellon revealed the god, Scourge, did not travel alone. Otherworldly minions accompanied the immortal deity on its journey. Together they traversed the stars and crossed dimensions in their subjugation of worlds.

Making camp several hundred feet from the portal, the armies settled and fell into their routine of inspections, preparations, and training, instructing the citizen militia how to do the same.

At the officer's camp, key figures gathered around a large bonfire. Severina, Karas, Heliosa, and Rennard ate and discussed their impending confrontation. Joining them, at Ulren's specific order, was the famous—or infamous—bard, Faustice. Renowned for his songs of glory and heroic deeds, as well as his notorious magical musical instrument, the bard entertained and annoyed the citizens all over Tormelund. His mighty flute hung from a sheath on his waist like a knight's sword. His legendary curly, golden locks of hair glimmered in the light of the fire, and his ever-cheerful demeanor exhausted all those around him.

"Fret not, dear companions, for we shall win this day handily!" Faustice declared and took a long swig of ale.

The others rolled their eyes or sighed in exasperation, unimpressed by his cheerful demeanor and golden armor.

"So sure, are you?" asked Heliosa. "Consulted the god of music on this?"

"Milady, there's no cause for rudeness," he quipped politely.

"Look, Faustice," began Heliosa. "I'm a realist. I can't afford to be the optimist."

"And that's why I'm here, my friends."

"Just don't go accidentally summoning a demon with that flute of yours," grunted Karas.

Faustice smiled and replied, "None of you have seen my trusty friend in action. You're all in for a treat."

"Bards," added Severina as she rolled her eyes, tearing another bite of bread off her slice.

Faustice stood and raised his mug. "To our glorious battle. May many songs of victory be born from it!"

The others gave less enthusiastic cheers with their mugs.

Faustice drew his flute—an ornate instrument of silver decorated in emeralds—and spun it through his fingers in a dazzling display. He tossed the flute into the air and caught it with grace and skill.

"And now let me treat your ears to my classic melody, 'Sevi the Slayer.'"

As one, they all exclaimed, "No!"

One dozen soldiers stood watch over the portal at any given time. Likewise, the entire army slept in rotating shifts so that a sizeable force would always be ready if the enemy breached the crack. Frayed nerves and high tension were the order of the day for the brave men and women in the combined army. They held their fear in check, knowing their loved ones needed them to be at their best. They were the first and last to stand against whatever stepped through the portal.

Deep in the night, a hush fell over the land. Even the steady hum from the portal seemed muffled. The blue light within flickered and wavered, as though shadows crossed in front of the light source. Movement from beyond.

The guards immediately called out, one blowing into a large horn, alerting the entire army. One-third were already awake and at the ready and began to charge their way toward the portal as the others woke and grabbed their gear, hurrying where they needed to be.

The strategy was already in place and the armies took up their assigned positions—a bottleneck funnel of soldiers that would leave little room for an enemy force to move. Heavy shield units were in the front, polearm and swordsmen in the middle rows, with archers in the rear. Spell casters and battle mages took up positions in the back some distance from each other so as not to interfere with each other's magic.

In moments, the stage was set, and the soldiers were in place. Rage and fear were etched on all their faces. Severina took up a position with the swordsmen, dead center, facing the portal. Faustice stood next to her, flute and smile at the ready. Heliosa and Rennard took their place with their fellow magic-users. And Karas commanded the forces from the rear. They were as ready as they could be given the unknowns of the battle.

Severina ventured a long look over the army, assessing the resolve of those she would share a battlefield with. She felt proud of their courage, proud to be among them, and honored to have been received by these people so openly.

Her eye caught some individuals in gray cloaks, their hoods up. She didn't recall seeing them in the camp or on the march from the castle. She swept her gaze in all directions and soon spotted several of the same gray cloaks sprinkled throughout the gathered forces. She estimated close to one hundred of these strangers. Perhaps she had simply not seen them prior. Perhaps they had joined up with the army after the camp had been established.

Wrath sent a tingling sensation to her gut.

Yes. I see them. I feel it too.

She noticed one of the hooded figures acknowledge and nod to another, then to another. *Something's not right.*

Before she could assess further, a massive explosion of sound erupted from the portal; a cacophony so immense it buckled many of the soldiers to their knees, clutching their ears. As they recovered, the crack jolted, sending ripples in the ground beneath their feet. The narrow opening fractured and splintered into several lighted spines, the base opening fully to extend some thirty feet across.

A brief moment of eerie silence followed, the army hushed in anticipation.

A low, deep rumble began from within the light, growing in volume and vibration. The soldiers gripped their weapons tight, flexing their muscles in preparation. Most of the seasoned military had seen all manner of foes. However, the otherworldly horrors that spilled forth from the glowing portal were nearly beyond comprehension.

CHAPTER 4

The putrid stench came first. It poured from the Void like a thick, rotten gas. The army coughed and choked, but held their positions.

The rumbling started once again, growing rapidly.

"Hold!" yelled Karas, though he doubted they could hear him over the growing din.

Then the portal filled with slithering, writhing creatures. Dozens fell into the field, all human-sized but possessing all manner of forms, and they immediately fanned out.

Colored of sickly green, gray, and mauve, the otherworldly monsters attacked the first row of soldiers, striking their shields with tentacles, mandibles, and misshapen claws. Each varied in their appendages, ranging from bipedal to tentacled to hunching on all fours. Their heads were bulbous and octopodal, slathered in thick ectoplasm with two dead black eyes protruding on either side. And there was no mouth. The nightmarish monsters lashed out and penetrated the mortals' defenses.

They ripped shields and slammed down on helmets despite the valiant retaliation with blades, spears, and polearms.

The creatures kept pouring out from the portal, and so in an attempt to stagger them, the archers targeted the portal and struck dozens of the beasts. Their arrows seemed to have no effect on them, and the slimy things kept pushing through like a leak in a dam.

Severina lost track of the gray-robed warriors as the battlefield descended into madness. Too far from the enemies to strike with Wrath, she called upon her honed magic and called down large bolts of fire from the sky to pound the foes in the center. The flames caused panic among the creatures as they spread fire to one another. Yet, they did not cease their assault.

She whispered a prayer of gratitude to Menavaria, then cast a powerful gust of wind to spread and fan the flames across the beasts. The fire kicked up but did not deter them from pushing into the soldiers.

The magic-users took their cue from Severina and began casting their attacks—being careful not to harm their own army.

The citizen army stood their ground, and what they lacked in experience they made up for in heart and bravery. Strategically spread out among the soldiers, they stood a fighting chance. Despite their efforts, their expedited training and lack of experience made them incur heavier losses than the soldiers.

The center of the battlefield became alight with lightning bolts, magic flames, bolts of ice, showers of acid, and more. While the spells harmed the strange enemy, they kept pressing on. Nothing seemed to phase or stop them.

More and more soldiers fell to their attackers with screams and shrieks of pain erupting all over the field.

Karas charged in on his horse, pushing through his soldiers toward the front line.

Severina took note of her friend on horseback and Wrath sent a brief chill down her arm. With a nod of agreement, she felt compelled to fight by his side and moved swiftly toward Karas.

Wrath at the ready, she reached the front line just before Karas and began hacking and slashing enemies.

Karas's horse crashed through several monsters to reach the front line. With a bit of room to move, he commanded his steed to spin in a circle while he decimated foes all around.

Together, their blades severed limbs and beheaded the creatures with ease.

Heliosa observed the field with growing concern. Instead of attacking, she chose to heal and protect soldiers with powerful magic granted to her by Quellon's grace. Waves of healing energy washed over a large group of soldiers to her left. To her right she sent a white light of protection, causing assaults against them to crash against a translucent protective shell. She couldn't protect them all, but she could give some a fighting chance.

Rennard exhausted most of his ranged attack spells and had to change tactics. He moved closer to the melee and focused on a soldier at the front, casting a spell on the brave woman, causing her to grow. She shot to five times her height, towering above friend and foe alike. Her armor and weapons grew with her, granting her a massive hammer with a head the size of a horse.

The warrior woman gave an echoing battle cry and started crushing and battering groups of enemies. Not stopping with the hammer, she also took opportunities to kick the beasts back at the portal.

Her fellow soldiers cheered, bolstered by this new giant hero.

Severina ducked to avoid a hammer strike and caught herself smiling at this new development, bumping into Karas, who sliced the head off a nearby creature.

"You are full of surprises," he exclaimed.

"This isn't one of mine. I thought she was a gift from you." She laughed as she cleaved one of the beasts clean in half.

Despite the giant, the monsters kept coming, and soon the battlefield descended into further chaos, the defense lines beginning to waver.

Unable to launch volleys for fear of harming their own, the archers drew swords and charged into the fray. Likewise, the spell casters switched tactics, imbuing the soldiers with enhancements to their weapons, armor, and health.

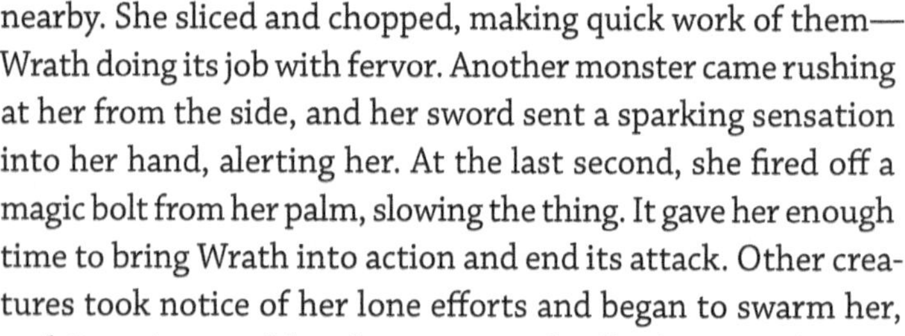

Severina spun away from Karas, targeting a group of beasts nearby. She sliced and chopped, making quick work of them—Wrath doing its job with fervor. Another monster came rushing at her from the side, and her sword sent a sparking sensation into her hand, alerting her. At the last second, she fired off a magic bolt from her palm, slowing the thing. It gave her enough time to bring Wrath into action and end its attack. Other creatures took notice of her lone efforts and began to swarm her, and Severina confidently spun in a deadly dance and made each being suffer whenever they dared attack. Eventually, she began taking hits: a claw to the arm, a tentacle strike delivering a stinging blow, and various other attacks that made blood bead on the surface.

As she struggled to fend off the evil invaders, movement deep inside the portal caught her eye. Something massive, taller than the giant soldier, approached the breach. Just the sight of the shadow of this thing infused her with a sick feeling, an overwhelming revulsion.

Wrath let her know it was afraid.

She took down another creature and turned to Karas, yelling as hard as she could to announce to him and the soldiers what many may have already guessed. "Scourge is coming!"

She barely finished the warning before a monster pounced on her back.

Karas faced the portal and witnessed the shadow approaching, and a sickening feeling sank deep inside him as the mysterious behemoth drew nearer. He pushed the feeling away and called out to his soldiers.

"Rally!"

The soldiers heard the cue to focus on their leader, but most were too deeply embattled to heed the call. As hard as they pushed to reach Karas, the creatures kept them tangled and struggling.

Severina fired another bolt from her palm and burned the monster on her back. The beast fell to the ground, where she finished it off with Wrath. She moved to rejoin Karas and noticed four of the gray-hooded fighters gathered together, huddled and not fighting. Before she could process the scene, she lost them in a sea of monsters and soldiers.

As she stepped up to Karas, Wrath sent a warning down her spine. Her mind raced, and she instantly looked around for the danger.

From behind Karas, she spotted a gray-hooded man rushing up on him. She locked eyes with Karas and pointed with a warning shout. Without hesitation, he spun, bringing his blade up in time to deflect the attack from the human. He quickly countered and drove his sword through the traitor's belly, sending him to his grave.

Severina and Karas exchanged confused looks for a moment before the battle closed in once again, separating the pair. Now, she spotted the grays stealthily attacking the soldiers. Slitting throats, slicing the backs of knees, thrusting daggers into backs. The entire army had been infiltrated.

And still behind them, the shadowy thing closed in on the reality tear.

A gray came at Severina from behind, Wrath's intuition tipping her off and giving her the chance to spin in time to block the dagger. This opponent adjusted to her counter and stepped back into a battle stance, giving a thin-lipped smile under a brown goatee. From his belt, he withdrew a short sword, his dagger in the other hand.

He came at her with both blades slicing incredibly fast, and Severina found herself instantly on the defensive. His footwork revealed formal training in swordplay, and he moved his dual weapons with an uncanny quickness, as though they were extensions of himself that left Severina barely managing to fend him off.

As the numbers thinned on both sides, the spell casters maneuvered themselves closer to the portal, remaining on the outskirts of the fighting. They had spied the juggernaut nearing the opening and, now in closer proximity, began casting all manner of magic in a desperate attempt to seal the portal and prevent whatever was drawing closer from crossing through.

Arcane bolts shattered against the opening. Conjured boulders appeared and stacked themselves against the portal walls, only to disintegrate before their eyes. Variations of fire, frost, and lightning were employed, but all failed to seal the portal.

Despite the noise of war laying thick over the battleground, a deep guttural, slick voice carried for miles around and shook the earth, cutting through the cacophony of noise with ease. The words spoken were in an unknown language, but the creatures seemed to respond to it with their own undecipherable noises.

A strange cloud emitted from the portal and remained in the opening, writhing and undulating in a bizarre pattern. Severina deflected the gray's attack and stole a glance at the new invader: a cloud made of large, unknown flying insects. Several breeds intermingled by the thousands to form the cloud and disrupt the view of a mass inside.

The gray came at her again, his grin somehow growing.

"It's finished," he hissed and lunged at her. They crossed swords up close, and Severina knew she'd made a critical error. In blocking the short sword, she'd left herself open to his dagger.

The gray exploited the flaw and thrust the thin blade beneath her armor and into her torso, just below the ribcage. Severina grunted, taking the hit, then fired off a magic bolt. Their proximity meant they both felt the hit, sending them staggering away from each other.

Karas slit the throat of a creature and checked on Severina. Upon seeing the dagger retreating from a fresh wound, panic gripped his attention. He watched as she regained her footing and came at her opponent once more, worried relief lingering that she hadn't fallen yet.

Distracted a moment too long, Karas didn't see the gray-hooded woman sneak up on him until her dagger was drawing across his throat. As his neck opened and his life spilled out, he spun fast, grabbing his assailant by the cloak and shoving her to the ground. With his last effort, he drove his blade through her heart, all while gasping and choking, the blood flowing too freely to stop even as he clenched his neck.

The insects began to spread out, all the size of a human fist, deadly stingers and mandibles striking panic in the ranks of the army.

At the portal, about thirty feet high, massive, clawed hands gripped each side of the opening, and the stench from the slick, putrid flesh forced dozens to wretch and gag. The voice from within cried out once again as the hulking figure started to rip the crack open wider.

The blue light from behind flashed brighter as the portal gave way to the force of the being within. Karas fell to his knees, eyes wide with terror as he witnessed the horror that came through. Despite the warmth of his blood, he felt chilled to the core, whether from blood loss and the oncoming rush of death or the revelation of what they were up against being revealed, he could not tell. But as his vision wavered, all he could see were the feet of friends and foes alike.

From within the portal, the insects spread out, revealing the god, Scourge. Standing nearly forty feet tall, solid black and slick with putrid fluid, the immortal being entered the new world. The creature had no face, no features whatsoever. The thing stretched out four appendages from its humanoid torso: three muscular arms and one grotesque tentacle. The beast's lower half broke into several massive tentacles, writhing and squirming to keep it upright and mobile.

As it made contact with the dead grassy plain, the ground turned dark with decay. This massive being was pestilence personified.

Across the battlefield, all fighting ceased, soldiers trying to come to grips with this celestial horror, and the minions pausing in respectful reverence.

A handful of soldiers and some of the citizen warriors fled in terror, discarding their weapons in their haste. Those less fortunate gripped their heads, screaming in dread as blood began to flow from their eyes before keeling over, sobbing, unable to comprehend the sight.

Severina shook herself out of a stupor and managed to shove her fear deep down. It could not end this way. Not if she had anything to say about it. Not after she asked so many to sacrifice their lives to save their home.

She noted the gray near her raising his arms in welcome to the god, an easy opening. She was about to strike at him, but instead opted for a bigger prize—something to rally what troops Tormelund had left. She pointed her palm at the approaching insect swarm and unleashed a huge bolt of fire.

The deadly flame lasted long enough to light up a large portion of the flying insects. As the bugs scattered in pain and panic, they spread the flames to their fellow insects, causing a chain reaction of burning death for the creatures.

The gray-hooded man kept his arms pointed at the sky, greeting his god.

The orange glow from the alight bugs revealed Karas's body, lying motionless in the dirt, and Severina's panic welled up.

She fought back tears as she raced to his side, his name falling out of her mouth in a pained cry. Her worst fears came to fruition as she discovered the gash in his throat and his lifeless eyes.

She hugged him tight, despite the enemies all around, carefully cradling his body and supporting his head as though it would lessen whatever pain he had felt during death. She forced herself to look about, ever-wary of her surroundings. The grays seemed consumed by adoration of their god's arrival.

Despite her newfound grief, Severina's firestorm proved to be the rallying cry the heroes of Tormelund needed, snapping them out of their shock and spurring them to action. The soldiers began hacking their way through the minions, magic-users launching spells at the enemy god.

Scourge moved farther out from the portal, head turning as though taking in the new world with nonexistent eyes. The earth shook with every slide the giant tentacles made.

The magically enlarged woman stomped on a minion, bursting it into a gory mess before setting her sights on the vile deity. With a fierce battle cry, she charged the god, her valiant act drawing cheers from her fellow, much smaller, soldiers as she raised her giant hammer for a fatal strike.

She swung with all her might, but Scourge's grotesque tentacle caught the giant weapon, encircling it and stopping its downward momentum, instead drawing it inward. The abrupt halt threw her off balance and, with the pull from the tentacle, she stumbled into the slick black flesh of Scourge's chest and shoulder.

She shrieked in pain and leaped back, left hand moving to wipe the residue off her flesh while Scourge paid her no more mind, advancing. The giant soldier staggered, now sobbing and screaming as her skin that had met with Scourge's began to bubble and decay. The pestilence spread like wildfire, covering her with a growing sick brown color of rot despite her attempts to clean it off.

She fell to her knees as the decay reached her neck and coated her entire left arm, flesh and tendons falling from her widening wounds. Soldiers and monsters scattered out of her way as she collapsed fully, her cries of agony echoing into the night sky, drifting softer into gurgling, then silence.

Toward the back of the fighting, Faustice had been anticipating his moment to shine—and this was it. It was all about the glory and showmanship, after all. He threw back his magnificent white cape, revealing gleaming gold armor, and, with flute in hand, charged toward the battle.

As he drew near, he pressed the magic instrument to his lips and breathed life into it. Together they blew forth a haunting, hypnotic melody that could have hailed from the nine hells. The soldiers heard but an ordinary flute, but the foes experienced a sonic onslaught to their senses.

Soldiers parted to allow him through as he walked toward Scourge. The musical tones landed on the god like a mountain, forcing Scourge to buckle over and hold its massive hands to where ears should have been.

And the bard kept playing as enemies fell victim to the disruptive sting of the melody. Scourge and minion alike writhed in pain and confusion.

A single bard had turned the tide. Faustice had certainly chosen his moment for the fullest effect on his growing legend. Surely, this would cement him into Tormelund's history for all eternity.

The soldiers, while furious that he withheld such a beneficial power, took the opportunity, striking down nearby enemies in fervor to not waste the time granted.

As the chaos of battle progressed, no one noticed three gray-hooded figures flank and sneak their way toward the musical menace.

Severina couldn't find the strength to leave Karas's side. Try as she might to stop them, her tears gushed. Karas had been more than a friend; he'd been a mentor. And now he was gone.

Out of the corner of her eye, she caught sight of the gray-hooded attacker contending with three of the surviving insects. He sliced one in half, then swatted and dodged the others. The bugs seemed frenzied and confused as the strange music rang out in the air.

Vengeance rose within Severina, pushing grief to the side. She wiped away her tears and found her footing after carefully laying her friend down. As she rose, she took stock of the battle before her. The gray-hooded man tangled with the insects some twenty feet from her, and Scourge loomed behind him, heading toward the battlefield off to her right.

She felt Wrath's vibrations in her sword arm, imploring her not to seek revenge, that there were more pressing matters at hand, urging her to focus on the god.

Shut up. I know what I'm doing. Severina hissed internally and broke into a run, ignoring the mayhem around her, and focusing ahead.

The traitor managed to glance at her just as she darted by. Her target was Scourge, despite her fury toward the gray-hooded warriors.

Rennard, having made his way toward the front with the other magic-users, could see Severina's path and focused his mind, bringing forth a simple but effective spell. His eyes glowed with arcane light and Severina's legs moved faster, and faster, and faster until she was sprinting at a rate twofold what an able mortal humanoid should be capable of.

Severina raced past friend and foe alike and, as she reached Scourge's nearest tentacle, she held Wrath out to her side.

The deadly blade sliced a deep gash along the entire twenty-foot-long appendage. Sickly meat and fluid spilled out in the wake of her attack. Scourge was still reeling from the agonizing sounds when it felt the sting of Severina's onyx blade, and it quickly jerked the tentacle away from the danger, splashing more viscera around it.

The god pushed through the sound, turning to see what mortal had dared strike it, but all it could make out was a puny blur darting around its form.

Faustice confidently drew nearer the god, flute blasting. He felt invincible. A god rendered helpless against his mighty flute, he felt like a god, himself.

In his self-reverence and focus on subduing the god, he didn't see the grays creeping up from behind. He was proud of how perfectly his entry had been executed, and soon he would be writing songs about this day.

A blade of a gray-hooded man pierced his neck and his dream faded, shattered by the stark reality that he would die. His playing ceased as blood filled his throat, spilling down his golden armor. Then a sword punctured his lung, entering just under the armpit. A third blade swiped the back of his knees, making him drop to the ground, flute tumbling to the ground. The attacks continued hitting one after the other, relentlessly.

The bard's ego suffered more than his body. The pain was insignificant compared to the loss of status and fame. He fell on his back, choking as he bled out, staining the white of his cloak... But he regained his flute, clutching it to his chest as he stared skyward.

Severina circled Scourge and repeated the deadly slice on another massive tentacle. The first one ceased movement and seemed to wither, changing to a dead-gray color.

Scourge, released from the aggravating music, changed tactics, knowing it could not spot the insolent mortal. Instead, it turned down its palms and rained putrid fluid upon everything close to it. Severina managed to steer herself wide of the splash radius. Like before, the ground decayed wherever the liquid touched, spreading a vomitus stench as it landed.

Another tentacle withered and went limp from the damage inflicted, making Scourge unstable.

Circling behind Scourge, Severina paused and analyzed her target, preparing for another deadly strike. Before she could resume her unearthly sprinting, the gray hood lunged at her from her right. His dagger slashed her right arm as she sensed him and tried to evade.

She switched to a fighting stance, Wrath at the ready.

"Why?" she barked.

"The world needs cleansing. A new start," he replied calmly.

They crossed blades, assessing each other's skills.

"Who are you?"

"We are the servants of—"

"I don't give a shit about your traitorous group. I want to know the name of the man I'm about to kill."

He grinned confidently. "I am the Harbinger. My blade is your end."

"I love a challenge."

She came in hard, deftly swinging Wrath with the precision of a jewel crafter.

The Harbinger dodged and parried every strike with maddening ease. "Imagine, the world cleansed! Reborn in his image! Is that not enticing? Is that not *perfection*?" He laughed, seeming giddy from the mere idea of the world being destroyed.

Knowing that he would be a lost cause to get information from, Severina utilized her magical speed. Whipping around behind him faster than he could comprehend, she stopped and thrust Wrath into his back, raising him from the ground a fraction. Ripping her blade free, she appeared before him again, thrusting her sword through his stomach.

"Looks like *my* blade is *your* end," she snarled softly, twisting her blade before withdrawing it and shoving him backward.

The Harbinger's eyes revealed his shock, and he collapsed, grunting and clutching his pierced torso.

No longer tormented by the pesky blur, Scourge gazed down upon the battling mortals with its featureless head. Clenching its fists and tightening its chest and torso, its skin began to pulse in rhythmic beats, undulating its flesh from the center down to its hands.

The terror of the behemoth approaching sent the army scattering out of its path.

Scourge's flesh calmed, except for its fists. They pulsed with pent-up energy—building and building toward an inevitable conclusion. And then the god opened its palms. From the newly opened fists poured a foul black-green liquid that splashed across the battlefield as it waved its arms back and forth.

The black-green liquid brought rot to everything it touched. The ground, soldiers, and even the god's minions who were unfortunate enough to get caught in the wake instantly decayed agonizingly slowly as the liquid touched them. Dozens of men and monsters cried out in their suffering, unable to scramble away in time, and from the wounds sprouted maggots and unknown insects.

The battlefield grew stained in the rot as Scourge moved farther from the portal.

Severina circled the god in frustration. Her remarkable speed kept her relatively safe, but she could not decipher a method of killing the thing. Hacking its tentacle appendages wasn't enough. In her rage, she sliced up a minion unfortunate enough to stumble into her path.

The army's numbers grew thin, Scourge taking out dozens at a time. The monstrous servants also suffered great losses, but Severina feared the scales were not tipping in their favor.

The mages' spells hit targets with less frequency and became sporadic. There are only so many spells one can memorize at a time, so the powerful displays of fire, frost, and more no longer lit up the night sky as they had in the earlier moments of the war.

Several of the casters switched to using artifacts and devices imbued with magic: rings, wands, staves, and more were wielded in an effort to take down the deity.

Heliosa found her way to Rennard, looking haggard and exhausted.

"You understand our situation, yes?" she asked.

"That our magic is practically useless against Scourge."

"But I do like your thinking with her," she said, indicating Severina. "Let me see how I may help her further."

She closed her eyes, whispering a prayer to Quellon. As though aware of the ongoing turmoil, a blast of bright white light instantly shot from her hands toward Severina, bathing her in pure light for a moment before vanishing.

A warmth enveloped Severina, who realized from the familiar sensation that a spell of protection had washed over her. She smiled at the traitor as he tried in vain to bury his swords in her whilst his free hand clutched the hole in his stomach.

Taking advantage of the new protection, she leaped onto one of the dead tentacles and ran up toward Scourge's torso—unharmed by the deadly slick coating of its flesh. She made her way to where the tentacle met its body, placing her within reach of the tender abdomen.

Observing the shifting battlefield, she noted that the soldiers had eliminated most of the grotesque minions, but the grays still worked their way through the army, slaying their own. Some were slain, but not enough of them.

Scourge sent its skin pulsating toward its closed fists once again and Severina knew what would be in store for the remaining army if she didn't stop the oncoming attack. She took a deep breath and leaped to the center of Scourge's torso, thrusting her onyx blade in deep. Her momentum paired with gravity allowed her to keep the deadly sharp sword embedded and slice a deep line across and down the being's core, effectively gutting the god.

Entrails and fluid spilled forth as rapids as she kicked herself free and landed hard on the ground below, rolling a few feet before springing back up, somewhat winded but still mobile. Scourge bellowed another deep cry that echoed for miles, this time filled with a slick gurgling. It scrambled to clutch its gaping wound, too late to prevent the damage already dealt.

Severina hurried out of the way as the mighty god stumbled and staggered, pushing her already burning muscles more to avoid the falling being.

Cheers roared from the army at the heavy blow, fleeing from the vicinity of where the wounded god may fall, striking at the inhuman minions as they retreated from the threatening spill.

The remaining grays had no time to mourn. With the battle all but nearly over, and many of its minions defeated or now seeming lost and unsure of what to do, there was not nearly enough chaos for the cloaked people to hide their actions. The act of one drew the attention of soldiers, and the news spread like wildfire as more and more soldiers caught on to the truth and began cutting them down.

Scourge let out another bone-chilling shriek and collapsed to its side. It lay still except for a subtle final breath and the death rattle twitching of its limbs.

Severina fell to one knee, heaving and panting. A mixture of relief and grief washed over her.

Having stumbled away from where he fought Severina, the Harbinger clung to life, laying in the blood-stained dirt and forced to observe the entire slaughter of his belief system and companions. The blood loss left him pale, and his cloak obscured him enough that he appeared dead, allowing him to be easily overlooked by the remaining soldiers.

Instead, they swarmed the last of the traitorous, gray-hooded bastards who joined their deity in death.

Scourge's body continued its death spasms, unnerving those closest to the giant dead body. It twitched and shifted, spilling more entrails before it, the ground becoming a marsh of putrid rot. However, from deep within the wound, a dim blue glow was revealed from the loss of innards—the same shade as the hue from the portal.

Rennard and Heliosa joined Severina's sides, looking over at the body, which rested about twenty feet away. The glow cast a dim and eerie light over the inhabitants of Tormelund.

"What is this?" whispered Severina. Wrath sent shivers down her spine and high-alert nausea deep in her gut.

"I'm afraid I do not know," replied a perplexed Rennard.

Heliosa took a step closer, fear rising in her. "I know exactly what this is," she said, voice trembling. She turned to face them. "There is a soul gem within."

"A what?" asked Severina, a frown creasing her brows.

"I've heard of such things, but I never imagined I'd ever see one," added Rennard in a hushed tone.

Heliosa turned her head toward Severina. "A soul gem is a rare scenario where an immortal being's soul is housed within an object, not the physical body."

"What does this mean?"

"Scourge isn't dead yet," Rennard revealed after a pause.

"Oh, of course!" Severina exclaimed.

Exasperated, Severina stepped closer to the god's body, flexing her hand on Wrath. She took stock of the survivors around her, all the people who had fought to protect their land and loved ones.

"We must have access to the gem. Cut carefully," said Rennard.

Severina turned to the body and sliced deep from the existing wound in a line across to the chest. More organs and gore fell from the carcass, increasing the strength of the blue glow. She hacked her way deeper into the body cavity, praying that the protection lasted as long as needed until finally the gem was exposed—a sapphire the size of a helmet.

Unsure of whether to touch the object, Severina used Wrath to pry it free, but even her mighty sword could not dislodge the sinister artifact.

"How can we destroy it?" she beseeched her magic-focused friends. Rennard had no answer for her, and Heliosa seemed to fall deeper into thought.

Wrath sent a warmth to her chest. She understood. *Thank you, my friend.*

Moving away from the tainted ground, Severina sat cross-legged on an unharmed piece of the field and closed her eyes. Folding her arms gently in her lap, she breathed deeply and calmly.

The soldiers, unwilling to approach her and finished with removing the traitors, began to carefully make their way around the field in search of survivors.

Rennard nudged Heliosa, snapping her out of her thoughts. They observed the warrior on the ground and sighed, knowing that Severina was attempting to communicate with her god for guidance, perhaps the only viable path. These were, after all, her god's domains.

Severina shut out the entire world, focusing inward. The putrid air disappeared. The shuffling, demoralized army faded. The slain immortal fell away to nothingness. In her mind, there was only serene communion.

She prayed to her goddess, Menavaria, as she had done so many times before. But what she was about to ask of her was quite possibly a grave insult. Menavaria might help her, or she could smite her just for asking. To be rid of Scourge forever, she would risk it.

"You've done well, child," came the powerful but soothing voice of Menavaria.

Severina opened her eyes to see the battlefield in a new light. Gone were all the remnants of war. The fields of grass, revitalized, swayed in a sunlit breeze, and before her, Menavaria, in all her glory, stood nearly double her height. Severina felt the love of her deity.

"You've made me proud once again," the goddess added.

"Thank you, my sister," she replied. Sister being the preferred moniker of the deity. After a pause, Severina mustered her courage and pressed on. "I have served you for most of my life."

"You have. Faithfully and adoringly."

"I don't believe I have asked for much over the years."

"You are sparing in your requests, to be sure."

"But I now must ask something of you," she stammered, her courage wavering.

Menavaria laughed. "Severina, the mightiest of warriors cannot ask for a favor? Be calm, child. I know what it is you seek."

Severina was speechless.

"Don't look so surprised. When one of my mortals faces an immortal in battle, you can be sure I'm going to observe. I know you need help with the soul gem within that foul beast."

"Yes, Sister. Scourge won't be truly dead unless the gem is destroyed."

"I am familiar with such things. Soul gems are a coward's path. One with fear in their heart. Do not fret, dear Severina. I'll do this for you and bring the good people of Tormelund safety and security once more."

"I cannot thank you enough."

"As with all things, there is a price to be paid," Menavaria said with sudden seriousness.

Severina stumbled, hastily answering, "Anything. Anything at all."

Menavaria laughed again, her smile warm and joyful. "I'm joking, sweet one. I will do this favor for you and demand nothing in return. You've earned at least that."

Severina opened her eyes to see her allies and friends gasping and gawking at something behind her. She turned and laid eyes upon the mesmerizing physical form of her goddess.

Menavaria was here. In her world. In her presence. She felt tears of rapture well.

Menavaria smiled warmly. She stood the height of two men and emitted a luminescence from within, giving her an angelic white glow.

Some of the soldiers stood motionless and silent, while others fell to their knees.

Severina rose to her feet and bowed to her goddess.

"I'll have none of that," she said pleasantly. "Now, let's see this soul gem."

Unlike when Scourge moved, there were no vibrations as she walked over to the carcass, looking as though she glided through the battlefield. She kneeled, staring at the gaping wound and the gem buried within.

An unamused expression flitted into existence briefly before she reached inside, grasping the glowing sapphire. With a mighty pull and grunt, Menavaria ripped the soul gem from its resting place and held it high in the air.

The Harbinger looked on in stark terror of this pure deity through lidded eyes. It felt as if her very aura pained him. His breath came in low, raspy whispers as he forced himself up with much effort, shaking as tears ran streaks down his dirt and blood-stained face. He was nearly finished, and now he had to watch as his god was desecrated and defiled.

Menavaria lowered the soul gem onto a boulder and drew her signature weapon: a one-handed battle hammer.

"And so ends the pestilence of Scourge!" she shouted, raising the hammer high. Severina felt her joy soar. At last, Tormelund would be free. This world, and many others, would be free.

The Goddess's hammer fell.

The Harbinger appeared with staggering speed for how injured he was, pushing the gem out of harm's way. A direct strike from Menavaria's hammer would undoubtedly have obliterated the gem, however, it just barely clipped the edge, smashing the boulder.

The concussive force of the blow, rather than annihilating the gem, caused it to fracture and explode. Splinters and shards fired in every direction, spreading deadly projectiles across the field.

The fragments pierced through the armor and tender flesh of soldiers and magic-users alike. Those that were able scattered and ducked.

Menavaria took multiple hits in the explosion, her physical being racked with shards. Severina watched in horror as her beloved goddess gasped and stumbled backward. At the same moment, Severina herself felt the bite of one of the soul gem shards pierce her chest. She fell to the ground simultaneously with Menavaria, attempting to crawl toward her god.

Rennard instinctively put himself in harm's way to shield Heliosa, pushing her to the ground and shielding her with his own body. He felt the sting of a fragment slice his arm, but all thoughts of pain left him as he witnessed Heliosa fall victim to the very same fragment, the shard striking her in the head, embedded deep, and ending her life swiftly.

The Harbinger took his last breath with a smile on his face, his fingers caressing the fragment of his god's soul lodged in his torso.

Severina watched the light fade from Menavaria, her body limp and lifeless. She screamed and reached for her goddess, but could move no more. The shard that struck her had embedded itself deeply, and all she felt was a numbing chill and the warm streak of her tears.

Severina heard Rennard cry out, but she knew not why. Out of the corner of her eye, she could see soldiers scrambling and fleeing. She spotted a few of them trying to aid Menavaria and they wept when they realized there was nothing to be done. The shards refusing to be removed.

Severina's broken heart began to slow. The shard buried inside had nearly crushed it instantly, and now, with each strained beat, she felt an iciness flood her body.

Soldiers stood over her, panic and anguish etched on their faces. They were speaking to her, but she could hear nothing. She grew tired. So very tired. A rest was what she needed. Yes, a long rest.

Severina closed her eyes.

CHAPTER 5

Severina felt weightless, as though she were falling end-lessly, but there was a warmth to it. A comfort. She opened her eyes to see that she was indeed plummeting through a dark, unfamiliar sky tinged with an otherworldly shade of purple. This strange sky held no sun, no moon, no stars, only a massive, ever-swirling vortex. A solid ground of golden wheat and gray ash rushed up toward her, and while she thought she should be more worried about that, all she could feel was serenity and a sense of belonging.

She crashed against the ground with a surprisingly pain-less thud, stirring small puffs of ash.

Lying on her back in a field of tall, swaying wheat, she gazed upward. The vortex seemed to be delivering small streaks of light that looked almost like raindrops in a storm.

The golden droplets struck the field around her and as far as her eyes could see. Gazing over to the site of one nearby fallen lights, Severina observed the glow fade and reveal an unconscious being. An elf who she didn't recognize.

She sat up to get her bearings, and no matter which direc-tion she turned, the field seemed to stretch on forever. She looked around and spotted dozens, perhaps hundreds, of other beings sitting or standing, all looking rather confused. Each large raindrop of light delivered a new entity onto the grassy field. All manner of creatures awoke and meandered about. She saw humans, orcs, elves, goblins, dwarves, and even some species she had never seen before.

An amethyst glow persisted over the entire landscape, as if an unseen purple sun cast its light over this world. Behind her in the distance stood a large grove of trees. Farther away she could see a large wooden lodge structure, a soft warm glow emitting from the doorway and windows.

She noted that in every direction she looked, the horizon was marked by an ominous wall of roiling darkness. Within the murky dark, a sinister storm of violent lightning strikes rained ever on, unrelenting. This chaotic darkness rose from the ground to the sky beyond her sight and stretched around the entire landscape like a barrier.

Where have I landed? What is this place?

She took stock of herself and seemed undamaged by the fall. In fact, even her wounds from the battle were healed. The gashes and gaping tears had vanished as if they had never happened. Her clothing and armor also appeared pristine and unmarred. Most importantly, she felt the weight of Wrath on her hip, sheathed and remaining with her. Relief washed over her.

Severina sent out a telepathic greeting, speaking to the blade as she'd done for years, but received no response. She tried again.

No lying down on the job. I need you.

Again, no response.

Wrath? Wake up. Come to me.

The silence sent panic through her.

Please, Wrath. Answer. Answer!

She felt a slight tingle in her right arm, so faint she may have imagined it. Did Wrath actually respond, or had she simply willed it to happen?

The sensation happened again, this time in her left hand. Both responses were weak, almost distant. She sighed in relief, thankful that Wrath was still with her in this unknown place. But joy grew clouded by worry.

What's wrong? Are you damaged?

Wrath sent a very faint sensation to her belly, creating slight nausea for just a moment.

I don't understand.

As her focus remained on the urgent conversation, Severina failed to see the robed figures moving about the field. Dozens of them made their way to the recently fallen and either greeted them or helped them rise. The robed figures were of varying races, from human to orc to kobold.

The sight of the robes forced memories of the battle to the forefront of her mind, and the loss of her goddess washed over her in a wave of grief and anguish. Images of Menavaria crumbling to the ground stabbed at her and she felt weak in the knees. A vital part of her being had been ripped from her, and her soul ached.

An agonizing cry tore from her into the dark sky above. She wept uncontrollably, thinking back to all the times in her life when Menavaria had come to her aid or observed her exploits. Menavaria had always been there where others had failed her. Despite Wrath on her hip, she felt utterly alone.

And she realized, in the moment of reflection, that her goddess's death was entirely her fault. It had been she who called upon Menavaria for help. She was the reason her beloved god was dead.

She fell to her knees, her sobs coming in heaves of pain and guilt.

I'm so sorry. I didn't know. I didn't realize what would happen. What have I done? Her internal struggle crushed her.

A tap on her shoulder snapped her back to her reality. She swiped the tears from her face and spun, being greeted by a large orc dressed in a simple robe. He smiled warmly, which unsettled her, and she instinctively reached for Wrath.

The orc laughed gently and waved his hands.

"I mean you no harm. I'm your shepherd, come to guide you."

Taken aback by his calm demeanor, Severina took a step back but did not draw her weapon. The weight of what she'd done still pressed heavily upon her, and she could only look up at the stranger with tear-filled eyes.

"Do not fret," the orc began. "I am only here to help."

"Where am I?" she managed to say.

"This is a good news, bad news situation. The key points are: You're dead. Your soul has come to a realm called the Sunless Crossing. This means one of two things: Either you are destined for resurrection back to your mortal plane, or your ultimate fate and afterlife has yet to be determined."

"Which is the good news and which is the bad?"

"That's up to you. Some souls are thrilled to learn they have a chance at resurrection. Some are absolutely horrified by it."

Dead... yes, that made sense. She had already accepted that she was dead. Nothing to be done about it. But the thought of all her friends and loved ones either being dead or suffering without her there to help filled her with grief.

She grew lightheaded. So many things were left unsaid to people she held dear. So many goodbyes she would never get to say.

"I understand how overwhelming this is, but believe me, you will get through this. And after your journey, you will learn the direction your time here will take."

"What journey?"

The shepherd only smiled and gestured for her to accompany him.

"Come with me. I have so much to show you. By the way, my name is Orvil. What's yours?"

"Severina."

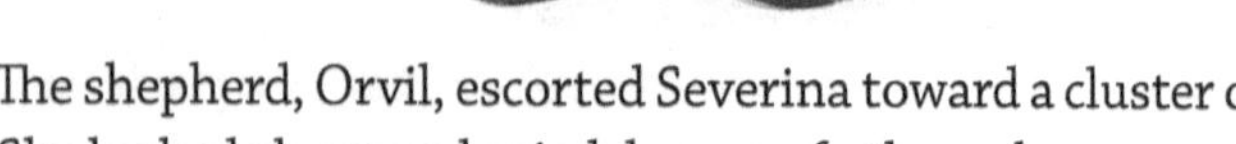

The shepherd, Orvil, escorted Severina toward a cluster of trees. She looked about and spied dozens of others she assumed to be shepherds guiding beings in the same general direction.

As they drew nearer, she noted many of the trees bore fruit. She spotted apples, pomegranates, pears, and plums. As they circled closer to the trees, she found herself tempted to pick and eat the delicious treats hanging from each branch.

She began to see more and more people ahead, each hosting expressions of confusion, fear, or apprehension. Shepherds were speaking to individuals or small groups, and those who waited outside seemed relaxed or were soon reunited by whoever they had escorted, each individual seeming confident and self-assured, or reflective and contemplative.

"Where are we headed?" Severina asked, trying to keep up with the orc.

"Welcome to the Atonement Grove."

"The what?"

"Here you will have your eyes opened to possibilities. Be mindful though, not all you see will be pleasant."

The orc led her on until they emerged in a large clearing. In the center rested a pond of the purest water she'd ever seen, crystal clear and devoid of any ash despite the weight of it outside of the trees. It had an alluring mystical quality that she couldn't quite put her finger on.

"Have a look in the water," he invited. "See what your reflection shows you."

Trepidation fluttered in her chest, but deep down, something within her knew this was the path forward. If she were lucky, maybe she'd forget what she had done to her beloved goddess with whatever she saw. Severina stepped close to the pond's edge and kneeled, leaning forward to catch her reflection in the shimmering water.

At first, she only saw the sad, disheveled half-elf woman she felt like. Sunken eyes, a downward smile, unkempt hair. Honestly, unlike the people outside, she looked dead. And she didn't care.

Severina sighed and focused on the sullen face looking back at her. Her eyes met her twin's in the water and there was nothing left in them but guilt and suffering.

Quickly she found her mind adrift, mesmerized by the subtle undulating of the still water. She felt overcome by a new sense of calm. Her pain remained with her, but somehow it felt pushed aside, compartmentalized. She drifted further away, succumbing to the water's hypnotic call. Memories of her death flashed to the forefront before older ones took their place, floating to the surface of her mind.

CHAPTER 6

Severina awoke with a start. She was nine years old, nestled under warm covers and a soft pillow in the back of a small, covered wagon. The cart had stopped moving, and through the slightly opened canvas, she could see that it was night. She heard her father conversing with other men, and though she couldn't hear the words, they all sounded fearful.

The horses neighed and grunted nervously. Then a strange animal noise rose in the distance, not purely animal though. Repeated calls gave them an intelligent feel, as if the things were signaling to each other out in the dark. If it was a language, she had no idea what it was.

Severina's heart raced and she pulled the animal skin blankets up higher, hiding within the warm folds. Her mother, a woman of elven descent, appeared at the back, throwing the canvas flap aside. She grabbed her sword from its sheath and looked at her daughter.

"Do not move. Don't do anything until we come for you."

"Mama—" But she was already gone.

Severina held her breath. Her only movement came from her index and thumb nervously rubbing the holy coin she kept in her pocket. It bore the symbol of two closed eyes and a third open eye set within the head of a battle hammer. Her mother swore she'd tell little Sevi more about this great and wondrous goddess when she was a bit older.

Then the attack came. Men cried out. Beasts snarled and grunted. Weapons clanged and rang out. The sickening noises of fatal wounds being delivered into tender flesh. She held her ears, trying to keep the sounds out. The seconds felt like hours, but the battle was over and done in but a moment.

She listened closely for any sign of her parents. Death moans and struggling movement on the dirt were all she heard. She poked her head out from her blankets, eyes fixated on the loose canvas flap at the rear of the cart.

A shadow crept across the beige cloth. Her heart raced, hoping it was her mother or father. Instead, the grotesque, skinless, dog-like face of an orc peered in at her. Blood ran from its nose and its black eyes seemed to dart randomly, unable to focus on any one thing. It staggered but still sniffed the air hungrily, the noise distorted by the freely running blood. Driven by its bloody instinct, the wounded orc snarled and started to climb into the cart.

Severina's mother stepped up behind the beast and immediately slit its green-skinned throat. The beast clutched futilely at its gushing neck and dropped out of sight, gasping and choking until silenced with one final thrust of her sword.

At last, she faced Severina, and that's when she saw the terrible gash in her mother's head. The wound bled freely from above her right eye, and despite that, she managed a faint smile, relief filling her weak voice as she called to her daughter, "Severi—" before her eyes rolled back and she fell out of sight.

Then nothing.

"Mama!" Severina cried out, then caught herself. Her parents had ordered her to stay silent and hidden. What if there were more of the creatures lurking about? She stifled her sobs as best she could and covered herself once more with her blankets.

She concentrated with all her strength to shut out the horrors outside the cart. She desperately wanted to go to her parents, but her mother's words kept her frozen in place. She had to obey. She knew it was for her safety. Still, the waking nightmare plagued her thoughts for the remainder of the night.

Daylight drew Severina back to reality. She had squinted her eyes closed so tightly after Mama disappeared. She could not face what lay in wait outside. The sun warmed the cart. The area remained still and silent. Nothing stirred.

"Mama?" she whispered. No response. She fought back tears. She had to be brave, like Papa always told her.

Be brave. Be brave, she told herself repeatedly. She crawled toward the rear of the cart, her heart beating faster with each move. The canvas flap swayed lazily in the morning breeze as she crawled toward it, hoping that one of her parents would greet her, tell her it was okay... She caught a glimpse of her mother's lifeless hand and sucked in air, shutting her eyes.

The sound of horses and a cart rolling closer snapped her into action. She returned to her hiding spot with haste, covering herself with the skins and covering her mouth. Outside, the horses came to a stop and someone jumped down and walked around the camp. Heavy footfalls. Boots. She froze, desperate to remain hidden.

In a flash of light, the back canvas was tossed aside, bathing the cart in sunlight. She held her breath. *Please go away. Please go away.*

She heard someone rifling through their belongings. After a moment, the stranger went silent.

"You can come out," said a male voice, gently. "I'm not going to hurt you. The monsters are all gone. You're safe."

Something about the voice. Fatherly. Soft. Welcoming.

Severina took the risk and slowly removed her covers.

The man before her was a portly human with a full beard and a warm smile. His eyes seemed kind. He wore not one piece of armor, only soft fancy clothes. He held out his meaty hand.

"Trust me. You're safe now, little one."

Severina timidly reached out her hand. She marked this event as the last time she would ever allow herself to feel weak and helpless.

A bustling city street found eleven-year-old Severina happily making her way through the crowds toward a dry goods shop. She carried a large burlap sack over her shoulder. From across the busy road, three young boys dressed in finery mocked and laughed at the ragamuffin girl dressed in rags.

Severina heard their slurs, but she kept moving. She had work to do, and Domlin was expecting her. The boys crossed the road and followed her at a distance, whispering to each other. She felt her anger rise, battling to suppress the fear that tried to surface. At last, she reached Domlin's shop, The Dragon's Hoard.

The Dragon's Hoard was a decent enough business, but it was more of a hobby for Domlin. He liked to maintain a clean, well-stocked larder of goods that he sold to his community at prices just barely above break-even. He even kept a few kegs on tap at the store counter for folk who wanted to visit for a spell. "The people of this town deserve to have a nice place where they can get what they need at a fair price and chat with their neighbors," Domlin would always say whenever someone suggested he raise his prices to match similar stores.

Truth was, he didn't need the money from the store. Domlin's real business was an import and export endeavor. Transporting large quantities of goods across the region was no small task. Wagons could only be built so big, and many of the roads between towns were unpaved. Make your transport too heavy and it was sure to get stuck in the mud. Send too many wagons and it became an operational nightmare, not to mention drove up costs. As a young adult, Domlin discovered he possessed a talent for the logistics of transportation and he had quietly become one of the richest men in the entire county. This was something only a select few knew for certain, as Domlin never flaunted his wealth, preferring the simple life, tending his shop, and caring for his adopted daughter.

Severina entered the store and closed the door behind her. "I'm back," she called out.

She made her way past an aisle of shelves stacked with containers of various grains, dried meats, sugar, and rarities from far-off lands.

"I have the nuts."

From behind a curtain, the stout, burly man stepped forth. His beard had grayed some since he rescued her that terrible day two years prior.

"Wonderful, child. Place it in the back if you would please."

As she ventured to the back room, she caught a glimpse of the ruffians peering in the window. Eventually, they left, but something told her this was going to be a problem.

Severina spent the day sweeping the store, stocking shelves, assisting customers with a smile, and helping Domlin where she was able. He had treated her like a daughter since the moment they met, and in this cruel world, she had not taken that lightly. Even though she still missed her parents every day, she appreciated the turn life had taken. She had a good home, food, clothing, and kindness.

She possessed one demon: her rage. Since that infamous dark day, she found herself quick to anger and lashing out when temperance was more appropriate. Domlin saw this streak developing in her and realized she'd need an outlet. On top of that, he knew this town had its share of ne'er-do-wells who would undoubtedly view Severina as a potential target. One day, after the shop closed, Domlin took her to the blacksmith, Kravell.

The late middle-aged man looked up and wiped soot from his brow as they entered. Severina, while never having met him formally, was pretty sure she'd seen this same man passed out in the gutter outside the local tavern a time or two.

"What can I do for you, Dom?"

Domlin placed a hand on Sevi's shoulder. "Lessons, Kravell. I'm hoping we can arrange some lessons for my daughter here... *paid* lessons, of course."

Kravell looked Severina up and down, then shook his head. "Got no time to babysit whelps."

He returned to his hammering. Severina felt the rage bubbling in her. How dare this lowly, dirty man be so rude? Why had Domlin brought her here? He could afford the finest sword masters in the realm.

"Please, Kravell," Domlin said, "She's... I think you and she have more in common than you realize."

At this, Kravell stopped and turned back. "The red sight?"

Domlin nodded.

"What's—" Severina started, but stopped when she saw Kravell approaching. The old blacksmith crouched to meet her eyeline, meeting her gaze appraisingly.

"Let me ask you something, child. You ever get mad?"

Severina nodded.

"You *ever* get *really* mad? I'm talking so mad you want to burn the whole world down? I'm talking ALL of it, every building, every town, every city... every *person*."

Severina took a step back, her mouth falling open.

"I didn't want you to scare her," Domlin protested.

But Severina wasn't scared. She was shocked. How could he know?

Kravell stood up straight. "The Red Sight is just a fancy term for a special kind of anger and fury. You don't even got to answer me, I can see it." To Domlin, he added, "Start bringing her to the field out back in the mornings, early. And I'll take the first week's pay upfront."

Despite Severina's impressed feeling regarding the old blacksmith's ability to get a read on her so quickly, she still held reservations about him as a combat instructor.

It took all of one training session for those reservations to dissipate into nothingness. Kravell was old, walked with a limp, and reeked of whiskey, but his remarkable skill with hand-to-hand combat as well as martial weapons became instantly apparent. More often than not, Severina returned home with an extra bruise or two, but she didn't mind. In fact, she was happier than she'd ever been.

Kravell began with basic brawling—fists, feet, dodging, tumbling. After 6 months, he knew this child was ready for weapons. He first started with the dagger. Her small stature aided in her skill, making her swift and agile. Soon he wanted to move up to swords, but she was still too small to wield a blade of that size. Instead, he upgraded her to a small mace and shield training.

One training session when Severina was having a particularly tough time mastering a maneuver, Kravell noticed her rubbing something between her index finger and thumb.

"What's that you got there?" he asked.

"What? Oh, it's this holy coin I've had since I was little. I tend to play with it when frustrated or nervous. It's supposed to be a symbol of some god... but, uh, my mother passed before she could tell me much about it."

"Let's have a look."

She held up the coin with two closed eyes and a third open eye set within the head of a battle hammer. Kravell chuckled.

"What's funny?" Severina asked.

"You're in the right place, girl. That there is the symbol of Menavaria, goddess of instinct and war. If you're going to walk the path of the sword, she's a good one to have in your corner. Now! Enough rest! Pick up your weapon and let's have at it!"

Months passed, and she finally grew into swords. He was thrilled to place a blade in her hands at last, eager to see how she progressed her skills. Now, three months into sword training, he found himself proud of this protégé. She excelled in this elegant weapon and, over time, he found that the discipline of the blade aided in quieting the beast inside her.

One day, they sat on the ground, huffing and puffing from the day's sparring session. Kravell took a long pull from a waterskin and handed it over to Severina. After taking a drink herself, she finally worked up the courage to ask something she'd wanted to know ever since the first day.

"You're such a skilled warrior... how... I mean, why..."

"Why am I nothing more than a poor, dirty, drunken blacksmith?"

"I didn't want to say it like that."

Kravell sighed. "I was a soldier once. I was a *good* soldier... great even. Believe it or not, I'm technically a knight."

Severina spat water out. "You're lying."

"I'm not. I still have the royal decree."

"Knights get land."

"And servants, and a keep, and plenty of esteem. Yes, I had all that once."

"What happened?"

"Bad habits. I fell into gambling and drinking. Let my rage get the better of me one too many times... I lost it all. That's probably why Domlin wanted you to specifically train with me.

Your anger, your rage. It can be useful, but if you aren't careful, it stops becoming a tool for you and instead becomes your master. Then *it* uses *you*. And you're looking at the result when that happens. Honestly, I'm lucky I'm still alive at all... had to give up all my vices."

Severina watched him pull a flask from his pocket and arched her eyebrow.

He shrugged. "Okay, all my vices save for one. I'm not a monk, for gods' sake."

Despite his best efforts, Kravell had grown fond of Severina. He'd never had children of his own, or a marriage, for that matter. He'd spent his social time in brothels and taverns, and so the time for fatherhood had passed. In Severina, he saw a chance to hold on to a glimpse of what might have been.

Severina, standing in the center of a training circle surrounded by wooden dummy enemies, looked at Kravell. Sweat poured from her skin and she panted heavily. Fresh slices and notches peppered the dummy targets.

"Well?" she inquired.

Kravell smiled and said only, "Again."

As she maneuvered through her routine, Severina brought her thoughts to the well-dressed ruffians. Their wealthy parents shielded them from any consequences of their actions, which emboldened them to harass anyone in town they chose. And it seemed now she was their target of ridicule.

She sliced and thrust in a deadly dance, selecting specific body parts on the dummies—a wrist to disable weapons, a knee to topple large foes. Only after the crippling wounds would she move in for the killing blow.

Kravell decided soon she would be ready for live targets on which to practice.

In the alley behind The Dragon's Hoard, Severina shook a broom free of dust and debris. The three wealthy boys, all a bit older and much larger than Severina, appeared. She didn't know their names, only that they meant harm.

"Do you smell that?" began the apparent leader, wearing a fancy cap. "Something stinks."

"Yeah, like a moldy girl," mused a different boy with a blue vest laden with ruby buttons.

"Look at her clothes," laughed the third lad, who wore silver rings upon his fingers. He had a reputation for shredding people's faces with those rings.

The leader quipped, "I bet she wishes she had dresses and finery and could sip tea all day. Don't you?"

Severina said nothing. She just let the words wash over her, fueling her. She squeezed the broom handle tighter.

"What's the point?" asked blue vest. "No one would ever want to court her."

"Yeah, she's right where she should be, down in the muck, cleaning up after respectable citizens," spat the ring bearer.

"You should leave," Severina snarled in a low whisper.

Ignoring her, the bullies pressed on.

"And her father can't afford proper employees. Has to put his daughter to work!"

"Wait—he's not even her father," exclaimed the leader. "Of course, he treats her like a slave. He doesn't love her. Her own parents didn't love her enough to keep her—"

Severina's broom handle slammed into the leader's mouth, cutting off his vile words. The rough handle delivered a shred to the roof of his mouth and planted splinters on his tongue. She withdrew the handle before the boys knew what had happened and wasted no time in launching a barrage of crippling attacks.

She smashed the right knee of the blue vest boy, dropping him. She spun and struck the ring boy at the elbow of his ring hand, sending him stumbling, clutching at his limp arm. The leader in the cap was too busy coughing and spitting out blood to avoid her next assault as she swiped the handle across his nose, dislocating it. He cried out and fell back on his ass.

"And this is a warning. Come by my shop again and I'll do much worse."

Domlin stepped out into the alley searching for his young ward and was shocked by the scene before him. He recovered his senses and quickly looked around for witnesses.

"Get inside, Sevi," he ordered. She snapped out of her fury-state and rushed into the shop. Domlin surveyed the damage as he fought back a grin, knowing these lads most likely deserved what they got, and bent down to help them to their feet.

The leader swatted Domlin's hand away. "We don't need help, peasant."

The powerful man stood straight and changed his demeanor to better suit the situation. "Well then, I suggest you do as my daughter says and never return. Maybe next time I let her finish what she started. Now get out of here. You're bleeding all over my alley."

Taken aback by the brazen comment, the boys turned tail and made a hasty exit.

Domlin knew this was only the beginning of their troubles.

The next day, four men of the town guard entered The Dragon's Hoard. Domlin already knew what was coming. They would take him before the magistrate over the incident.

The front guard opened a scroll and read, "By order of Magistrate Perkins, the child Severina is to appear before the court to answer accusations of assault against—"

"The *child*?" protested Domlin. "She can't go to court. She is but eleven."

"That is the order, sir. You may accompany her."

"Severina was the victim. Why does she have to—"

"The accusers tell a different tale. Where is the girl?"

"I'll get her. We'll comply, no problem. This is a big mistake though."

Severina and Domlin were taken into the local keep, the metal gate slamming down behind them. The guards escorted the two through a courtyard, a foyer, and finally into a large chamber filled with benches. A raised table stood at one end, with two smaller tables in front of it. Behind the large table sat Lorien Perkins, the local magistrate. She dressed in finery that seemed more suited to a ball than a court hearing and her long hair rested mainly atop her head in a fancy up-do. Though she'd been a magistrate for many years, she maintained a youthful appearance.

"Bring the child to me," commanded Lorien.

Domlin was relieved not to see the accusing parties. If this hearing was only between them and the magistrate, he might be able to talk their way out of this mess.

The guards led them to the front and motioned for them to sit behind one of the tables. Severina nervously settled into an uncomfortable chair, hands clasping her trousers beneath the table to try to hide her uncertainty over having no idea what to expect.

The magistrate looked them over. Her countenance was not quite scornful, but nor was it pleasant. Domlin couldn't get a read on her.

Addressing Severina, the magistrate began, "You had quite the day yesterday."

Severina was at a loss on what to say or do. Domlin gave her a gentle nudge and a nod.

"Y-yes, your majesty," she managed to say.

Lorien smiled. "Magistrate will do. I'm not royalty. You, my dear, are being accused of assault against three of our city's most prominent families. They are saying it's an unforgivable outrage. They are saying it's a level of audacity deserving of the most severe punishment."

She let the statements hang in the air for a brief moment.

"But *they* are not the magistrate, *I* am. And *I* say, it's long overdue someone taught those spoiled brats a lesson."

The magistrate's expression softened into a calm smile, while Severina and Domlin traded looks of confusion and shock.

Magistrate Lorien continued, "Those boys have caused more than enough trouble in my city. Bravo to you, Severina."

Still apprehensive, she replied, "T-thank you, Magistrate."

"The families are furious, which is quite amusing to me."

"But they are powerful, with much influence," reminded Domlin.

"That may be, but *I* do not answer to them."

"But surely you can see my concern for Severina's safety now."

"Yes. I have no doubt the child can handle herself in a scrap, but there is concern over your shop. These families do have powerful friends that can make your life hell. Even if I were to add protection for you both, I'm sure they would find a way to do you harm."

"Can't you use your influence to stop them?"

"If only I could rely on my power. Governmental politics is a many-layered, oft untrustworthy monster. Sure, they'd smile to my face and promise fealty. But I could never trust that they'd actually comply when my back is turned"

Domlin sighed, frustrated at the seeming lack of direction. "Then what are we to do?"

Lorien rose from her chair and made her way down to their level. Her slender figure glided down the steps with her dress undulating gracefully behind her. She approached them warmly, smiling broadly.

"I may have a solution if you'll hear me out."

Back at the shop, Domlin couldn't stop pacing.

"Is this madness? It feels like madness."

"But it would solve our problems, right?"

"It would. It would. But are you prepared for such a change? Am I? It's just too much to consider."

"We have to be quick though. She said so."

"But *marriage*!? It's so much so fast. I don't know how I feel about someone marrying me for my money."

"It wasn't just your money. Like she said, *this may fall together quite nicely*. She has the noble title and the legal authority, but it sounds like her estate's coffers are running a bit dry. You have no title, but plenty of coin. And she *did* mention she's always found you handsome..."

"She was just saying that—"

"No way! She was smiling and everything! But ... what do you think of her? Do you find her attractive? Do you think she's a good woman?"

Domlin sighed and said, "Yes ... on both accounts."

"Then why not? Security. Wealth. A better life. And we'll still be together."

"But what about you, Sevi? Are you good with having a new mother?"

"She... she won't be my mother. That will never happen. But I get a sense she is kind and that will be enough... I think."

"Well, this is certainly an adventure I didn't expect." After sighing heavily, Domlin took her hands in his, smiling at his daughter.

"If you're sure about this."

"I am." Severina gave an assured nod.

"Then I guess I'm going to be married!"

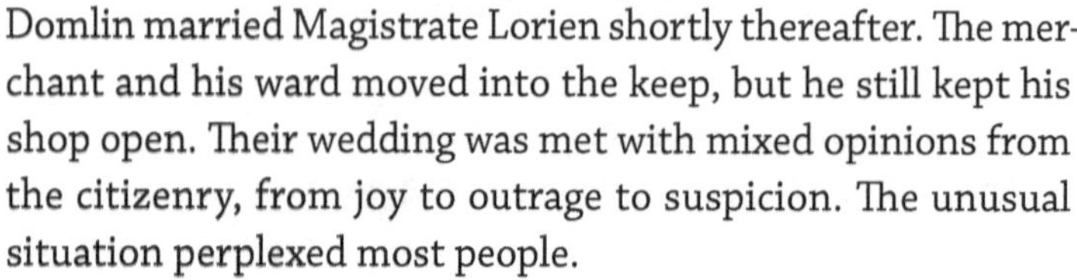

Domlin married Magistrate Lorien shortly thereafter. The merchant and his ward moved into the keep, but he still kept his shop open. Their wedding was met with mixed opinions from the citizenry, from joy to outrage to suspicion. The unusual situation perplexed most people.

Within a few months, the townsfolk found other musings to dwell on and gossip about and the new family was no longer the headline of the day. Inside the keep, life together was an adjustment. In the beginning, Lorien had Domlin and Severina sleeping in their own chambers, far from her own. But she insisted they had meals together and scheduled many activities with them. She definitely had a process in mind for them to eventually become a family and perhaps even find love.

The ire from the influential families of the bullies dissipated in light of the new circumstances. Now they were forced to address Domlin and Severina with respect. Feigned or sincere, it did not matter. Their former target had escaped their clutches. She knew peace in her life for the first time in a long time.

As Severina grew into adolescence, her beauty blossomed, as did her social skills. She found she suddenly had many suitors. While she found herself curious and wanting to be near these gentlemen, she mostly found the whole idea of courtship amusing and couldn't take it seriously.

Lorien had become a dear friend and a genuine motherly figure, though Severina could not bring herself to address her as such and remained Lorien in name. Lorien helped her navigate womanhood as she discovered new things about herself almost daily, and Severina was eternally grateful for this loving support. She spent most mornings lovingly brushing Severina's hair and having their treasured whispered girl talk.

Domlin and Lorien had grown in both friendship and love. Their relationship had shifted from a marriage of convenience to a genuine love story, with him courting her even though they were married, and she let him. Through acts of kindness and romance, he showed her his character, and now Domlin and Lorien shared quarters and were inseparable most days.

Domlin had hired help to run the shop, freeing his time to devote to his marriage and assisting Lorien with her governance. She appreciated his business acumen and sought his advice regularly on such issues.

And when the day was done, they cherished their time together: Dinners in the manor house. Nights in the town. Rides in the woods. Celebrations in the ballroom. Their lives became filled with romance.

The Duke and Duchess of the realm, Hollister and Winter, gave the couple their blessing and welcomed the merchant and his adopted daughter into their inner circle. In fact, as Domlin's business acumen grew more evident in matters of governing, the royal family was overjoyed to have him in the fold.

Now fourteen, life was good for Severina. Finally.

But that peace was short-lived, for Severina was dealt a new complication to contend with on the day she turned fifteen. For on that day, Severina discovered magic.

She had been out for a birthday ride, a solo adventure to settle her mind before the evening's festivities, when she came across an overgrown trail cutting through a densely wooded forest. She had every intention of riding right past this foreboding trail, but then the strange lights of red, purple, and yellow burst in the sky just beneath the treetops. The mystical balls of light danced around each other, soaring and diving in the air.

Severina couldn't help but be drawn to the oddity. She dismounted and led her horse into the overgrowth. The shadows crept in and blocked out more and more of the sun as she pressed onward. The dancing lights were too wonderful to resist, and she felt no threat, especially with her sword sheathed on her hip.

Soon the path opened wide once again, revealing a simple cabin off the path, hidden in the underbrush. The humble structure with the thatched roof rested at the center of a clearing. In front of the home, a gray-haired woman danced and spun gracefully, dressed in animal furs, weathered cloth, and no shoes. Her wrinkles showed the beginnings of age, though she still held a mostly youthful appearance. Severina guessed the woman was a bit older than Lorien.

She froze when she spied Severina staring dumbfounded at her. The dancing lights above her head dissolved instantly. The two looked each other up and down.

"Well, are you going to join me or not?" she asked.

Severina stepped into the clearing, curiosity overcoming any fear of this magical stranger.

"The look on your face tells me you've never seen such things," she continued.

"Who are you?" Severina asked.

"I thought my rumored reputation would precede me. I am Ursen... or as some have called me: Ursen the Wretched."

Indeed, Severina had heard the name. Stories of the witch of the wood had been told to frighten children for decades, but Severina couldn't imagine them being true.

"You don't look like you eat children," replied Severina.

Ursen grinned. "Not this week anyway."

"How are you able to do that with the lights?"

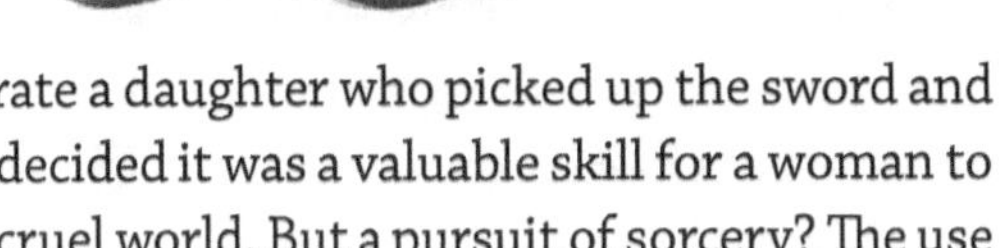

"Child, let me show you wonders you've never dreamed of."

Lorien would tolerate a daughter who picked up the sword and trained, had even decided it was a valuable skill for a woman to have in this often cruel world. But a pursuit of sorcery? The use of magic had been outlawed many years before and Severina was sure she would receive a lecture on how "the dark arts were unbecoming of a proper lady."

Severina knew the law all too well. Magic use of any kind was banned, punishable by jail and possibly death. She understood what consequences might await her, but the allure of magic was too great to resist, and Severina found herself spending more and more of her days in the enchanting hut of Ursen the Wretched.

Ursen was a woman of nature and preferred the company of flora and fauna over people. She was amused by her namesake, laughing that her reputation as "wretched" helped keep others away.

She would often jest, "It's been a while since I met a person I didn't instantly want to banish to another plane of existence… so for that reason alone, I guess you're worth teaching."

Ursen started the child off with the simplest of magic: igniting a fire, creating artificial light, and dancing smoke. To her credit, Severina was by no means a "natural" at the arcane arts. She had to work for every inch of progress. She found the challenge invigorating, and every stumble in her training only hardened her resolve.

Severina practiced constantly every minute she spent in the woods. Unable to reveal her new skills to her family and friends, she needed every moment with Ursen to count.

"Teach me more," Severina pleaded with fire in her eyes as they sat together outside Ursen's hut, enjoying the sun.

"Slow down, girl," she laughed. "We have time."

"I don't have time, Ursen. Life is not promised."

Weeks became months, and months became years. Severina managed to keep her magic pursuits hidden from her adoptive parents, but she suspected Ursen had concocted some form of magic to aid in this subterfuge. Whatever the case, Severina was grateful to be able to study wizardry as well as swordplay. She experimented with the various casting methods. Spells could be channeled through "focus" items, such as wands or rings. They could also be born of verbal incantations and material components. However, Severina found herself gravitating toward the method many found to be most challenging: spell memorization. Through meticulously writing arcane runes in one's spellbook and committing them to perfect memory, a magic user could theoretically cast spells instantaneously with little more than a flick of the wrist. Severina immediately saw the value this skill could have in combat. Taking this route, while the most difficult, just seemed right to Severina. It felt as if she was casting the spells from her soul.

Severina pushed herself harder and faster in her studies, obsessed with learning all she could. Ursen warned her against rushing her lessons for fear she would not be able to properly control the magic, but the stubborn teen wouldn't listen. More than a few times Severina accidentally leveled distant sections of the forest or scorched trees with her lack of control. But she would not be deterred.

Ursen had graduated the teen up to orbs of fire, auras of deadly frost, and even calling down lightning. Secretly, she was curious how far this girl could go with her skills; how far she would push herself. In her heart, she knew she'd teach Severina everything. Every bit of knowledge she had to give. And what a marvel she would become.

By the time Severina turned seventeen, she was a force to be reckoned with. Deadly with the sword and mighty with magic, she felt confident she could handle any threat life threw at her.

Until her parents informed her the Duke and Duchess's son wished to court her.

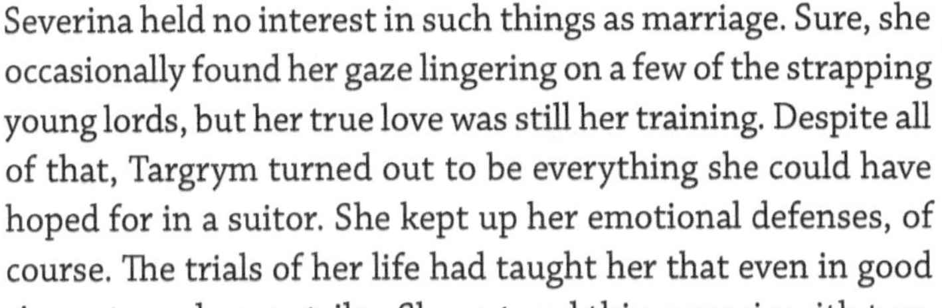

Severina held no interest in such things as marriage. Sure, she occasionally found her gaze lingering on a few of the strapping young lords, but her true love was still her training. Despite all of that, Targrym turned out to be everything she could have hoped for in a suitor. She kept up her emotional defenses, of course. The trials of her life had taught her that even in good times, tragedy can strike. She entered this scenario with trepidation and a bit of curiosity.

Hollister and Winter felt Severina was a strong and strategic match for their son. This young girl rose to prominence from a tragic childhood.

Severina was fast becoming a "woman of the people," and Hollister very much liked the politics of that. Winter cared more for her son's happiness and seeing him with Severina assured her she'd made the right choice.

As for Targrym, he admired the fierce spirit within Severina. Her boldness was matched only by her beauty. Their introduction was formal and stuffy, with both sets of parents hovering and making the room awkward.

He was certainly handsome—trimmed dark hair, piercing eyes, a firm jaw, and a cultured demeanor, and it was easy to find him attractive and charming.

Once the niceties fell away and people settled into conversations, Targrym leaned in close to her and whispered, "Shall we leave these elders to their tedious chat?"

"I thought you'd never ask," she replied, taking his hand with a stifled laugh.

They walked the garden of the castle, wandering slowly as the conversation warmed them.

"Apologies for the awkward arrangement," he began.

"I must admit, I was surprised. I'm not royalty. I've got no high blood."

"That's actually what drew me to you. No pretense. No snobbish lineage."

"And your parents?"

"Oh, they are quite fond of you."

"This just feels so surreal."

"And that's why I like you."

Targrym proved to be a patient and respectful suitor, letting their relationship develop at a slower, more natural pace. Severina found herself impressed by his resilience in holding off the Duke and Duchesses's insistence they be "married yesterday."

Consumed with her swordplay training and her secret magic tutelage, Severina had no intention of making room in her life for love or romance. She liked to tell herself it was because she simply didn't have the time, but part of her knew it was largely due to a fear of allowing herself to get close to someone on such a deep level. It had taken years for Domlin to get past her emotional walls, and although she loved Lorien, she had not let herself bond deeply.

Fear of abandonment still held Severina prisoner. And so, it was with Targrym that she felt the void would be filled. She liked him quite a lot, and he seemed to truly understand her— at least the parts of her she allowed him to see.

But he eventually won her over. He wasn't pushy, gave her space, brought her thoughtful small gifts, and never asked her to change. He asked all the right questions, making a great effort to get to know her. As she slowly lowered her walls, their courtship progressed smoothly and naturally.

Of course, Domlin and Lorien were overjoyed. Their daughter would have a secure and happy life, and in the end, that's all they wanted for her. Even if the young man had been a pauper, if he made her smile, that was enough for the two of them.

A year passed and Targrym proposed. It happened on the eve of Severina's 18th birthday party. Her parents had created a celebration for the entire town. First, a festival in the town square with games, dancers, plays, and a feast. In the evening, the local social elites made their way by invitation into the castle for a more intimate affair. The guests were treated to the finest wines and meads, a feast fit for a king with exotic meats and fruits, and a famous band of bards brought in from afar.

Severina was overwhelmed with joy. Never in her life had she felt secure and safe enough to let herself feel this level of happiness. So when Targrym bent the knee and revealed a stunning diamond ring in front of the entire crowd, her tears came in uncontrollable bursts.

"Severina, daughter of Domlin and Lorien, would you kindly do me the honor of becoming my wife so that we may live out our days in the same joy we share this night?"

Her voice trembling, Severina answered as only she would, "Hell yes!"

The crowd, including her parents and the Duke and Duchess, laughed and cheered with a resounding, "Huzzah!"

He twirled her about as the bards played on. Everyone congratulated them and shared in the dance. Domlin wiped away tears of elation. Lorien took his hand and laid her head on his shoulder.

But their joy didn't last. A month later, war broke out along the kingdom's western border. King Aslor called up all his commanders, generals, and able-bodied soldiers to the front lines. This included both Duke Hollister and Targrym.

Severina wept on the day of her beloved's departure. She didn't know when she'd see him again, if ever. The parting was torture. The fear of abandonment rose with her like a poisonous phoenix, overwhelming her. She refused to let her fiancé see her this way, especially when he had war and death to contend with. She kept her crushing sorrow to herself.

Targrym left on horseback with his father and a contingent of warriors, all ready to die for king and country. The echoes of their wives and mothers mourning followed them away from their homes.

For days, Severina didn't leave her room. She didn't show up for training, keeping the blacksmith waiting in the castle courtyard. She didn't venture into the woods for training with the Ursen. She barely ate. She spoke to no one.

Eventually, at Domlin's insistence, Severina emerged from her room. After a much-needed bath and a hot meal, she began to feel herself again. Melancholy overshadowed her every moment, but she went through the motions of the day. Wedding planning. Sword training. And a return to her secret visits in the woods.

Most in the town felt sympathy for her. Many wives shared her fate and felt a kinship with her. While Severina appreciated all the kindness and well-wishes, she felt unable to shake the depression and worry in every moment. Was Targrym safe? Was he alive? Would he come back to her?

News from the war front came via town crier every few weeks or so. The king's forces were believed to be having success in repelling the invaders, but both sides had suffered heavy losses, and it quickly became clear that the toll of this war would be significant.

Hearing news from the front was about the only time she left her chambers. She gobbled up every scrap of information, every rumor, anything that might indicate the status of her betrothed.

She carried on like this for over a year. Her 19th birthday was a subdued event, with no one in the village feeling like celebrating anything. Food had grown scarcer as supplies were desperately needed at the front line. The news coming in from the war became almost repetitive: Sometimes they won battles, and sometimes they lost. The one fixed constant was death. All news, good and bad, came with death.

Severina's despair was matched by that of the townsfolk.

Finally, a letter from Targrym reached her. It was months old, but she relished every word. He spoke of longing for her and of the plans for their wedding upon his return. He touched on the horrors of the war, and she imagined the true atrocities were simply too terrible to write about. She held the letter close and let hope wash over her.

She continued her trainings with renewed vigor. After so many years working with the blacksmith, she was now able to best him more often than not. Likewise, in the forest, Ursen watched her pupil's prowess grow until she became a powerful sorceress in her own right. The thought of reuniting with her fiancé gave her the focus she needed to excel.

Severina even rekindled her wedding plans, calling in seamstresses, bakers, caterers, and designers. This would be a wedding for the ages. A celebration of love and homecoming. She only hoped the reunion would be swift.

Then one magical day, some eighteen months into the war, the town crier announced victory for King Aslor. The military crushed the enemy at last and the men were on their way home. The word went out through the entire realm.

Finally, Targrym returned home. He set foot in the village with only half of the men he'd left with, his father not among them.

Severina rushed into the town square where all the families embraced their loved ones and wrapped her arms around Targrym. He returned her warmth and kissed her passionately.

The Duchess had no such reunion waiting for her, and few others shared her precise pain.

Swept up with a mix of joy, relief, and grief, the town remained torn between celebration and mourning. Revelers embraced the downtrodden and mourners leaned on their joyful friends.

The weeks gave way from rest and recovery to rebuilding and replenishing. The village rallied to ramp up the sowing of crops, the tending of farm animals, and the nurturing of vegetables and fruits. And with Severina's and Targrym's wedding fast approaching, the people had something to look forward to.

For modesty and propriety, Targrym stayed in his parents' castle during the preparations, but he'd make the two-hour ride as often as he could to spend time with his beloved. On the days he was not by her side, Severina felt longing for him. Lorien took note and let Severina know that's what love felt like.

Her joy was restored and Severina's heart overflowed. Life had taken such a turn, and she marveled at how her path had changed so much. She still missed her parents, but Domlin and Lorien had stepped into the roles with more love than she could have ever hoped for.

Just days before the wedding, Severina decided to surprise Targrym with lunch at his castle. She packed bread, cheeses, meats, and wine in a basket and rode out in the morning.

She smiled as she entered the courtyard and handed the reins of her steed over to the waiting stable boy. She glided into the castle, servants bowing respectfully, and she asked them to never do that.

She rushed up to Targrym's chambers and found the study empty. She dared to approach the bedroom. A scandalous move to be sure, but they were about to be husband and wife, anyway. Rules and decorum be damned.

She opened the bedroom door and her world shattered. There, in the bed that was meant to be hers soon, lay Targrym with another woman. She dropped the basket to the floor, alerting the couple to her presence. They sprang from the bed to dress.

"Severina," he struggled to say as he put on his pants. "What are you doing here? I was not expecting—"

"Clearly you weren't," she quipped coldly.

The woman's clothes were the modest servant's attire.

To the woman, Severina asked, "How long have you two been intimate? Do not lie to me."

The woman knew all too well Severina's reputation and skill in combat. "Since before he left for war, ma'am."

Fire in her eyes and ice in her veins, Severina turned to Targrym. "This is what you think of us? This is what you think of me? I thought you loved me."

"I do, my sweetheart. I do. This was nothing but a tryst. A fling. It means nothing."

The servant looked stung.

"How could you do this to us?" cried Severina.

"We can move past this. I want to marry you and live out our days together. We can still have all we dreamed about."

"No. No, it's over."

Seeing his plans crumbling, Targrym shifted to a stern demeanor—hoping to set her straight and salvage the relationship.

"Severina. As your royal and husband-to-be, I decree that we shall get married, and we shall be happy. And you will forget all this nonsense."

The audacity of the comments stirred a rage within Severina that had long laid dormant. Not since that day in the alley with lordling brats had she allowed it to bubble this close to the surface. It roiled within her, stronger and hotter than ever. She clenched her fists tight and shut her eyes.

The servant backed away to a far corner of the room, unwilling to step between the pair.

"Severina, do you hear me?" he commanded. "You will do as I say."

"No!" she screamed, and before she realized what she was doing, a bolt of arcane violet energy burst from her hand toward her fiancé. It struck Targrym in the chest, tossing him back against the wall. As he collapsed, the magic dissipated, leaving a sizzling scar on his chest.

The servant screamed at the display and fled the room, rushing past Severina, who was fixated on Targrym's unconscious body. The servant's cries echoed down the hall and through the castle.

Targrym stirred, shaking his head as the realization came over him and he saw the wound. His gaze shot up to his bride. Severina stood trembling, staring at her own hands. He sat up quickly, outrage taking hold.

"Magic?!" he barked. "You're a sorceress?!"

"I—I'm sorry. I didn't mean..."

Targrym stood up and shouted, "Guards! Guards!"

Severina panicked and bolted. Fleeing down the hall, down the stairs, into the foyer, only to be confronted by five guards.

"Halt!" ordered the leader, swords drawn.

Severina was weaponless, except for her magic, and she dared not use that again. Instead of fighting, she pivoted and ran deeper into the castle. She fled into the dining hall and the kitchen. She rushed past the surprised cooks and maids and out the side door, the guards not far behind.

The stables came into view. *Almost there.*

Halfway across the courtyard, more guards spilled forth from the stables, another five. She turned, but the original guards were nearly on top of her. She froze. She panicked. The guards closed in.

Targrym stepped out onto the front porch, still shirtless, his smoking wound on full display.

"Surrender. It will be easier for everyone. Your parents included," he said in a subtle threatening tone.

His mother, Winter, came out onto the porch, still dressed in her black mourner's garb. "What is the meaning of all this?" she snapped, looking at Severina, the guards, and then finally her son, before spotting the burn mark on his chest.

"What? What happened to you?"

Targrym nodded toward Severina. "She happened."

Winter's eyes narrowed, the kindly widow gone. "Explain."

"Apparently, my bride is a damn wizard. She can cast spells," he yelled, throwing his hands up in frustration.

The guards moved in and took hold of Severina while she was distracted listening to Winter and Targrym.

Winter turned to her, anger etched on her face. "Why, Severina?"

"Ask your son and his lover," she spat.

The picture became clear to Winter now, and she turned to face her son. "Go back inside and get dressed. By the gods, you are royalty. Act like it."

"But what about her?" he complained, gesturing sharply to Severina.

"Leave her to me. Now go," Winter said sharply, leaving no room for argument.

Targrym looked frustrated with more to say, but obeyed his mother and left.

Winter stepped down from the front entrance and approached her future daughter-in-law.

The guards held Severina tight, though there was no need. She would never harm Winter.

"I understand your anger, Severina," she began, standing very close to her now. "I really do. In your position, I would have done the same, though not with magic. I am not armed with such gifts."

"I'm sorry. I really didn't mean to. I saw them together in his bed. In *our* bed. I lost myself."

"That is unfortunate for us all. You do understand we must abide by the law. You will stand trial for assaulting a royal and for using magic. There will be no wedding."

Severina fought back tears. "And what of Targrym? No consequences for him?"

"What he did was both foul and cruel, but no crime was committed by him. It's simply in a man's nature."

"I don't accept that. How is that right?" she pleaded.

"Child, you are a female and a witch. Righteous justice awaits you now."

She acknowledged the guards and said, "Bind her hands and gag her so that she may cast no more magic. We've had enough mischief for one day."

Severina spent her time in the prison below the Duchess's castle. Her parents were allowed to visit her, but only to look in on her and verify she was well and not being mistreated. Lorien sobbed while Domlin held back tears. They were shaken and confused.

"Magic, Sevi?" was all Domlin could say, his disappointment thick in his tone.

Targrym ventured down once as well and only smirked at her. Gone was the loving fiancé she'd known; replaced by a sinister creep who now mocked her predicament. She kicked herself for being so utterly fooled by this man.

Winter even visited her and was kind in the way she could be. "I'm sorry it has to end this way. I truly would have loved having you for a daughter... We could have overlooked a scorned fiancée's retaliation. But the spellcasting is... It is unforgivable. I'm sorry."

Food was given to her, the gag removed only for eating, then quickly replaced. The guards were under strict orders to not allow her any opportunity to use magic.

In just a few days, the trial commenced, held in the town at Lorien's keep. Magistrates and royals from all over the realm came to witness the story of the decade. Sitting in the high seat at the end of the great hall in judgment was the king's wizened advisor, Khybus who wore robes of orange and blue that cascaded down to the floor.

He stroked his long gray beard as Severina was brought in by Winter's guards. They escorted her to a circular dais with a railing that sat before the judge, and the guards locked her chains to the railing, restricting her movement before removing the gag.

Severina looked around. In addition to the royalty present, she spotted her parents seated not far away. Their expressions were a mix of despair and anxiety.

Khybus leaned forward and spoke in a gravelly voice, "Am I to understand you weaponized a spell against the Duchess's son, your fiancé, Targrym?"

"Yes, your honor," she replied sorrowfully.

Khybus leaned back and looked over the young man in question.

"He seems relatively unharmed. That bodes well for you, child. Tell me what happened."

Severina relayed the entire tale, start to finish. And when she was done, she looked to Khybus for his reaction.

After a long pause, he said, "And you learned the casting of spells from the hermit in the woods, Ursen the Wretched."

She did her best to hide her shock at those words. *How could he have known her name?*

"No. I don't know that name," she replied.

"Lying can only harm you," he began.

At that moment, guards escorted a bound and gagged Ursen into the room. Gasps rose from the crowd. Some were shocked a sorceress lived nearby, while others knew of the hermit but couldn't believe she was still alive.

Ursen looked lovingly at Severina for a brief moment, expressing all her emotions through her eyes before turning her attention to Khybus.

"Please, I do not know this woman," Severina urged, shaking her head.

"Your loyalty to your teacher is misplaced. She attacked the guards on sight. We know who and what she is. And she will be executed for her crimes."

She glared at Khybus. "Then why bring her out to stand trial?"

"Oh no. You misunderstand. She is not on trial. I wanted to see the reactions of you both. To show you that even those believed to be powerful are not above the laws of the realm,"

Khybus admitted, flicking his wrist toward the guards, who proceeded to drag the hermit from the chamber.

"She did nothing," Severina pleaded. "She's just an old woman."

"With a fierce fireball."

"Please, just let her go."

"Impossible. Now, what to do with you?"

Severina cast her eyes downward, awaiting judgment. She felt ashamed for putting her parents through this and outraged at what Targrym did.

Khybus cleared his throat.

"Targrym's behavior was most unbecoming, immature, lecherous, lewd, and cruel. But not illegal."

The crowd murmured in agreement.

"You, on the other hand, not only broke our most exalted law, but attacked a member of the royal family."

"And I'm sorry for my actions," she admitted.

"I'm taking that into consideration as I decide your fate. Is there anyone present who wishes to speak on the accused's behalf?"

The murmurs of the chamber fell silent and people looked amongst one another. To Severina's shock, no one stood up for her.

At last, her parents rose. Domlin struggled to find the words at first before patting the railing before him. "Sir, my daughter has made mistakes, but she's a good person. Her heart is pure. I beg for mercy. She will promise to never use magic again, and she will make amends to the Duchess's family. Please."

"Pure of heart?" Khybus chuckled. "I suspect Targrym and his new scar would disagree."

Lorien spoke up. "Please. We are more than happy to compensate. Whatever it takes."

Severina stood motionless, but inside she was a raging storm of emotion. She'd lost her fiancé, the life she had wanted, Ursen, and now even her town abandoned her. And she noted the shame on her parents' faces. Everything was crumbling.

She turned to her parents and mouthed "I love you" to them and they did the same in return, but their expressions appeared deflated and melancholy. She found herself on the verge of breaking down into tears.

At last, Khybus cleared his throat and a hushed silence fell over the crowd.

Deep in Severina's gut, her instinct had told her to be prepared for anything. And if this went south, she felt she would be ready for anything. Would she go free, or would she accept whatever fate this judge dealt her?

Khybus's expression looked grim. "I, Khybus, advisor to King Aslor, having heard all the evidence of the case, as well as testimony from the parties involved, declare I've reached a decision."

Everyone waited on bated breath.

"Severina, despite the circumstances of your situation and the extreme emotional trauma of what happened on the day of the incident, you are still responsible for the illegal use of magic that caused harm to Targrym. The crime of magic assault is compounded by the fact that the victim is royalty. I have no choice but to sentence you to death."

The crowd gasped and Severina fell to her knees under the weight of his words.

"It brings me no pleasure making this decision, but the law stands above all else."

Severina felt her rage emerging again. The injustice of all this. The smug look on Targrym's face. Everyone, save her parents, turned their backs on her. The fact that just because she was a woman, she was being treated as less than.

"No," she whispered, shaking her hung head. Slowly she stood, flexing her restrained hands as guards approached.

"No!" she shouted, uttering a spell that snapped her bonds, freeing her hands.

The guards raced toward her, the crowd gasping and some moving toward the doors, others enraptured by what may occur. She spoke more enchanted words and added hand gestures, blasting the guards away from her and sending them skidding across the floor.

She looked over at her parents. Domlin wept and Lorien looked away in shame. If they supported such actions visibly, publicly, they would fall to scrutiny too.

Targrym came at her suddenly, sword in hand. He swung, and she narrowly ducked in time. "Die, witch!" he shouted, swinging again.

Severina gripped the railing, swinging herself over it to escape his reach.

"Stop this!" she shouted.

"You've brought shame to me, to my family. Made a laughingstock of this region!" he roared, vaulting over the railing to pursue her.

Hesitation held Severina back from all but putting distance between her and Targrym. This would only end with her death if she didn't protect herself though, and with no weapon on hand, magic was all she could utilize. She shouted the words and performed the hand gestures to launch a fireball at her attacker and the fiery orb struck Targrym, engulfing him in punishing flames.

He shrieked and flailed about, crashing into a crowd of people. As they scattered, several of the people caught fire as well, their delicate finery the perfect fuel. The wooden pews the victims scrambled over began to burn. Panic became the order of the moment, everyone racing toward the exit.

Winter remained within the witness station, looking on in horror as her son rolled about on the floor, alight with unnatural flames that slowly ate away at him. Whether intentional in her pause or not, by the time she drew closer, her child was dead, and any closer risked her being a victim to the still-consuming flames too. Retreating, she made her way around the thick of the crowd, attempting to exit and quickly becoming lost in the sea of people.

The crowd stumbled and staggered their way toward the exit, shoving one another from their path and trampling those who fell in their desperation to flee.

Two guards rushed to Khybus's sides, ushering him down from his seat and toward a back door where they could exit unimpeded by the common folk. All the while, they urged him to hasten, to not pause and exchange blows for worsening the situation.

Severina took her eyes off her frightened parents as the king's advisor rushed by. Her rage fully in control now, she summoned another spell and fired lightning from the palms of her hands. The bolts sparked and bounced through the air before hitting the old advisor. Electric shocks pierced through him, sending him into spasms. Severina did not relent in the attack until he had collapsed.

Other guards rushed her, tackling her to the ground in fear her fury would be directed elsewhere. They all went sprawling across the smooth stone floor, shifting the aim of her lightning and blasting the high ceiling above them all with the tail end of the spell. The trailing bolts cracked the stone ceiling, and no longer supported and secure, large chunks began to shift free, threatening to rain down on the fleeing crowd.

She saw her parents then, toward the back of the crowd as though they had been waiting for a moment to pull her with them, but still they hesitated to abandon her. Above the panicked crowd, the ceiling broke away, dropping several massive pieces down. Screams erupted, people dropping to cover their heads, and Domlin took to shielding Lorien with his own body.

Grappling with the fear of losing her parents again, Severina hurled a random spell at the falling debris, screaming out as the guards wrestled her still. Her magic landed true, blasting the stone chunks into dust, which rained harmlessly upon the terrified people.

Despite the display, one of the guards punched her hard in the face, blinding her momentarily. The other drew his sword while kneeling next to her, wiping blood from his askew nose.

Stunned, but not unconscious, Severina turned her rage upon them. Always at the ready, she launched two arcane blasts, one for each man. At point-blank range, the magic spheres impacted with uncanny potency, sending the men reeling and choking air into their lungs.

Severina raced to her parents, grabbing them both by the arms and helping them along. No opposition remained, and they joined the crowd outside.

A mixture of glares and thanks came from the survivors, but no one dared make a move toward her. Murmurs in favor were quickly stomped out by those sowing the seeds that she started it. That she was the cause. That *magic* was the cause.

Severina continued to pull her parents to safety, getting them as far from the burning building as possible. The trio came to a stop, the alleyway devoid of life, commotion breaking out where the smoke danced into the sky.

Domlin paused before he pulled himself free, panting heavily, his eyes welling with tears as he struggled to speak.

Lorien eased her arm from Severina's grip, rubbing where she had been gripping tightly, brow knitted with too many emotions. Her eyes were bloodshot, likely from the smoke and fighting back tears.

Severina saw that she was thinking frantically, doing mental calculations. After a few dragging seconds, she looked at Severina and lost the fight against the rushing tears. Quietly under her breath, she said, "I am so sorry, dear, for everything I am about to say to you. Please know I do not mean it, but it is the only way to save our lives. To save yours..."

Before Severina could register this, Lorien screamed and clutched at Domlin, panic overtaking her expression. "Get away from us! Get away, you wicked sorceress!"

A painful realization dawned on Domlin's face and Severina saw the hurt in his eyes. He cupped her cheeks, pressing a quick kiss to her forehead before whispering, "I love you... I'm so, so sorry..." And then he joined in the shouting, "Be gone! Be gone, wretched spellmonger!"

"Run, Sevi!" Lorien whispered in a desperate rasp.

The survivors that didn't help in staving off the angry flames had taken to hunting down Severina, and upon hearing the yells, followed them, a stampede of footfalls fast approaching.

"Magic is a dark art—forbidden! And you have shown us why that is. You are no daughter of mine!" he yelled, shoving her backward to force her to move, to escape.

Severina wept as she stumbled back from her parents. Their sad eyes and feigned expressions of shame were the last thing she saw of them. She turned and, catching the fast-approaching mob, cast one last spell—teleporting her away from the nightmare and safely to her room. Packing the essentials needed, including her sword, Severina raced down to the stables. The commotion within the town left the place empty, and she was able to saddle her steed unimpeded.

She charged out of the stables, hearing the mob's confusion and rage drawing closer as they worked to locate her.

In no time, she was on the open road, moving onto a smaller path that took her away from the high traffic of the main road and helped to hide her movement among the trees. Only then did she allow the agony to take hold, sobbing for hours as her horse carried her away from her life.

CHAPTER 7

Severina mourned for months. Traveling in a daze, lost in guilt and grief, she barely knew which direction she rode. She ceased taking care of herself, only eating and drinking because she felt death was too easy and she didn't deserve the peace. She kept herself alive—barely—in order to wallow in suffering.

She didn't bathe. Didn't brush her long hair. Didn't change or wash her clothes. The horse led her far and down random roads, but Severina managed the cognitive thought to avoid towns and cities, keeping to the side roads and trails.

For four months she wandered in a Westerly direction, remaining hidden from others. At some point down the road, her horse broke free and fled, abandoning Severina to her journey in solitude. She stole or hunted food when she needed and occasionally bathed out of necessity. But did not, could not, face herself and what she'd done to those she loved. Nor could she allow herself to dwell on their final words to her, no matter how false they were.

She eventually found herself in the realm of Tormelund. A peaceful area of moderate climate and a variety of terrains. Farmland dominated much of the flat prairies. A high-peak mountain range provided natural protection to the north. And a coast to the west added commerce, food, and tourism to the economy.

Still on foot, Severina came out of the wilderness one fateful day onto the busy stretch of road between Durren and Seafare. To her left, the ocean. To her right, the capital.

She wandered toward the coast, still in a daze, ignoring passersby as she entered the sprawling seaside town. The smell of hot food drew her toward a modest tavern on one of the side streets. There was no luxurious ocean view, more of a working-man's bar—rough and crass.

Severina stood outside for several minutes, wrestling with her need for food and the lack of money.

Like most of the structures in town, the tavern was made of hardened mud and thatch that had been painted white with blue trims. Whilst a fitting theme for the seaside town, the structures kept patrons inside warm against the biting ocean wind.

Severina decided to move on when an older woman flung the door open. She was thin, lanky, and perhaps a bit awkward in her own skin. Her red, frizzy hair hung in her face as she peered at the disheveled person in the street.

"Well, come on then. Get in here and get some food in ya."

Severina paused, unsure what to do.

"Now look, missy," began the woman. "I don't have time for nonsense. You either want to eat, or ya don't."

Severina couldn't resist the wonderful smells washing over her from inside. She came to the door, and the woman turned up her nose at the smell of this stranger.

"For fek sake, ya need a bath. I'll just sit ya away from the others so as not to scare away my business."

The place was called The Seagull's Shanty and had many tables and a long bar. A staircase led upstairs to a set of six rooms for rent.

The woman led Severina to a corner of the bar, far from the five customers enjoying their meals and drinks.

"Now sit right here and I'll bring ya somethin' hot to fill yer belly."

Severina felt completely out of place. She hadn't spoken a word to another person since she was chased from town. Couldn't even seem to recall what social graces were anymore.

In moments, the woman placed a steaming bowl of stew before her, accompanied by a tankard of ale.

"Eat up, lass," she began. "I'm Elena. This is my place. And you are…"

Severina took the spoon and started shoveling the delicious meal into her mouth with no thought of manners.

"You look like someone who ain't seen much kindness of late. Well, just so happens, I got some extra layin' around."

Severina kept eating voraciously, stopping only to wash meat down with swallows of ale.

"Well, seein' as ya not much a conversationalist, I'll leave you be. Ya need anything, just let me know, dear."

Elena left her to tend to her customers. Severina quietly watched the woman work for much of the afternoon; welcoming new customers, filling drinks, serving food, collecting and washing dishes, sweeping the floor. Elena never stopped moving.

Severina gradually grew more comfortable in the presence of others. Elena checking in on her helped, as did the constant hot food placed before her.

As the sun set, business slowed. Elena took a break and sat on a stool on the other side of the bar from Severina.

"Ya got a name, lass?"

Severina felt compelled to answer this kind person, but she couldn't find the words. At last, she managed to stammer, "I... I don't h-have money."

"Well, that's an odd name," Elena joked, grabbing a rag and starting to dry newly cleaned bowls and mugs.

"Listen, I don't know what ye been through, but I can tell it's been hell on ya. I'm assuming ya got no place to go."

Severina nodded.

"Then ya can stay here tonight."

Severina shook her head, protesting.

"Now, no arguin'. It's settled. I'll not have a young lady such as yaself walking these streets alone at night. The town may look pleasant, but there's sure as shit a rough element."

They sat in silence.

Severina fought with herself and forced herself to speak at last.

"Th-thank you," she whispered.

"No need to thank me, child. I'm just doin' what every good person should."

Elena looked Severina over, scrutinizing her. "If yer ta sleep in one of my beds upstairs, ya got ta have a bath. I'll not have my sheets ruined by whatever mess ya been rollin' around in."

Severina nodded in agreement. "Severina."

"What's that, dear?"

"My name. Severina."

"That's quite lovely. Pleasure to meet ya, Severina."

Severina found a smile had developed, the first one she had in ages. She settled into watching Elena again as she left to handle new customers, and the smile remained.

Severina felt she'd started a journey that day. Toward what, she didn't know. But for a brief moment, she forgot she hated herself.

After several baths, Severina began to feel somewhat herself. Elena took away her old clothes, most likely burning them, and left her fresh items to try on. The long tunic acted as a dress and she used rope to tighten the loose fit at her waist. It was ill-fitting and not at all fashionable or practical, but she was grateful nonetheless.

One night turned into three and Elena had given her a room, clothing, and meals. But most of all, she'd given her kindness.

By the fourth morning, Severina felt some of her strength returning, both physical and mental. She was able to hold conversations with her new friend now, though she remained reserved about her past. Elena respected her boundaries and seemed happy just to have a new friend.

Severina offered her services as a barmaid, cook, or cleaner—whatever she needed—in exchange for the room. Elena welcomed the offer and allowed Severina to earn her keep.

Days turned into weeks and business was good, leaving them both tired by day's end. Once a week, Severina noticed a charming man in chain mail armor enter and chat with Elena. She'd hand him a small leather pouch, and he'd be off.

When Severina inquired about the man, Elena brushed it off. "The price of doing business in Seafare."

"Protection pay?"

"We don't call it that, my child. More like a community fund."

"But if you ever decided to stop contributing?"

"Well, then I'd get a visit from a different man. And it wouldn't be pleasant. It's just the way things work around here."

Severina let it go. She was no longer in the business of stirring up trouble.

One morning word spread that Ulren Grizzletooth, the dwarven king of Tormelund, would be visiting Seafare that very day. Rumors said it was to personally greet diplomats from some far-off region. The lower classes were never privy to much information.

Sure enough, around midday, the king's convoy arrived and cleared a path to the docks where a large vessel, lavishly adorned in gold filigree, had docked hours earlier.

Curious, Severina made her way to the port and stood watching with the crowd.

The king's carriage arrived, and the dwarf stepped out in all his regalia. He was met with enthusiastic cheers, and he waved broadly, calling out welcomes and thanks to many in attendance.

A party of well-dressed humans exited the ship and met Ulren and his entourage, exchanged pleasantries, and headed for the waiting carriages. The guests boarded their carriage, but as Ulren stepped up to his, and turned to wave, an arrow sliced through the air, narrowly missing the king's head.

The crowd broke into terror, bustling to put distance between themselves and the carriages, while some took to looking around for the assailants. Another arrow struck the carriage door as the king ducked in swiftly, and both carriages headed to the capital with haste, guards flanking each side until Ulren was safely returned to the castle.

More guards took up stations along the ship, and the crowd immediately dispersed.

Back at the Seagull Shanty, Severina relayed the incident to Elena.

"King should've known better. Seafare is gettin' rougher by the year and he does nothin' about it."

"The people seem to love him, for the most part."

"I think his heart is in the right place. He just overlooks the details at times... details as in the little folk like you and me."

Severina pondered. A part of her wanted to make a plan to end the criminal activity herself, but her only task now was to work for Elena and keep her head down.

Yet the next day she found herself with her sword in hand, practicing her swings and parries. The blade once more felt natural in her hand, an extension of her arm. She practiced in all her spare time. Weeks passed, and she felt somewhat adept once again, her years of training reigniting within her.

In reaction to the assassination attempt, King Ulren declared martial law in Seafare, requiring everyone to be indoors at dusk. This brought the ire of the local businesses that needed evening customers to survive as the restriction reduced the profits of the businesses that once thrived. The demand from the local crime syndicate, however, remained the same, still wanting their normal share despite the diminished income of many establishments.

In weeks, tensions grew. Business owners were getting roughed up for lack of full payments, and some shops closed down entirely. Although extra guards were on duty, they could be paid to look the other way when needed.

Severina could feel the tempers boiling on all sides and was grateful Elena had been able to keep the crime lords happy. Full payments kept being sent. However, when the charming man visited, Severina made sure to be in the barroom to keep an eye on her friend's safety.

Over the weeks, Severina returned to studying her magic. Though she didn't possess any of her spell books, she'd committed several to memory and diligently copied them down in a new tome. Each evening by candlelight, she added spell incantations and potion instructions. Soon she had an array of magic available to her. Instinct told her she'd soon need it.

The day came sooner than expected.

She woke to sounds of struggle and rushed downstairs to find Elena on the floor, beaten badly.

"Elena! What happened?" she asked, hurrying to her friend's side and wincing at the visible wounds, dreading what other ones hid beneath the clothing.

"I've been keepin' a secret, my dear. I haven't been able to make full payments for over a week now. This was their warnin'."

Severina helped her into a chair and fetched water and rags. As she cleaned up the cuts and scrapes, she spoke in a low, serious tone.

"Don't open the tavern today. Stay closed. Stay out of sight."

"Why? What's happenin'?"

"Please, for me. Just do as I ask."

Elena noted the sword on her hip.

"Don't do anything rash, Severina. Please."

"I won't," she lied.

Later Severina stood at the mouth of the alley she knew would take her to the crime lord's base of operations. She'd heard all the stories about how the butcher shop was a front. About how in the backroom, where the meat was carved and cured, stood a door that led to the source of all the organized crime in Seafare.

She took a deep breath. This felt good. Felt right. But the creeping self-loathing wouldn't let go, and she pushed it aside as best she could. Elena needed her. The whole town needed this. She stared down the alley at the back door to the butcher shop five stores down and noted the guards, four of them, casually lounging about outside the butcher's back door.

She drew her sword and walked into the alley. People passing by paused to gawk at her. Was this woman really going *there* with a weapon drawn?

The lazy guards noticed her approach, weapon at the ready. They stirred and slowly stood, laughing.

"Well, what have we here?" mused one of the men.

Their leather armor had seen better days and underneath it, their clothes with shabby and unkempt. They drew their swords, low-quality weapons most likely stolen from victims.

"Young lady looking for a good time," smirked another guard.

Before another could speak, Severina leaped the last few feet to close the gap. She brought her blade down, severing the sword arm of the first guard. He screamed as she kicked him back into the guard behind him and they both went sprawling to the ground.

As the guard to her left reacted, she shifted her stance and thrust the sword into his chest. His jaw fell open in pained shock as a guttural moan escaped his lips. She twisted the blade, ensuring it was painful, and then pulled it out. The man was dead before he hit the ground.

She spun and slit the throat of the guard attempting to sneak up from behind. Her attack landed true, and he collapsed, gagging and choking on his own blood.

The last uninjured guard scrambled to his feet, clambering over his comrade with the missing arm. As Severina stepped toward him, she stuck her blade through the throat of the moaning, one-armed man on the ground, silencing him.

The last guard held up his sword, hands shaking.

"Where's the boss?" she asked coldly.

The whimpering guard pointed to the butcher shop doorway before dropping his sword and running in the opposite direction. She was about to cast a spell, perhaps launch a fireball at him, but thought better of it.

Instead, she opened the back door and slipped inside.

The back room smelled of meat that had turned. She noticed closets where some were properly cured, as well as a butcher block that hadn't been cleaned in ages. Cuts of beef, pork, and venison remained in the open air on the block. The stench was repulsive.

She spotted the rumored door and pressed her ear to it, listening. Silence. She quietly opened it and discovered a flight of stairs leading down. She descended, closing the door behind her.

Down some thirty feet, the stairs led to a path cut into the dirt. Supportive wood slats and mounted torches lined the short hall, which ended at an open room. She heard voices down the corridor and slowly made her way, remaining in the shadows as best she could. From her stealthy advantage, she was able to get a look at the occupants.

Seated around a table, counting coins, was the charming local man she'd seen many times around town, a large half-orc in shining plate mail she'd never seen before, and a finely dressed gnome who sat on a stack of boxes atop the chair to be able to see above the table. By the sound of things, the gnome called the shots.

"Since the proprietors of Hook and Line have come up short for the past month, it's time to remove them and put in our people," said the gnome in an authoritative voice. "How can a bait and tackle shop in a fishing town not turn a profit? I'm tired of their excuses."

"The usual?" grunted the half-orc.

"Nah. Make this one look like an accident. But don't burn the place down or anything."

The gnome turned to the charming man. "What about the Shanty? She gonna be a problem?"

The charming man rubbed his bruised knuckles. "Not at all. She got the message. She won't be short again."

"Good. Now—"

The gnome's speech was cut short as Severina's blade emerged out the front of his throat. Blood splattered across the table as the half-orc and the human man jumped back in shock.

They looked past the corpse of their boss to see Severina.

"You! I know you from the tavern," said the charming man, drawing twin blades.

"You're dead!" shouted the half-orc, drawing a massive broadsword.

Severina held her hand out, sending a lance of fire straight into the half-orc. The blast knocked him back into a wall and he screamed in agony as the flames consumed him and then spread to the wall.

The charming man came at her with both swords dancing. She deflected the attack and swung low, slicing his knee. He grunted from the blow, staggering to regain his balance before falling. Without giving him a chance to recover, she swung fast and true, severing one of his arms at the elbow. He howled in shock and pain.

The blaze started by her spell began to spread through the room and the table above the charming man went ablaze. Severina noted the fire, then took a swipe at the man's other knee, immobilizing him. He dropped his remaining sword and clutched his wound.

"You bitch! You'll pay for this!"

She sliced the leg out from the corner of the table nearest him and watched as the table tipped and fell on him, coating him with fire, and Severina walked away as his screams echoed down the smoke-filled hall.

Once outside, Severina spared one last look at the building, which had begun to leak trails of smoke drifting upward. Some townspeople had stepped outside to see what the commotion was about, but Severina was too deep in her rage to care about witnesses. Her eyes glowed with white light as she called a massive lightning bolt down from the sky to decimate this den of predators. As she stalked away, a name... a title was whispered in hushed tones among the witnesses:

"Stormbringer..."

"Ya smell like smoke," said Elena curiously.

"Do I?" Severina responded as she took a cloth and wiped a spot of blood off the tip of her sword.

Elena looked out the doorway to the bustling street. Alarm bells rang out and water brigades rushed up the street. She noticed smoke rising from a few blocks over.

"Severina, what did ya do?"

Severina began washing dishes. "What do you mean? I've been here with you the *whole day*." She smiled, locking eyes with Elena as she said those last words.

"Tell me, dear. Tell me ya didn't do anything stupid."

Severina held her gaze. "I didn't do anything stupid. After all, I'm just a barmaid."

Elena narrowed her eyes at the young lady and sighed.

"You have nothing to worry about, Elena. In fact, I don't think you'll ever have to worry about trouble again."

Elena went pale and her voice trembled. "Ya didn't."

"Just a gut feeling."

Elena let it go, hoping what Severina said was true. "I don't know where ye've come from or what yer runnin' from, but I am surely blessed ya stopped in front of my shop."

"I'm the lucky one, Elena. You saved me, mostly from myself."

The next day, King Ulren's elite guard entered the Seagull's Shanty. They politely but sternly collected Severina and took her by carriage to the castle in the capital city of Durren. Her heart raced as she contemplated what might be in store for her. *Reward? Punishment? Banishment?*

The guards escorted her from the courtyard into the foyer and then to the right into a great hall lined with pews facing an ornate, raised dais. Atop the dais stood a throne of simple wood etched with skilled carvings.

On the throne sat King Ulren Grizzletooth. He appeared in deep thought as he watched Severina approach.

The guards stepped aside as she reached the front of the dais.

"I hear tell your name is Severina," he began in a deep, commanding tone.

"That is correct, your Highness."

"And you are a simple barmaid in Seafare."

"Also true."

"And yet... why are there whispers and rumors circulating about you conjuring a burst of lightning to annihilate a butcher shop?"

She could play it coy, or she could be blunt and honest.

"I went there because everyone knows the butcher shop hides the headquarters of the criminal underground in Seafare. I killed their leader, their muscle, and their collector. No one in that city will be victimized by them again," she stated bluntly.

Ulren was taken aback by her honesty and struggled to find his next words, so set off guard by her response. In the end, he simply released a hearty laugh that filled the hall.

"I must say, in a position where I hear lies told to me by the day, your honesty is refreshing."

Now it was Severina at a loss for words. "Um, thank you? Sire."

"I would be very curious to hear how you single-handedly dispatched these thugs."

Severina retold the story in great detail, leaving nothing out, and the king looked her up and down incredulously as she came to the end of the tale.

"Stormbringer, indeed."

"Storm-*what*, your majesty?"

"That's what they're calling you. The Stormbringer... Severina Stormbringer ... has a nice ring to it."

"I... uh..."

The king leaned forward. "You possess a level of courage, or perhaps stupidity," he added with a grin, "that is rarer than the most valuable of diamonds."

"Thank you. I don't know what to say."

"Of course, this does present a bit of a quandary." The king's face took on a contemplative expression. "By all reports, the men you've killed were undeniably awful. But we also have laws in this realm, and I'm pretty sure you broke a handful of them in your ... righteous rampage. On top of that, it doesn't make my appointed constables look very good, you so efficiently doing their job for them. We're going to have to do something... something very public, to remedy this..."

Severina braced for the worst. Lashing? The stocks? Hard labor? Death?

"There is only one solution," continued the king. "Severina Stormbringer ... I'd like to offer you a job."

"A job?" Elena repeated. "King Ulren offered ya a *job*?"

"I know! I still can't believe it."

"But doing what?"

"Well, there are still a few details to be clarified. In short, I will be something of a contracted mercenary for the throne. The incident at the butcher shop will be recorded as my first 'official' mission."

"A contracted what?"

"I'll be tasked with handling problems that require solutions ... outside the realm of traditional or official methods."

"That sounds a bit ominous, lass."

"Not at all. It's for the greater good. Isn't the king a good man?"

"He seems to be."

"I don't think he will ask me to do anything wrong or evil."

"Sounds like yer either being naïve or tryin' to convince yerself this is a good thing."

"Elena, please be happy for me. This is a step in the right direction. I have a path to redeem myself."

"When I said that, I meant more like performing acts of kindness around town, not being a killer for hire."

Severina winced at that. "I hope you know me well enough to know that I would only take a life if I felt it absolutely necessary."

"Do I know you that well? I had no idea you were even capable of such violence."

Severina sighed and made an attempt to lighten the mood. "On the plus side, your financial prospects are looking up. You'll have your spare room back to rent, and no one coming around to extort you. I think the Seagull's Shanty is about to see some serious profits."

"But where will you live? At the castle?"

"No. The king can't be seen having direct contact with me for the most part. They've rented me a place near the center of town. I'm on the king's payroll. So strange to say that."

"This is all happenin' so fast. Are you sure ya don't want to stay longer and think on it?"

"Don't worry. I'll pop by every day I can. We'll still have our visits and chats." Severina gave Elena a warm, squeezing hug.

"Lots to do. I need to buy clothes and furniture and supplies. So much to do." She headed for the door, but stopped and turned.

"Thank you, Elena. I will never forget what you did for me."

"Be careful, Severina. Don't be so eager to race down this new path that ya lose yerself along the way."

Severina blew her a kiss and left Elena standing alone. She looked about the empty, quiet tavern and sighed.

Weeks passed and Severina outfitted her apartment with beautiful decor. She had custom leather armor made for herself, as well as a new sword crafted from the finest metals money could buy.

Most importantly, she learned quickly that magic was not only perfectly legal in Tormelund, but there were also mage guilds all over the realm. Towers and castles designed entirely for the learning and practice of magic were present, and her delight overcame the shame that still sometimes crept within. She was determined to carve out a life here. And she would gain the love of the people with her acts of kindness. Never again would she be abandoned or rejected.

Although there was not a single wizard or sorceress in Seafare, she was told of a guild in Durren. She quickly worked to gain an audience with the guild council and demonstrated her magic prowess. Impressed, the guild gave her standing as an initiate, assuring her it was just protocol because while her skills were on par with a more experienced mage, tradition was tradition. They told her she would be allowed to test out through the ranks: Apprentice, Adept, Master... until she hit her ceiling. For the time being, she was given access to the basic books. She accepted the delay, understanding how guilds and organizations operated.

In the early days of this new role, King Ulren sent her to only *investigate* potential crimes or people, not to engage or interfere. After some months, his tasks increased in difficulty: escorting valuable caravans, protecting high-level targets, and the occasional intimidating message delivered to an enemy. The work was largely above board and rarely strayed into morally gray territory.

She reconciled those less savory missions by telling herself it was all for the greater good. The king's right hand, Karas, had become a single point of contact for most jobs. Over time, the two became friends, often competing with each other in tests of their skills as warriors. It was a toss-up, for both were masters of the blade.

Severina made it a point to get as familiar with the lands of Tormelund as she could. She would often take weeks-long rides simply to survey the terrain. If this realm was to be her home and under her protection, she needed to know every hill and valley like she knew every wrinkle and crease in her spell book.

One day, when she had ridden to some of the most remote reaches of the kingdom, she found herself overcome with a strange tugging sensation. It was as if something was trying to pull her in a specific direction. Ever the curious soul, Severina heeded the pull and followed it, eventually being led to the ruins of what had once been, presumably, a crypt. All evidence of who had been buried there or what gods this structure had been dedicated to were long gone, erased by weather and time.

The pull brought her to a dilapidated wall at the back of the crypt. And resting there, leaning up against the stone as if it had been specifically placed there for her, was the most beautiful sword she'd ever laid eyes on. It had no gems, no filigree, no ostentatious embellishments, just a blade of some impossibly dark black material; but it was perfect nonetheless. The pull intensified and her ears filled with a drum-like resonance that pounded louder and louder until her fingers wrapped around the hilt. In an instant, the tugging and the pounding in her head stopped. Severina felt a calm confidence wash over her. A single word appeared in her mind: *Wrath*.

Yes. Yes, this blade is Wrath. And it was meant for me. She didn't know how, but she *knew* it. From that day forward, Severina was never seen without her trademark black-bladed sword.

As time moved on, her visits with Elena lessened in frequency. The king's work kept her away from home much more often than she had thought it would. But whenever she was in town, Severina made it a point to visit her dear friend. They laughed and reminisced about her early days and the condition she had arrived in. They spoke of their futures and the joys they hoped to have.

Severina's musing about the future never included romantic love. She never spoke of a desire for the comfort and warmth of a partner. After the betrayal of Targrym and the events that she had set into motion, her heart seemed forever closed off to those sorts of relationships.

This did not mean she lived her life as a monk. Every so often, she would take on a casual lover, but she always made sure to break things off before emotions got too strong. Best to avoid the messy entanglements of love, she reasoned. To Elena that seemed a lonely existence, but to Severina it was self-defense.

Despite the open-mindedness of Tormelund toward magic, Severina kept her powers close to the vest, using them sparingly and only when in dire need. However, a day came when she would be forced to stop holding back. A hostile blue dragon appeared in the skies above the kingdom's northern lands, and the standard military units were no match for the devastating powers of the beast. Its lightning breath felled nearly an entire garrison and Severina had no choice but to unleash every drop of her arcane power. In the end, the dragon fell, a smoldering husk. And she was left burned, wounded, and exhausted … but triumphant. On that day, Severina ceased to be the king's best-kept secret and instead became the famous Savior of Tormelund.

The citizens of the realm adored and praised her wherever she went. It was the happiest she had allowed herself to be since fleeing her old life. She clung to this joy, nurturing it in the hopes it would last.

Severina looked up from the shimmering pool toward the leafy canopy. A sense of understanding rose within her, giving way to acceptance. She'd lived her life and now it was time for the next adventure.

The Atonement Grove gave her new eyes to better see this world and accept leaving the old one. Out of sight, her Shepherd waited, and she started toward him, exiting the grove in a satisfied silence, the Shepherd not wanting to interrupt her thoughts.

Outside of the thick trees, a new glow in the distance grabbed her attention, an enormous plateau with what she assumed were buildings atop it.

Orvil followed her gaze, a smile tugging the corners of his lips in realization. "Welcome to the Sunless Crossing, officially."

CHAPTER 8

"That is our destination," Orvil stated, indicating the soft glow in the distance. "Nox Valar, the heart of the Sunless Crossing."

They walked together around the groves of fruit trees toward the plateau and Severina spied dozens of others. Most of them were walking in a slightly different direction than where she seemed to be being led, and scarce others were heading in the same direction as her.

"What is it?" she asked.

"It's a massive city of souls that is home to millions hailing from countless mortal realms. You've come here for one of two reasons: either you are destined for resurrection, or your ultimate fate is undetermined, and there is no afterlife for you at the moment."

"And the pond? It ... somehow allowed me to see it?" she asked.

"Yes. All new arrivals must take their turn in the Atonement Grove. Only once they have come to terms with their death are they able to see Nox Valar."

They pressed on in silence, Orvil allowing Severina time with her thoughts and Severina contemplative. Occasionally, she looked around at the other souls on the same journey, curious. None looked familiar, and she began to wonder why she hadn't seen any of her companions, or enemies for that matter. They all died around the same time.

Eventually, their path through the field led to a dirt trodden road, a rough route to the city that many had walked before her. While never becoming a crowded journey, they were never entirely alone, and Severina would glance at each passerby, hoping to spy a familiar face.

After what felt like hours of walking, Severina and Orvil came upon a gathering of people near the side of the road. They wore familiar gray robes and huddled closely together, whispering. Several Shepherds stood nearby, perplexed and losing their patience.

As Severina passed the group, her eyes were drawn to them again as a feeling in her gut triggered. Could it be Wrath alerting her? She paused and looked closer at the group, Orvil noticing the halt after a few paces and turned, looking between the group of gray cloaks and Severina with uncertainty.

She recognized one man instantly upon closer scrutiny: The Harbinger. Her sense of calm evaporated as her eyes filled with malice. "You!"

Severina pushed aside those in her path and grabbed the Harbinger by the collar, who looked stunned to see her.

"Murderer. Traitor," she hissed and punched him square in the face before anyone could stop her, releasing him so that he could stumble back from the strength of the blow.

The Harbinger took the hit, smiling in return. "One does what one must in troubled times."

"What does that even mean?" she barked.

The Harbinger simply shrugged with a smirk, seemingly enjoying how easy it was to get a rise out of her.

"I will kill you," she growled.

"Good luck with that," he laughed, waving a hand to have the others around him back down.

Orvil carefully placed a hand on her shoulder, positioning himself between them, facing Severina. "There are more important things. Trust me, this will accomplish nothing."

"You don't understand."

"I assure you I do. Let's go and I can teach you about this realm, if you are ready."

Severina couldn't back away. This bastard had caused so much strife, so much pain.

"Step aside," she ordered, rage bristling.

"Severina, if you start a scene here, we will have to stop you, and the Nyxian Guard will also get involved. You don't want that, I *promise* you. Just walk away with me," he urged.

She was beyond listening, hand on Wrath's hilt and ready to draw it. The sentient sword felt alive in her hand, but she paused upon hearing a familiar voice.

"He's not worth the trouble, Sevi."

She spun round to see Karas standing nearby, in all his armored glory. He smiled warmly at her.

"Karas!" Her hand relaxed, eyes doing a quick search for any of the wounds she saw on him, and seeing they were nonexistent, she raced to him and embraced her dear friend. "I thought I'd never see you again."

"Our worlds may have changed, but I see you're exactly the same," he mused.

She didn't want to release him. His presence comforted her more than she could express. At last, they separated, and she had to force herself not to shed tears of joy.

"When you fell I thought all was lost."

"No, Sevi. Not for you. I knew you'd find a way to vanquish Scourge."

"And look what it cost me," she mused.

"Small price to pay for saving the world, I'd say."

The gray-robed figures began to move along, uninterested in the reunion, the Harbinger smiling all the while.

Severina pointed to them, a glare firmly set on her brow. "And these pricks tried to pave the way for our world's destruction! They slaughtered their own kind to give Scourge a foothold in our world. They deserve to—"

"Die? Yes, I quite agree. And that seems to have been the case. Justice fulfilled."

"Am I just supposed to let it go? Just watch them walk away?"

"Sounds like what you crave is revenge."

Severina pondered this for a moment, then offered, "And what if I do? Revenge feels like the right move. Justified."

"Come on, Sevi. We're all dead. That life is over and done. I know it may be hard, but think… What's the point of satisfying a bloodlust that belongs in another world?"

She was taken aback by his words, and, after some thought, sighed. "I hate it when your logic makes sense."

She watched the group continue and even controlled her rage when the Harbinger turned and gave a gleeful wave, despite her urge to cut that arm off and force-feed it to him. A gentle tingling in her arm let her know that Wrath approved.

Keep your opinions to yourself, Sword.

"If you two are ready," began Orvil. "Perhaps we could continue?"

In the background, Karas's Shepherd, a slender elf woman, nodded in agreement with her colleague before taking her leave.

"Karas, please continue with Orvil if you would. Given you've met someone you know, it would be unfair for me to ask you to come with me separately. He shall take over as your shepherd for the remainder of your journey." She bowed slightly, perhaps an old habit of politeness given the soft way her voice carried.

Karas looked between the two shepherds and then to Severina before he nodded to the shepherds. "That... Thank you, greatly. I appreciate it."

With the confirmation given, the elven women took off deeper into the fields, easily gliding through the fields away from the trio with unexpected speed.

Hours passed quickly as the two friends caught up on the details of the battle and their experiences in this new realm. Severina grew melancholic as the conversation reached the climax of the battle when Menavaria took to the battlefield. The loss still crushed her heart and bled guilt through her veins. Logically she knew her goddess's death was not her fault, yet her thoughts fed her a different story, and she felt the sting of shame, nonetheless.

"Have you seen any of our other friends?" she asked as they walked, desperate to change the topic.

"I thought I caught a glimpse of Faustice when I first arrived, but lost track of him in the field."

"I have to hand it to him; that conceited, arrogant shit came through on the battlefield. That flute of his..." she begrudgingly admitted with a hefty sigh.

"Aye. Bards." Karas rolled his eyes, a smile cracking his briefly annoyed expression.

"I hope we actually don't see more of our friends here. That would mean they survived."

In the distance, a black dot amongst the gold cut across the field and moved toward them swiftly. The Shepherd noticed it first and slowed their pace, notably not alarmed.

Severina and Karas noted the slowed pace and followed the Shepherd's gaze, watching the swift black thing draw nearer. They could see defined arms and legs, and a single large wing.

"What's going on?" asked Severina.

"Not sure. They aren't in armor though, curious," Orvil replied.

As the approaching figure came into focus, they could see a tall, muscular form with a thick head bearing two curled horns. The being's single wing, on the left side, had a bat-like structure. The most striking feature was that the figure's body appeared to be made entirely of black stone.

The thing came to a stop a few feet away, not seeming out of breath, despite the exhaustive pace he'd kept.

"Apologies for my tardiness," he said with a deep, grainy voice that was equally authoritative and comforting. "Severina, I am here to guide you."

Surprised by these words, Karas turned to his friend, only to find her just as perplexed.

"And, ah, who are you?" Orvil asked, quickly looking the being up and down.

The dark stone being looked at Orvil, sighed and seemed irritated. "Someone was supposed to tell the Shepherd who collected her... I forgot to give the message, never mind that now." He turned his focus to Severina. "Forgive my manners, dear Sevi. My name is Vrath the Onyx. I'm to be your protector and guide here in the Sunless Crossing."

"I already have a guide." She cocked a thumb at Orvil. "And how is it you know who I am?" she asked.

"Also, what *are* you?" added Karas, completely thrown off by this unfamiliar creature.

"I am a gargoyle," he replied, as if that simple answer should explain everything. When he noticed her stunned expression, he frowned briefly. "Has ... your shepherd not told you any-thing?" His gaze shifted to Orvil, who was suddenly flushed, stumbling over attempts to start multiple sentences at once.

"An easy day for you, I suppose, Shepherd," he mused, shrugging it off as his attention shifted back to the pair. "Gargoyles are the protectors of this realm. Sometimes we move around and journey elsewhere, protecting structures or locations. I am the same, but different. I was made to protect a person. *You*, Sevi."

"Me? Why me?"

"I cannot say why. It is what I was tasked with upon my birth, my creation, and so I shall follow it."

"I don't understand any of this," Severina admitted, crossing her arms.

"Neither do I," added Karas. "If you are her protector, where have you been? We really could've used you back in the mortal world."

"Good point," she agreed. "Why are you here now? I could have used a protector thousands of times in life."

"It's … complicated. I can explain more as we travel."

"This place makes no sense whatsoever. We're doing just fine with our Shepherd here escorting us to that city place."

"Nox Valar," the Shepherd repeated.

"Yes. That place. So, Vrath, was it? You may consider yourself relieved of duty."

"That is quite impossible," Vrath said matter-of-factly. "I've protected you from afar as best as I was allowed." His gaze shifted a fraction lower before quickly returning to her face. "But now that we are in the same realm, I'll never leave your side. Ever."

Severina and Karas exchanged looks, silently asking the other what their move should be. Karas flexed his fingers, stealing a glance at Orvil, who was still somewhat flustered, but otherwise unbothered.

Severina's hand moved, gently resting on the pommel of her sword. Once the connection was made, a sensation bloomed into existence in her torso. Her hand snapped away, and she touched where the sensation had begun, gaze shifting to the gargoyle.

"My sword," she began. "*Wrath* is my sword."

"I was trying to imprint *Vrath*, but I suppose you heard it in your mind as Wrath…"

"I'm sure there's no emotional baggage to unpack there," mused Orvil.

Severina, Karas, and Vrath all shot him looks and Orvil cringed, adding in a murmur, "That was meant to be an inside thought, not an outside one."

Severina turned back to the black stone gargoyle. "Why help me? You don't even know me."

"But I do, Severina. I've known you since you were a child. I've been there at every triumph and every tragedy. I was helpless to intervene for many years. But once you grew into adulthood and began adventuring, I found a way to provide some aid."

She gazed at her beloved sword. "This sword has gotten me through the hardest of times. I cannot thank you enough. There are no words for this."

"How did you forge the sword?" asked Karas.

Vrath said nothing, only indicating where his missing wing should have been.

"You gave up flight for her," Orvil muttered, an edge of disbelief in his words. "Cut your wing clean off to make that blade. There are very rare few who have made such a sacrifice."

Severina's brain whirled, wracked by this new knowledge. Never in all her years had anyone sacrificed so much for her. Tears welled in her eyes.

"Why would you do this? Why give up something so precious?"

"I am sworn to protect you at all costs. It was the only way I could truly influence your safety. I could not be by your side, but I could deliver a gift such as this."

"But you can no longer fly."

"A sacrifice I was willing to make. I have no regrets, Severina. It was my choice to do this, and I was happy with the outcome. Please, I am happy. You did wondrous things with Wrath in your hands."

She approached the gargoyle and threw her arms around her guardian—as best she could, given his massive size.

"I don't know what to say except thank you. I don't know how to ever repay such a kindness, but I will try my best."

"How about we start with you allowing me to escort you to Nox Valar?"

Orvil hung back for the remainder of their trip, letting the two souls and the gargoyle chat among themselves.

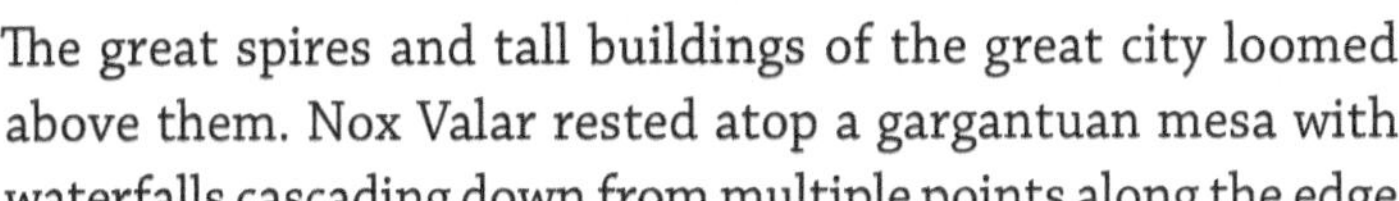

The great spires and tall buildings of the great city loomed above them. Nox Valar rested atop a gargantuan mesa with waterfalls cascading down from multiple points along the edge of the city.

Severina had spent their journey bombarding Vrath with endless questions, desiring to know every aspect of her life he had secretly observed and how he interfered or wished to interfere. The patient guardian dutifully answered and engaged, happy to finally be in her presence physically.

"My greatest sorrow," he had added toward the end of the inquisition, "is that I could not take away the times when loved ones let you down or deserted you. I watched each incident tear you down further and further. And I was helpless to stop it."

"Don't hold on to anguish over it. I have come to terms with it."

"We can protect against physical harm, but rarely can we aid in preventing emotional wounds."

As Nox Valar neared, the wonders of the city steered the conversation.

"What will happen once we enter? And *how* do we enter?" asked Karas.

"Stairs... A lot of stairs." Vrath gave a deep, rolling chuckle. "You will join a line and wait until you have an audience with the Keepers of the Eternal Sands. They will reveal how long your stay will be in the Sunless Crossing before you can venture toward your final afterlife," he answered, looking to Orvil for confirmation, receiving it with a nod.

"How long we stay?" asked Karas. "We don't just go immediately?"

"I'm afraid that doesn't happen often. Most souls remain in the Crossing for some time," Orvil chimed in.

"Why?" asked Severina.

"A multitude of reasons. Some because they have ties to the material living world that might resurrect them. Others because they have inner turmoil or unfinished business to deal with. The main reason is that there are lines for everything, and so you must wait your turn. Even for entry to your afterlife." Despite his earlier lack of information sharing, Orvil answered the questions with an ease one could only get from experience.

"So, I am not in control of how long I must remain?" inquired Severina.

"Not entirely, though there are means to speed up your process, should you be unsatisfied with the timeline. There are ways to earn coins with shorter wait times. Heck, there's even a sanctioned gambling option where you can wager crossway coins against others."

They came to a stop outside the gargantuan archway cut into the base of the cliff. Severina could see a wide tunnel leading away and upward through the mesa.

Vrath turned to Orvil and said, "I can guide them to the Keepers and get them settled in the city if you would like to be absolved of your duties here."

Orvil glanced between Severina and Karas. "Normally, I would insist that I fulfill my duty and see them to the Keepers… but we are overflowing with new souls right now. Today has seen a serious influx across the fields. If you're certain you can handle it, then I'll take you up on the offer."

Vrath exchanged a formal handshake with Orvil and a soft promise to take them straight to the Keepers before the shepherd gave a parting nod to the souls and turned back toward the endless swaths of wheat and grass. Severina and Karas watched Orvil go for a few moments before looking back up at the imposing stone archway.

Vrath took a step forward and said over his shoulder, "Welcome to Nox Valar, city of souls. Take your time. This part can be a bit overwhelming."

CHAPTER 9

Despite the exhaustive and near-endless stairs they had to climb, it felt worth it by the end. The streets of Nox Valar held wonders beyond their dreams.

Creatures and beings from hundreds of worlds mingled and blended, forgotten were the prejudices of the living. Here, a species that might have been considered monstrous in the living world was just another group of the citizenry. Anyone could be a business owner, pursue a craft or hobby, or relax and wait out their time.

Severina and Karas couldn't stop looking about. In every direction, new and shocking aspects of the Sunless Crossing assaulted their preconceived notions of normalcy.

The buildings themselves helped shape the odd nature of the place. Most every building was hewn from white and black stone. However, each neighborhood held little details and accents that belied when it'd been built and by whom. The doors told a *lot* about the people within. Some doors were built fifteen feet tall and half as wide. Some had doors Severina doubted she could even fit her fist through.

The purple hue of the realm remained ever-present but was punctuated by bright artificial light from businesses, homes, and various gathering places. The newcomers soaked in all the beauty of it. Nox Valar was a place of awe!

Vrath led them through the streets toward the center of the massive city. To Severina's knowledge, the living world she came from didn't have a city of such size. The time it would take to cross from one side to the other would be arduous on foot and bearable on horseback.

However, they did not complain. Around every corner, something new and fascinating met them. There were areas dedicated purely to the arts, with some large buildings set aside for theater with music of all sorts ringing out. Everywhere had people gathered in the streets, pursuing hobbies, learning a craft, gambling, and socializing. For the two strangers, this seemed like paradise.

"How is it that everyone gets along?" asked Severina.

"There are still those that have rivalries and prejudices, but most toss them aside given the nature of where they are and how they got here. Don't believe everything your eyes tell you, though. There is still treachery and pettiness in the dark recesses. I'm afraid there's no changing that."

"What do we need to know to look out for?" asked Karas.

"All in due time, friend. Enjoy the sights of the city for now. It's your first impression and I want it to be full of joy and wonder."

As they neared their destination, Severina and Karas heard a familiar voice call out. "Praise Quellon! His luck has certainly delivered today."

They turned to see Heliosa, clad in her robes and divine talisman, racing up to them. She embraced them both, bringing a smile to Vrath's face.

At last, she separated and looked them over. "I was hoping to find my friends. Prayed hard to Quellon for it."

"The god of luck always comes through for you," said Severina, smiling.

"Not always. I ended up dead, after all," Heliosa quipped. "But you still won the day."

Heliosa noted the downtrodden expression on Severina's face and understood the reason.

"It was a high cost, but worth it for Tormelund to be safe once more," Severina added.

"Menavaria's sacrifice will not go unpraised. I suspect the citizens of Tormelund will sing songs of her epic battle for eons to come."

"That is comforting, believing she will not be forgotten."

"Neither will you, my friend," Heliosa replied, placing a hand on Severina's shoulder.

"How long have you been in the city?" asked Karas.

"Just a few days from what I can tell from the Keeper's Temple." She threw a thumb over her shoulder in the direction they were heading.

Vrath stepped forward. "Pleasure to meet you in person, Heliosa."

Heliosa grinned. "And who do we have here?"

"Vrath the Onyx, at your service. You may know me better as Wrath, however." He gestured toward Severina's sword.

Heliosa's eyes lit up with curiosity. "Oh, how marvelously intriguing."

"Have you already had your audience with the Keepers of the Eternal Sands?" Vrath asked.

"Not sure who they are, but when I arrived in Nox Valar, fellow clerics of Quellon met me and escorted me to our temple."

"So, you have not met with the Keepers and been told how long your stay here will be?"

"No. Should I have?"

"Yes, and it is most unusual that didn't happen."

"Do you want to come with us?" added Severina. "Apparently, it's what everyone has to do here."

"Sure. Sounds like a plan, and if I'm meant to do it, might as well tag along!"

"Have you seen any of our other friends?" asked Karas.

"No. You're the first ones I've seen," she said, shaking her head.

Karas nodded and added, "Let's hope that's a good sign that the others survived.

"One thousand and sixteen?" scoffed Heliosa, looking down at the sandy bronze coin in her palm. "I'm one thousand and sixteenth in line?!"

"Could be worse. I'm one thousand and seventeen," said Severina.

"I'll give you one guess what number I got," chuckled Karas.

"This will take an eternity," grunted Severina.

"Not really," countered Vrath. "These initial meetings aren't long. The Keepers see hundreds of souls per day. I imagine you'll be at the front of the line in two to three days."

"How do you even track the passing of the days here?" Karas asked.

With an arched eyebrow and a slight smirk, Vrath pointed upward, behind Karas. He turned to look up at the massive temple of the Keepers. Atop the roof, a large hourglass sat, wide strips of glass running up the length of each side, and within, they could see some of the interior of the temple, the rest obscured by height, or the slowly rising sand that fell from the tower's apex.

"The temple itself is an hourglass," mused Heliosa, proud she already knew.

Vrath explained, "The sands fall until the tower is completely full. That marks the passing of one day."

"What do they do then, turn the whole temple upside down?" asked Karas with a grin.

Vrath shrugged. "The sands simply disappear and start falling again."

"Incredible," Severina marveled at such magical artificing.

The word had barely escaped her mouth when two massive gargoyles, one crimson and one purple, approached the party. They wore imposing matte white plate armor, a massive great sword on the hip of each.

"Severina Stormbringer?" inquired the purple gargoyle, a female.

The friends looked at one another, uncertain and surprised.

Severina cleared her throat, looking between the two gargoyles. "Yes?"

"Please come with us. All of you may accompany," the red gargoyle said, a male.

Vrath smiled and nudged Heliosa, leaning down to whisper, "It appears the luck of Quellon is with us." The comment worked to bring another smile to the woman's face.

The party was led back to the tower of the Keepers of the Eternal Sands.

"What's going on?" asked Severina.

"These Nyxian Guards are taking us to the front of the line. That's my guess at least," Vrath theorized.

"So... what's a Nyxian Guard?"

"In short, these are the guards that serve the governing bodies of the Sunless Crossing. It's an extremely difficult position to earn, and before any of you get any ideas, none of you can become one. You became ineligible as soon as you died... Sorry, Sevi." Vrath gave a sad smile.

Severina looked as though she wanted to protest, but in a new kingdom with new rules, she wasn't about to overstep. Especially within the presence of the Guards.

"Okay, but why Nyxian Guard and not something like Nox? Valar? The Nox Valar Guard?" Karas asked, curiosity causing his brow to furrow.

Vrath fell quiet for a moment before grinning. "You, my friend, ask the right types of questions... In short, they are named after the goddess who made this realm, Nyxia. According to the most prominent legend, she created this realm, this purgatory, for souls. We aren't sure if it was to protect them, make them reflect, give them a second chance..." Vrath shrugged, looking toward the gargoyles leading them who had glanced back a few times, looks of fondness apparent at the discussion.

Vrath cleared his throat. "But whatever the case, her name was respected enough back whenever she was around that us gargoyles decided to take and honor it, becoming the protectors of the realm, and the souls within it."

They were led inside the temple after a short discussion was had at the door between the Guards, and each member was waved inside. There, they were met by thousands upon thousands of time-keeping machines. Dials and ticking gadgets hung on the walls and rested on tables, taking up much of the floor space. They recognized some of the objects, but most remained a mystery.

The guards led them deeper into the tower and up flights of stairs until at last they came to a large set of double doors stretching some twenty feet up.

Two more guards, standing at the doors, opened them as the party approached.

"Beyond those doors lie answers. Please heed them carefully," said the purple gargoyle. With that, they turned and left the tower.

"That felt unnecessarily ominous," noted Karas.

Severina looked at her friends, took a deep breath, and led them into the chamber.

CHAPTER 10

everina and the others entered the semi-circular chamber that was large, but not extravagantly so. Above them, magical lights undulated and danced around, their light illuminating several desks stacked high with books and time-keeping devices.

A single window at the center of the back wall stood the height of an average human, allowing the purple glow of the Sunless Crossing to permeate the room. Despite the window being open, the room was a surprisingly comfortable temperature, not chilled as one would expect, and the occasional echo from the city streets below wafted in.

Several beings stirred behind their desks, some jotting notes in large tomes, while others consulted charts, muttering as they made notes on pads.

An older human in decorative robes made his way to a large chair against the wall in the center of the desks.

"Who have we here? Ah yes, Severina Stormbringer and her friends. Please, do step forward so that I may get a better look at you. Don't be shy."

They did as asked, stepping closer and into the light cast by the open window.

"Karas of Tormelund, valiant and loyal warrior. Heliosa, devotee of Quellon. And of course, Vrath the Onyx, the gargoyle who cut off his own wing. I bid you all welcome."

"Thank you," the souls murmured, still cautious about this entire procedure.

"I am Drake de Leone. Now I suspect you're wondering what all this is about."

They nodded in response, and Drake took a deep breath.

"See, resurrection magic is a curious thing and an invaluable boon for mortals. The gift of returning a dead friend, loved one, or hero back to life? Wondrous! This realm sits between life and the afterlife, however. This is where all souls come to wait out their time, just in case resurrection comes knocking. That is where we, the Keepers of the Eternal Sands, come in. We process each and every soul that comes into the Crossing the moment they start falling as a golden dewdrop with no form. We check the charts and determine how much time must pass before each soul will either be resurrected or can move on to their intended afterlife."

"Wait, why wouldn't a soul immediately move on?" asked Heliosa.

"Besides having to wait until the chance of resurrection passes? It could be any number of factors. Most everyone is waiting for their afterlife, and if everyone could do it instantly, the temples would be a chaotic flurry trying to admit every soul. Some of which wouldn't be ready to pass... And so there are lines for the temples, to also give people time to resolve anything outstanding," Drake said, pausing for a moment to let that information digest.

"Not only that, but just because you think you have a god and an afterlife waiting for you doesn't make it necessarily so. Some gods have tests for their followers, a task or a challenge they need to complete or overcome. Some souls worship no gods at all… or perhaps their god is dead."

Severina winced at that last statement but redirected her emotions toward pragmatic ends. "So, you have information for us about our time here?"

"Indeed. Now, keep in mind that you are all considered heroes in the realm you hailed from and tales of your heroisms will circulate longer than we can even hazard a guess. Because of this, automatically you all have two hundred years *minimum*," Drake stated, pausing as the group seemed stunned, a mix of pride and worry fighting for dominance on their faces.

"However, here is what I advise… Karas, be ready to leave in thirty-three years, seven months, and four days. Heliosa, you are already initiated into your temple here. A bit of a breach of etiquette on their part, but we can overlook the transgression this time. It would be a safe bet to assume you have five days."

"Well, that certainly is an unexpected development," said Heliosa, unsure whether to smile.

Severina turned to Drake. "And what of me?"

Drake took a deep breath before answering. "It should have been explained to you that there is an institution here called the Godless Monarchy…" He paused and, upon seeing her confusion, sighed. "Well, it serves as the governmental authority for the realm. The highest positions in the Godless Monarchy are that of The Sovereign and The Arbiter. Now, The Arbiter is always a gargoyle. They are the Defender of the Sunless Crossing and Commander of the Nyxian Guard."

Drake tapped the desk a few times. "The role of Sovereign is always held by a mortal soul that meets strict criteria: First, they must have had their mortal life cut short. Second, they must have no afterlife awaiting them. And third, they must have no chance of resurrection. Bonus points if they have no attachment to any god."

Karas, Vrath, and Heliosa all looked at Severina.

"What?" she asked.

"Check, check, check, Sevi," Heliosa replied, miming the actions of ticking off a list.

Severina turned back to Drake. "Please don't tell me you are talking about *me* becoming your Sovereign. I just got here *today*."

"Bit of a high opinion of yourself, eh? No, we are not asking you to take the throne, Severina. Our current Sovereign has many years remaining. The question we are asking you is: would you like to do some good? Would you like to be of service to the millions of souls here within this realm? There are many roles to fill within the House of the Sovereign. But for now, the question is simply, *would you like to help us*?"

Severina looked down at the floor, thinking aloud. "Yes, I no longer have a god... Yes, I had many decades left in my natural lifespan..." She looked up and added, "There's really no chance of resurrection?"

"There is a possibility."

"But you're not saying it's impossible. It may still happen."

"Yes. Your friend, Rennard, still lives.

"Well, there you go."

"Our invitation stands, nonetheless."

Severina sighed. Confused and frustrated, she just wanted peace in her afterlife. And again, the guilt for Menavaria's death crept up and choked her.

Seeing her expression of sadness and confusion, Drake hoped to alleviate her trepidation. "Joining the House of the Sovereign has its perks. You will be respected and can help make a real difference in the quality of people's time here. It's a chance to continue doing great things."

She barely heard any of it. She wanted this madness to end. "Can I go?" she asked. "I need to think."

Drake's expression turned dour. "There is one more matter to discuss, I'm afraid."

"Get to the point, Drake. Please," Karas pushed. The seasoned warrior could sense the sudden shift in the mood. He heard the change in Drake's timber, so subtle most would never notice it. A lilt that many people involuntarily have in their speech when they fear violence is imminent.

"You have picked up an unwanted companion."

"A *what*?"

"Embedded in your chest is a shard of the soul of the deity you called Scourge. It is the very thing that killed you. Unfortunately, a fragment of his soul still resides within that shard."

Severina felt like she'd be stabbed in the chest all over again. "Tell me what this means," she demanded.

"We are not certain yet. This is an entirely new scenario for us. Unrecorded anywhere and unheard of."

"Can you remove it? Can you get it out?"

"We don't know what will happen if we attempt to remove the shard. If we remove it, we may unleash it into the realm. Or removing it could obliterate your soul. We are unsure without further evaluation."

"And if it stays in me?" Severina asked, fists clenched at her side as she tried to remain calm.

"It is likely trying to reform itself into a full soul. It might try to overtake you and control you. It might burst out of you. Again, we aren't sure."

"What can we do?" Severina felt emotions begin to swell. Fear, anger, panic... all vying for her attention. Maybe she was imagining it, but she could have sworn she heard a voice—a rasping whisper clawing at the back of her mind, urging her to run far away.

"The first thing we must do is isolate you. Whilst the consequences of that shard of soul are unknown, it is too dangerous for you to roam the city."

"You want to make her a prisoner?" Karas asked.

Drake held his hands out apologetically. "Obviously we don't want it to feel that way. But what would you have us do? There are millions of souls out there counting on us to keep them safe."

"I will not be locked away while you scholars read and hope to find a cure for this."

She wasn't imagining it. There *was* a voice. It poured thoughts and ideas into her mind. It told her these people meant her harm. They meant to lock her away in darkness. They meant to persecute her for the freak that she was. The voice was making a lot of sense. Instead of death, they wanted to isolate and study her. Severina's expression turned hard, steely, cold.

Drake's tone became apologetic as he saw the shift. "I understand how it may not be the most enticing option, but it is the only way, Severina. For now, at least, until we understand more."

Vrath stepped forward. "Drake, surely we can find a compromise here."

"There is nothing else we can offer at this time, Vrath, truly." To Severina, he added, pleadingly, "Will you please come with us of your own accord?"

Severina closed her eyes and shook her head, whispering a small, "No."

Drake let out a disappointed sigh and waited a few moments, giving her a chance to reconsider. Awkwardness began to saturate the room, and with a shake of his head, he snapped his fingers. The double doors opened and six Nyxian Guards entered the chamber, approaching with calm purpose.

Severina looked to her friends, steely purpose in her gaze; one that invited them to follow in what was to follow. As she turned back to Drake, her eyes lingered on the window a moment longer than usual. "I'll find the solution myself. *Without* being locked up!"

She bolted for the opening, her friends right behind, Heliosa seeming giddy, Karas resigned but amused, and Vrath sighing before joining.

Severina leaped out the window, not knowing or caring what awaited her. She landed hard on a cobblestone street, rolling with the momentum. As she glanced over her shoulder, she spied her friends all making the jump as well.

Her right shoulder ached, but it didn't feel as if anything too detrimental had befallen it. Perhaps a benefit of being dead.

The others were up and with her a moment later. Without a word, they fled into the crowded streets, not daring to look back.

CHAPTER 11

The bustling streets made their fleeing difficult, the group having to dodge through crowds and moving carts. Vrath took the lead, having them duck down alleyways as often as possible.

They ran endlessly for what felt like hours, being led through markets, business districts, and art communities. Every place he could think of with confusing twists and turns to lose the pursuing Nyxian Guard.

Finally, he came to a stop in a quiet, secluded alley, the sky shielded by overlapping roofs. They all settled down, but no one said a word. Everything had happened so quickly, they were still processing the decision to run in the first place.

"Are you daft?" asked Vrath, angry concern evident. "They are the best chance of removing that cursed shard and saving you."

The voice at the back of her mind was gone, as though it never existed. The coldness or anger Severina felt earlier had vanished. She was convinced this was the right move.

"Didn't you hear him? They have no idea what they're doing. I will not put my soul in someone else's hands. I will determine what happens to me on my terms."

"I understand. The news was a shock, but please think this through."

"And what if they do remove the thing? I am to be in line to service some throne I know nothing about, potentially even sacrificing myself for it? What does that even mean if we're already dead? This place is madness!"

"This place—" Vrath started sharply, then paused to take a slow breath. "Nothing has been explained to you, and that isn't your fault."

"I don't appreciate being forced into anything," she snipped.

"It's an honor, Severina. One that isn't forced upon people."

"They can keep it."

"Severina—"

"Are you going to help me or not, Vrath?"

The onyx gargoyle sighed. "I am sworn to protect you, and that is what I'll do. Even when you make mistakes."

"Thank you." Severina rolled her eyes, an edge of sarcasm in her voice.

Karas kept scanning each entrance to the alley. "What is our next move?"

"We need a place to hide and lie low," Vrath said, turning his attention to the calmer members of the group.

"I could ask my temple," offered Heliosa.

Vrath shook his head. "No. They won't want to get involved in this. I know a place. Follow me."

Back in the tower, Drake looked over his fellow Keepers, all still diligently working.

"Give me the room, please."

The other Keepers gathered their notes and exited, talking to one another about the earlier scene. Once the door closed behind the last person, Drake sighed, rubbing a hand down his face. "Kanen."

From the shadows stepped a figure wearing light armor, the hood of their cloak pulled low.

Without raising his head, Drake handed the figure a folded piece of parchment, sealed with wax. "The nation is called Tormelund. The capital city is Durren. Find the mage called Rennard and tell him he cannot resurrect the girl—Severina. Explain it could bring catastrophe to their world."

Kanen looked up, revealing an ashen face with sunken eyes. He spoke in a deep rasp. "Preventing the destruction of one's world is usually motivation enough. However, should the mage defy this request?"

"In that unfortunate situation, you make *certain* he cannot perform the rite."

"Understood." The Pale Horseman turned and left the chamber with nary a sound.

Faustice loved a crowd. In the theater district in Nox Valar, he had found his people. These entertainers understood him, just as he understood them. It was all for the show, for the performance. Did anything else really matter at all?

Here, his flute was far more than a weapon. It could be just a flute. Just a harmless instrument to instill joy in the listeners. And that is how he intended to live out his eighteen years before being able to cross over into his afterlife.

It was his time for the stage once again. He leaped upon it and spun to face the audience, arms spread wide in welcome. It was a good crowd, at least fifty music lovers.

"Thank you all for coming. I adore you!"

Cheers rose and Faustice soaked it all in. He'd never been happier.

"Tonight, I give you the Sonnet of Scourge. A little something I wrote about my last epic battle that sent me here to all of you."

More cheers.

Faustice broke into a fast-paced, brisk melody that got the crowd dancing. Between notes, he rhythmically sang the lyrics he'd painstakingly created.

> " Gather friends and hear the tale
> Of the Scourge that came to Tormelund.
> With pestilence he pierced the veil
> And ruined the fields of the land.
>
> When at last he came on the fateful day,
> He never dreamed the heroes that stood
> To crush his minions and make him pay,
> For the battle belonged to the good.
>
> And the hero who dealt the killing blow,
> Faustice with his flute afire.
> Echo his name so all will know,
> The people's savior to inspire."

He danced and dazzled and reveled in the adoration the crowd heaped upon him. Never had he been so praised, so loved. He had found his place at last.

As he soaked in the applause, smiling and bowing, Faustice swore he caught a glimpse of some familiar faces and a one-winged gargoyle sprinting down a side street.

"What trouble have you gotten yourself into?" he muttered to himself before the shouted demands of "Encore! Encore!" pulled his attention back to his beloved fans.

The Harbinger saw the great tower with its waterfall of sand drawing nearer, indifference saturating his mood. Apparently, he was about to learn just how long he'd be stuck in this place. He'd been driven by his purpose for so long that it was almost nice to have some time to simply exist.

However, as the tower drew near, the Harbinger felt a sudden sensation of dread build up within him, then felt a sinking feeling in his gut. Every step forward felt like a bad idea. These feelings grew stronger until they became more than feelings. He swore he could hear actual words forming. Words saying "Stop!" and "Turn back!" And then, like a dam bursting, a booming voice thundered in his head.

I command you to halt!

The Harbinger froze in place. That voice. He knew that voice...

My Lord?

I am here.

But, how? I saw you destroyed.

Almost. I still exist in the eight shards of my soul, one of which you carry within yourself.

The Harbinger felt the small, jagged tip of crystal poking out from his chest.

Do not go to that temple. They will lock you away. I am attempting to speak to all the shard carriers, to warn them away. It is difficult, being fractured as such. Some are more open to hearing my call than others.

What should I do, my lord?

Some of the shards are within your fellow believers. I will guide them to you. Find a place to hide and begin rebuilding your flock. We will then gather the shards so that I can be reborn. The great and powerful Thulsader shall reign again.

It will be done.

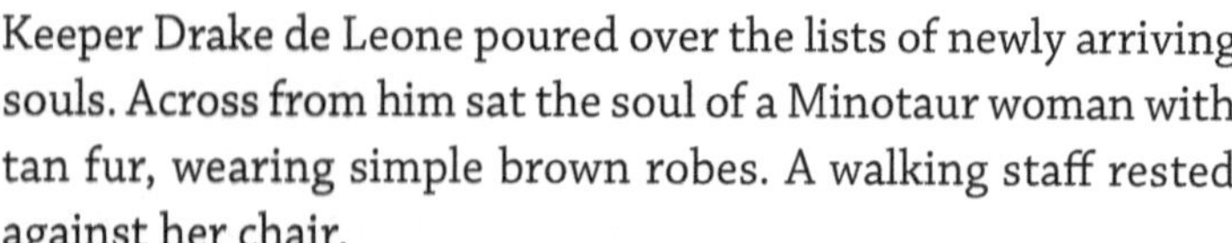

Keeper Drake de Leone poured over the lists of newly arriving souls. Across from him sat the soul of a Minotaur woman with tan fur, wearing simple brown robes. A walking staff rested against her chair.

Drake looked up at her. "Shepherd Yesha, this recent influx of souls..."

"The ones all hailing from that battle? As you know, it happens from time to time. A mortal realm has some epic, cataclysmic hullabaloo," she rolled her eyes, "and we suddenly have a little inundation. Nothing my people can't handle."

"Except this one is a bit different," Drake countered. "See, in this particular, what did you call it? Epic cataclysmic hullabaloo? Two gods were killed... one more so than the other. One of them had their soul broken into multiple shards of crystalized divinity, and those shards have all embedded themselves in souls that now walk the Crossing."

"Well, hell... and I'm going to go ahead and guess these shards are not pieces of a soul to a kind, loving, benevolent god, are they?"

"No, they most certainly are not. And we are having difficulty finding the shard carriers. We have one, an amiable dwarven woman, who has agreed to remain under our care until we can figure out the best course of action. There was a half-elf woman who came here and then ran away."

"You couldn't stop her."

"No, and of course she happens to be the leader for her side of the conflict."

"It always is, isn't it?" Yesha huffed, unimpressed.

"We have people searching for her. What I'm more concerned with are the ones who have not come here at all. Divine energy has a very specific signature to it. Our sorcerers have been able to glean that there are eight shards, yet we've only seen two carriers. The others are either being prevented from coming here, or, worse, they are *choosing* not to. We need every shepherd on the lookout. The shards are jagged blue crystals, probably lodged within the bodies of the soul. I've already alerted the Nyxian Guards and they are surveilling the city. We're counting on your group to survey the fields."

The Minotaur woman stood with a firm nod. "We're on it."

CHAPTER 12

Vrath led the group to a district of the city where Nyxian patrols rarely saw what happened on the streets. It existed in this unique scrap of land with the edge of the mesa bordering it on one side, and as chance would have it, the surrounding architecture was packed so tightly that it created an almost solid barrier. If someone wanted to see the ongoings of the streets, they had to navigate the narrow and twisting alleys and be inside the district before they could observe the goings on in the neighborhood of Shade Cliff.

He acquired a vacant apartment that had three bedrooms and a living room. After they settled in and rested, Vrath gathered them together.

"Now that we're in this fine mess, what are your plans?" he asked, looking at Severina.

"I was hoping you would have thoughts on this," she responded.

"Well, the wizards of the Godless Monarchy are the most qualified to remove the shard. But clearly, that is not an option."

"Nope."

Vrath shook his head, sighing deeply. "Fine. This is going to take time, but I'll check my sources. In the meantime, you three need to lay low."

"I'll keep her in check," quipped Karas, giving Severina a serious look as she went to playfully hit him. Her fist slowly lowered to her lap, a small frown creasing her brow.

The onyx gargoyle ducked down shadowed alleyways, navigating a maze of corridors, until at last he stopped in front of a non-descript door. He knocked.

The wooden door opened after a few moments, allowing him passage into a dark room.

A voice reached out from elsewhere in the dark chamber. "My one-winged friend, what brings you to these dark corners of our fair city?"

In total darkness, he could make out the silhouette of a short, halfling woman seated at a simple table near the corner. Next to her stood a guard of considerable size; nearly as big as him.

"Please, sit," she offered. "Apologies for the dark. I was recently injured, and any light causes great pain."

Vrath sat across from her and noted that she didn't appear to have any visible injuries or ailments. Until she opened her eyes. Her pupils were damaged and corroded.

"What happened to you?" he gasped.

"I ventured where I didn't belong."

"The Storm again, Alina?"

"Yes, of course. The Storm of Broken Worlds is the only place I can get what I need."

"That's a heavy toll to pay. Is it worth it?"

"For the trinkets of dead gods? Damn right, it's worth it. But you didn't come here to mock my maladies. Why have you come?"

"I need to find wizards."

"Pfft, go to any street corner. This city is lousy with 'em."

"The service I need performed is unique."

At these words, Alina leaned forward in her chair. "Do tell."

"Ever hear of a soul gem?"

The Harbinger and his companions had found lodging without much trouble in a massive tenement tower, a whole floor to be exact. It seemed no matter how crowded the city grew, there were always vacancies. While his people settled into their accommodations, he secluded himself in his room. He needed time to think, to be alone with his thoughts... well, not quite *alone*.

You did well. You have begun to rebuild the flock, and now it is time to begin reuniting the shards.

I am yours to command, my lord.

You are to be my vessel in this place. I will guide your hand to ensure proper extraction of the shards.

Yes. Yes, anything you need from me. I am your loyal servant, always.

I will not lie to you, favored one. The path ahead will be full of pain and difficulty. But you shall be rewarded with power beyond your dreams.

I am ready to serve.

The thing about being alive that Faustice missed most of all was the food and drink. Oh, there were plenty of both to be had in Nox Valar. One could eat and drink the day away. And while it tasted amazing, it just didn't deliver the same satisfaction. It was probably a subconscious thing.

At this point in the evening, after a show like the one he'd just put on, Faustice would typically find himself quite drunk. Alas, the wine here just didn't hit him like it had in life. His thoughts drifted back toward what he'd seen earlier. He swore it was Severina and the others he saw sprinting through the streets, and part of him wanted to find them and ask what was happening. But he had no idea how he'd even begin to seek them out. Admittedly, the other part of him was glad to have an excuse to not inconvenience himself.

A bit of laughter pulled him out of his reverie. He was reminded of exactly where he was at the moment and grinned. *Well, at least this place has something going for it,* Faustice thought as he reclined on the large tavern patio. He currently found himself surrounded by a variety of beautiful individuals hailing from dozens of different worlds and ancestries. They all made small talk among themselves in little huddles, but Faustice noticed the fawning glances aimed in his direction. He smiled and sipped his wine.

"Variety is the spice of ... death?" he chuckled to himself at the thought. Truly this was paradise. Why would he ever want to leave this place?

He stood after a very long time enjoying the adoration. "Unfortunately, I must bid you all farewell until tomorrow."

The crowd groaned and moaned their displeasure at his announcement. Several people hung nearby, all giving him their best "Want some company?" expressions.

He kissed the hand of a lovely humanoid woman with blue skin and subtle gills positioned behind her ears. "Care to join me for a more private concerto?"

She blushed and nodded with a coy smile. He kept her hand in his and began to lead her away, but then he paused and looked at a striking red tiefling with feminine features and piercings along her curved horns.

He smiled at her. "And you as well, if you'd like."

She stood to join him and they left in search of a more private setting.

CHAPTER 13

The mortal realm of Tormelund had already begun to recover in the wake of the battle against Scourge. Almost immediately, the fields started showing signs of healthy growth. Animals stopped falling ill, people as well.

Ulren commissioned a marble monument to be constructed at the battlefield to forever commemorate the brave souls who had died to save the world. Likewise, he had individual statues made for Karas, Heliosa, and Severina carved and set for permanent display in the center of Durren. He wanted no one to forget their sacrifice.

King Ulren spent those first days after the battle holding in his emotions as he addressed the citizens of the realm with grand speeches, but the moment he found himself alone again, he would dissolve into sobbing. He truly missed Karas and Severina. Despite the overall success of the battle, he couldn't help but feel like he'd failed them as their king.

Rennard grew into a valuable asset and friend, remaining by Ulren's side through every speech, every meal, and sitting outside his chambers listening to him sob. Rennard had seen right away the heavy toll the losses had taken on Ulren and knew he would need support.

The wizard quietly assumed control of the king's security detail. While many might assume the danger would lessen, intuition told Rennard to increase the vigilance. He burned up considerable, valuable magical resources to craft a necklace of protection for the king, claiming it to be a sentimental item that would comfort him. In reality, the large opal on the necklace was enchanted with protections stronger than any shield of metal.

King Ulren declared a day of remembrance and celebration when the commemorative statues were unveiled. It felt as if half the kingdom had crowded into the streets of Durren that day. After an inspirational speech from the king, feasting and merriment commenced.

Rennard, allowing himself a moment of respite, wandered along carnival rows with some colleagues from the arcane university. They indulged in the finest meads, ales, and wines, and devoured meats and breads from the best butchers and bakers in town.

As he stumbled into his chambers that night, half-drunk from the day's indulgences, he found himself growing morose, missing his dead friends. His head hit the pillow with a final thought: *I'm going to bring them back.*

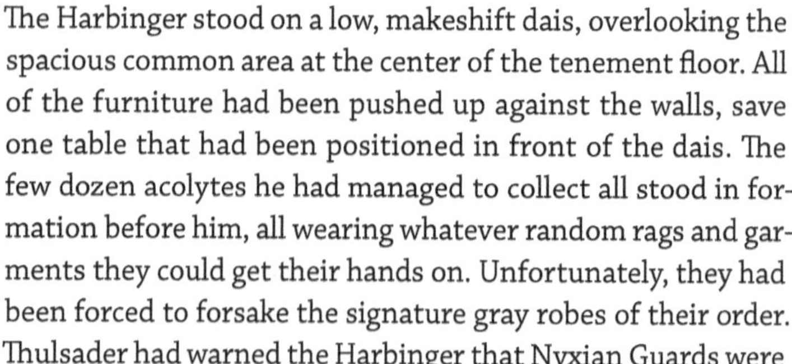

The Harbinger stood on a low, makeshift dais, overlooking the spacious common area at the center of the tenement floor. All of the furniture had been pushed up against the walls, save one table that had been positioned in front of the dais. The few dozen acolytes he had managed to collect all stood in formation before him, all wearing whatever random rags and garments they could get their hands on. Unfortunately, they had been forced to forsake the signature gray robes of their order. Thulsader had warned the Harbinger that Nyxian Guards were apprehending anyone in those robes, looking to see if they bore a shard.

That one there. He has a fragment in him.

The Harbinger felt his eyes being pulled by the voice in his head toward one young man, standing dutifully near the front of the group. He beckoned the one Thulsader pointed out to come forward, and the young man stepped out from the group with no hesitation.

"You have been blessed, haven't you?"

The young man nodded. "Yes, Harbinger! Our great lord has seen me fit to bear but a fraction of his glory."

He opened his robe, revealing a bare torso. A mere inch of jagged soul gem could be seen protruding from his lower left abdomen.

The Harbinger nodded. "You have done well fostering our Lord. But it is time for you to set down your burden, my child."

The Harbinger gestured at the table and the young man responded by dropping his robe and climbing up onto it. He allowed his wrists and ankles to be bound to the table legs. The Harbinger stepped down and drew a long dagger. The young man's breath quickened, but despite the hint of fear, he made no sound or complaint.

The Harbinger plunged the dagger into the man's stomach, causing him to scream in agony. As the Harbinger worked to free the gem from the man's sinew, it began to glow with an eerie blue light.

Keep going. Free the shard.

I'm trying.

With a final effort, he yanked the fist-sized shard free.

The young man's body went still, his screaming stopped, and he smiled. The Harbinger thought he looked as if he were about to speak, but no sound came out. Instead, the Harbinger and the others watched in horrified awe as the young man's body dissolved into black dust. A murmur rippled through the crowd.

Quickly brushing off the shock of what had just happened, the Harbinger held the blue shard up for all to see.

"With our brother's sacrifice, we move one step closer to Restoration!"

The Harbinger placed the dagger and the shard down for a moment to remove his shirt. He then picked both up and held them aloft.

"We are *all* servants. Our lord calls each and every one of us to purpose. We may be asked to sacrifice much of ourselves, but it is all for a greater good."

He plunged the blade into the side of his own torso, gritting his teeth against the pain. He slid the knife to create a larger wound, grimacing all the while. Satisfied with the wound his blade had cut, he withdrew the knife and began pushing the shard into himself. The agony was otherworldly, and he had to fight to retain his consciousness, gritting his teeth the whole while.

At last, he managed to insert the entire shard into his torso. The acolytes gasped as his wound miraculously began to close and heal itself. He staggered backward, still reeling from the pain. He slowly donned his shirt and then sat at the head of a long table.

As the pain diminished, he felt a surge of power and a clarity of thought.

He looked at his followers and uttered, "Six more."

Alina listened intently as Vrath told the tale of Severina and her heroic efforts in a battle that claimed the lives of not one but two gods. When the tale was ended, the halfling woman leaned back and stroked her chin.

"It'd be easy to criticize her for the rash decision to flee the Keepers... although I can't honestly say I wouldn't do the same thing in her situation. She was told nothing of this realm, and so all is new. Confusion is expected, but perhaps unfortunate in this scenario... But that bell has been wrung, so no sense fretting over whether it was the right choice or not. However, I can say you most *definitely* made the right choice coming to see me about this."

"You can help us?"

"I know of some who might be able to extract the shard without destroying her soul."

"Who?"

"You know my information is not free."

"What's the price?"

"Do not fret, I'll give you the friend discount."

Vrath remained suspicious. "We're friends?"

Alina continued, "Of course. All I need you to do is bring me the head of Ballindor the Sly."

"That bastard hasn't moved on yet?"

"No, and he owes me much. We did a deal in good faith. The whole 'rivals working together' thing. Well, I supplied the goods, and he refused to carry out his end of the deal."

"Which was?"

"To assassinate a different rival. And now he's making me look bad with his mocking disrespect."

"Why am I not surprised this went south? What did you think was going to happen?"

"Admittedly, I had a moment of weakness and thought we could forge an alliance or something. I will not make that mistake again."

"You know I cannot *literally* bring you Ballindor's head."

"Yes. The whole turn to dust thing..."

"And his soul will just return to the Crossing again in a few days."

"There are still consequences to 'death' in this place, Vrath, you know that. Maybe he'll forget who he is this time upon unraveling. Besides, it's about sending a message more than anything."

"And that message being?"

She smiled, adjusting her scorched eyes to look at the gargoyle as best she could. The effect was haunting.

"Do. Not. Cross. Alina... that's the message, Vrath."

"Why ask me to do this? I'm not one for violence. You know that."

"Yeah, but ... didn't you just tell me you have a close friend with you who can kill gods?"

"She's supposed to be laying low..."

"Which is why I understand what a big ask this is of me. And in return, I guarantee I will get you the people who can save her soul."

Vrath looked at her, defeated. "We'll see it done."

"And just who the hell is Ballindor? And why do we have to bring his head to this woman?" Severina stomped around the tiny room they all shared.

"We're not literally bringing his head. She just used it as a figure of speech," Vrath said.

Heliosa snapped her fingers. "Ah! The other Quellon clerics told me how when you die here, your body turns to ash. But they also said you just come right back."

Vrath sighed. "Yes. If a soul dies here, they are reformed in the fields. However, should a soul die too many times, they begin to unravel."

"Don't like the sound of that," noted Heliosa.

"This is absurd," added Karas. "I'm not a mercenary for hire, neither is Heliosa."

"How well do you know this Alina?" asked Severina. "Can we trust she can actually help?"

Vrath had expected this reaction. "I've … *collaborated* with Alina several times over the years. She's never let me down or stabbed me in the back… except for that one time, but there were extenuating circumstances. Regardless, she's someone who places a high value on the value of her word. She says she can help you, and so I believe she can."

"I don't like any of this," grunted Severina.

Vrath's tone got stern. "Severina, *you* made the snap decision to leap from that window and run from the Keepers. We are your friends, so we followed you. I am telling you now, your choice is either seek Alina's help or return to the Keepers."

"I know. I'm just complaining," she replied, then cracked a smile. "What's the worst that could happen? We're already dead." She paused, then laughed for a moment, causing everyone to look toward her.

"Are you alright?" Heliosa asked, concern creeping into her voice.

"Yeah, I just realized that … I guess I'm a mercenary again." Severina sat down, shaking her head with a smile.

Drake pinched his nose in frustration as the Nyxian Guard, a hulking female gargoyle of amber-hued stone, finished her report.

"So, you managed to search nine of the gray-robed fanatics, but none bore a shard? And since then, you have stopped seeing any of the gray robes altogether?"

"That is correct, Keeper," she replied.

"They got wise to us... this situation keeps getting more dire. I may have to elevate the potential threat level and alert the Godless Monarchy."

A knock at the door interrupted their conversation. The Nyxian Guard opened the large double doors, allowing a more junior Keeper to poke their head in.

"I have a ... sensitive message for you, Keeper Drake."

Drake waved them in, and they hurried over to whisper, "Alina from Shade Cliff would like an audience with you."

"Oh really?" Drake said with piqued interest. To the Nyxian Guard, he said, "I apologize, Captain Nadja, but could you please give me a private moment?"

The gargoyle left the room without so much as a word. When enough time had passed to ensure Drake's exiting guest and arriving guest wouldn't cross paths, he sent the junior Keeper to fetch Alina.

The halfling woman entered the chamber, escorted by her bodyguard, a thick veil shielding and protecting her eyes.

"I see your life remains as ... *dangerous* as ever," Drake said.

"Playing it safe is for the living," Alina replied. "Thanks for getting rid of the prong. This could have been awkward."

Drake cringed. "Don't call the Guards that, Alina. They're only doing their duty. More than I can say for *you*."

"If I'm so bad, why aren't I in chains, Keeper?"

"Because you've been useful in the past. Too useful to report. Now, are you about to continue being useful, or do I need to bring the captain back in here with a few of her comrades?"

Alina cocked her head to the side in amusement. "I hear you're looking for a girl with a god shard."

Faustice woke to see his two companions dressing. "Aw, no need to run off so soon."

The pair blew him a kiss and hurried out of the room, their footfalls pattering down the stairs. The noise had barely disappeared when a large orc man in leather armor stepped into his doorway.

Faustice reached for his flute, scrambling more upright as he found it was missing from his end table.

The orc man held up the magical instrument. "Got a job offer for you, flute boy."

"Well, sir. You've got me at a disadvantage, so I shall readily hear you out."

"Ballindor the Sly is hosting a party tonight. He wishes to hire you for the entertainment."

"And what exactly is the payment? This place is confusing."

"You get used to it. For tonight, your payment will be status. Do this gig and you will be given prominence, power, and roots to establish yourself here and make your time in the Crossing an absolute pleasure."

"Well, that is a compelling offer. And if I refuse?"

"Let's just keep this pleasant, shall we? The offer is most generous."

"Indeed. I'm feeling the hospitality already."

CHAPTER 14

allindor's party was held at an exclusive tavern called the Regal Trove. The occasion: to celebrate himself, of course. Everyone in his social orbit knew they had to show their face at this event, lest they fall on the bad side of this unsavory yet influential fellow.

The Nyxian Guard worked tirelessly to keep the populace of Nox Valar safe, yet the city was just so impossibly big that it was impossible to prevent some criminal elements from flourishing. That was the reasoning some people gave... And Ballindor was one such element. The self-styled crime lord had his hands in illicit activities across multiple districts and neighborhoods.

Shade Cliff had historically been easy pickings, but this upstart, Alina, was a problem. She was beginning to be a perpetual thorn in his side, and too many whispers were floating through the streets. Whispers insinuating that perhaps Ballindor's time on top was coming to an end.

And thus was born the motive to hire this new flashy bard that recently arrived in town. Ballindor knew that in this place where everyone was already dead, violence could only achieve so much. It wasn't as easy as killing your competition; you had to win over the hearts and minds of the people you aimed to exploit. A hot new bard singing songs of Ballindor's great deeds could be just the thing to help him win people over.

Among the faces in the crowd were Severina, Karas, Heliosa, and Vrath. Since they were nobodies, hiding in plain sight seemed like a good idea. From the center of the crowded chamber, they were able to assess the security of the establishment.

Outside the club, around the corner tucked in an alley, eight Nyxian Guards awaited orders to move in. The mission: arrest Severina. Inside, agents infiltrated the building as partygoers, ten in all, none of which were gargoyles. Two of them were magic users, equipped with a telepathy spell connected to one of the Nyxian Guards outside. At the most opportune moment, they would call in the Guards outside.

Hundreds gathered inside the tavern. The spacious building held décor from several eras and realms, giving it a strange, eclectic feel. At the far end stood a stage with its curtain drawn.

Backstage, Faustice twirled his flute in practice for the big show. Center stage, he spotted the host for the evening, Ballindor himself. He was shorter than expected and Faustice couldn't see his face, only an ostentatious cloak and thin fingers laden with gaudy rings that he waved about as if practicing his speech.

The troubadours at the opposite side of the stage began to play, and the crowd went wild with cheers. The curtain raised and the man of the hour stepped forward, arms outstretched.

Severina's jaw dropped when she saw Ballindor the Sly for the first time. This supposed crime lord looked like nothing more than a twelve-year-old elvish boy.

She turned to Vrath and hissed, "A child?! We're expected to kill a child?"

"Don't let his physique fool you," he responded, leaning in so she could hear him over the crowd. "He's been here over sixty years. His life was cut very *very* short."

"I'm not killing a kid. What's the matter with you?"

"He's no kid. I'm telling you, he's the most dangerous criminal in the city. Because his life was cut so short, he's been here an extremely long time and will probably remain long after you're gone."

"This is insane."

"He's an elf, which means he would have lived possibly a few hundred years. And he's only been here just over sixty. Do the math. His reign is just getting started."

"I'm not doing it," Severina said, shaking her head.

"If you want help, we have to!"

She looked at her friends, who watched their argument. "Where are you at with this?"

"No way," said Heliosa.

"Vrath makes some good points, but I can't do it," stated Karas. "I mean, look at him. He's adorable."

Vrath slapped his palm to his forehead, exasperated.

"I'm leaving," growled Severina, but paused when Ballindor began to speak.

He waved to silence the crowd. "Thank you all so very much for coming to my party. Your well wishes and adoration have truly humbled me. Tonight, I have a special guest for your entertainment. He's a newcomer to the Crossing. He plays a mean flute. You know him. You love him. And he is my newest employee. Give a big hand for..."

Severina froze. "It's not..."

"Faustice!" Ballindor waved him onto the stage.

Faustice charged out full of energy. He performed a one-handed cartwheel and stuck the landing center stage as Ballindor stepped away.

"Thank you. Thank you. And especially thanks to Ballindor for having me here tonight."

"Oh hell, what now?" sighed Karas.

"I wondered where he got off to," added Heliosa.

"Here's a little something I wrote recently. I hope you enjoy the Sonnet of Scourge."

Faustice launched right into the song.

Severina perked up. "What did he call it?"

"The Sonnet of Scourge."

She rolled her eyes. "Bloody bards…"

Vrath started making his way toward the stage, veering to the side to be less conspicuous—if that's possible for a gargoyle of his size. The audience was so enraptured with Faustice's flute that nobody noticed anything out of the ordinary, just another fan wanting to get closer.

Severina couldn't believe he was actually planning to go through with this. She followed and waved for her friends to do the same. They had to shake off the hypnotic melodies coming from the flute.

The Nyxian agents would have spotted Severina and her companions moving to the side if they were not also hypnotized by the tones and melodies cascading from the golden instrument like waterfalls of pure bliss.

Vrath reached the side of the crowd and had a clear path to the steps leading backstage.

Severina grabbed his arm. "We're not doing this."

"Do you want Scourge removed or not?" He tugged his arm free of her grasp and headed for the steps.

She couldn't stop him physically, but with magic, perhaps she could. She moved her arms and hands in a specific pattern, but Heliosa stepped in front of her.

"Do you trust him?"

"Get out of my way!" she barked.

"Do you trust Vrath?"

"Yes, dammit. Yes, I do."

"Then trust that he knows what he's doing."

"I aim to find out, and stop him if he moves wrong," Severina snapped and followed after him with Karas and Heliosa in tow.

Vrath slipped behind the curtains and Severina rushed the stairs and charged backstage to find him already holding the elf child by the torso, lifting him off the ground.

"I said unhand me!" he yelled. "Guards! Guards! Help!"

Severina looked to the right and spotted Ballindor's security lost in the song. They didn't hear a thing beyond Faustice's music.

Ballindor now saw Severina and the others. "You daughter of an undead whore! Let me go!"

"That's quite a mouth on you, kid," she said.

"Kid? I'm older than you, you raggedy trollop!"

"Damn, the mouth on this one," said Karas, having just arrived.

"That's what I said."

"Where's Heliosa?" asked Vrath.

Karas turned to see her hypnotized, mid-step at the bottom of the stairs.

"Damn bard."

He stepped down and shook the cleric free of the spell. Returning with Heliosa in tow, he noticed Severina unaffected by the flute's magic.

"How are you not falling under the spell?"

"No idea. But I'm grateful."

It was as faint as a whisper on the wind, yet Severina thought she heard her mind say, "You're welcome."

Ballindor screamed out again. This time, Faustice heard him and glanced to his right to see the gathering of his friends and new patron, pausing in his playing.

Thinking the song finished, the crowd erupted with cheers, as did Ballindor's security.

"Guards! Guards!" he yelled, and the two human guards finally took note of the situation. They drew their swords and charged forward.

The guards came in hard, swinging aggressively. Karas and Severina drew their blades and countered the attacks with ease. They turned the momentum against the guards and pressed them backward.

"Time to go!" yelled Vrath.

Unhidden by the curtains, Severina and Karas each dropped a guard with strikes that would have undoubtedly been fatal in the mortal world. A chorus of gasps and screams rolled through the crowd at the sight of violence. More security guards began to try pushing through the throng toward the stage. At the back of the room, a cloaked agent placed two fingers to their temple, sending a telepathic signal to the enforcers waiting outside.

Seconds later, the front doors of the tavern slammed open to reveal a squad of the heavily armored Nyxian Guards.

Faustice yelled at Severina and her friends, "You're ruining my big night!"

Ballindor, still struggling in Vrath's one hand, shouted, "You know these assholes, Faustice? You set me up? You're a dead man! You're dead when I get out of this!"

"What can you do? I'm already dead!" Faustice shot back. "But I had no hand in this!"

"Can we go, please?" yelled Severina.

Vrath sighed and said, "That's what I've been trying to do this whole damn time!"

They headed back down the steps into the panicking crowd. Ballindor kicked and screamed as he flailed about in Vrath's grip.

Despite their physical might, the Nyxian Guards found it difficult to enter the building against the tide of scared revelers trying to flee. Even the two incognito wizards that were already inside had trouble focusing their spells with all the constant pushing, bumping, and jostling.

The Nyxian Squad Leader, unable to make any progress through the actual doors bellowed, "Enough of this!" as he stepped to the side, smashing a window open and climbing through, with many others following, either smashing more windows or following through the newly opened ones.

Severina and her friends froze for a moment at the sound of multiple windows shattering. They turned to see the eight armored guards enter the building.

"Any ideas?" she asked as they huddled together and backed themselves toward the stage.

"Ha! You're all screwed now," laughed Ballindor.

Four undercover agents, now unbarred as patrons exited the establishment, rushed them with swords at the ready. Severina and Karas parried and countered, lining them up for a killing blow.

"Don't kill them!" shouted Vrath. "They are Nyxian Guards."

Severina deflected two more attacks and yelled, "So?!"

"Do you want to be labeled an enemy of the Sunless Crossing?!"

There was wisdom in his words. Karas and Severina shifted their fighting stances to defensive, as more agents joined the fray. They now held off six attackers, with more on the way.

Vrath swatted away an agent on the side while Heliosa focused and cast protection spells on both Severina and Karas. As they took hits from their multiple attackers, they felt no pain.

"Thanks!" Karas shouted.

The hulking Nyxian Guards stepped in, pushing aside the smaller, unarmored agents. They swatted away Karas's and Severina's swords and punched them with gauntleted fists. Thankfully, the protection spell kept them from pain, but the blows still knocked them back.

"What can we do?" yelled Heliosa.

Vrath punched a Guard across the jaw, sending him sprawling.

Beautiful flute music filled the air. All fighting ceased, the gargoyles looking for where it was coming from in confusion. Heliosa and Karas began to feel the effects of the gorgeous melodies once more. Severina acted quickly, shaking them to snap them out of it and motioned for them to leave.

Unfortunately, the hypnosis appeared to only affect the cloaked agents, leaving the gargoyles amused. They turned back to their targets with heavy fists raised.

Severina and Karas both ended up sprawled on the ground. Glancing toward Severina, Karas saw a familiar fire light up in her eyes and knew she was about to unleash hell.

From her position on the ground, she swirled her hands and muttered an incantation… but nothing happened. Severina again gestured with her hands and started to call out the words, but stopped. A confused look crossed her face.

"What's wrong?" asked Heliosa.

"Cast the spell!" yelled Karas.

"I can't remember the spell!" Severina yelled.

"Cast a different one!" Karas replied urgently.

Try as she might, only one spell kept coming to the surface; a terrible, brutal spell involving arcane energy, one that would surely cause wanton violence and suffering. It was as if her own mind was trying to force her to cast it. No! She couldn't cast that. These guards weren't *evil*. They were just doing what they thought was right.

"I got nothing," she hollered as the guards bared down on them, removing their weapons and keeping them restrained on the floor.

The leader bellowed, "Yield."

"It's about time!" yelled Ballindor.

"Surrender, Severina. It's for your own good."

"Brute force isn't exactly a great method for convincing me they have my best interests at heart!"

"Very well," the guard said, disappointed. He nodded and his colleagues moved in, cuffs in hand.

A thunderous boom cracked through the chamber, causing the gargoyles to double over, clutching at their ears. The sound came again, bringing all the Guard to their knees in pain. Yet Vrath remained unaffected. Severina turned to the stage, knowing what she'd find. Sure enough, Faustice was playing a different tune on his magic flute. An aggressive tone that sent piercing noise into the minds of his chosen targets.

"You realize you're now in the shit with us, right?"

He stopped playing, realizing what he'd done. "Shit!"

While the Guards still writhed in pain, Vrath hoisted Ballindor over his shoulder and led them out the collapsed wall and into darkened alleys.

"Dammit to hell!" Faustice cursed once more before sprinting after them.

Ballindor screamed for help and noticed no one in the streets came to his aid. In fact, some even lobbed jeers and taunts at the imperiled crime lordling. Apparently, he was not quite as loved in the streets as he had hoped.

The group didn't slow down until they reached the quiet, darkened alleys of Shade Cliff once more. Ballindor looked as if he might try screaming for help again, but Vrath grabbed his face with one large black stone hand. "Yell again, and I will pull your jaw off."

Ballindor stared up at the gargoyle with wide, terror-filled eyes, but remained silent.

Severina could only think one thing over and over: *what have we done?*

The Harbinger sat in his private chambers, meditating. While no one else occupied space in the room, he was far from alone.

You must be the one to remove her shard. If another does it, they may destroy it. We will need all eight pieces if I am to reform.

I understand, my Lord.

We need to keep collecting the others as you search for her. Every shard you regain will only increase your power.

It will be done.

You are my true chosen one, Harbinger. Do not fail me.

The Harbinger opened his eyes and stood, exiting his private chambers and marching down the hall to the common room. A group of acolytes held a bound and gagged soul who struggled against her captors. She had been a Tormelund soldier in life, and now she was forced to her knees for Scourge.

The Harbinger approached with slow, deliberate steps.

One of the acolytes addressed their leader. "It was just like you said; the Keepers let this one go for a little stroll. They must have trusted her. Only had one Keeper with her as a chaperone. We dusted the Keeper, no problem."

"And no one saw you?" the Harbinger asked.

"No. We are certain of it."

The Harbinger gazed down at the former soldier. "You've got something in that head of yours that I need."

The woman's eyes flared wide with terrified realization. The Harbinger wondered if the fragment of Thulsader inside her mind was taunting her at this moment.

"Don't worry," the Harbinger cooed. "You can rest now, faithful servant of Tormelund."

The Harbinger swung his blade swift and true, slicing the top half of her head clean off. The small fragment glowed once revealed in the dome that rolled about on the floor.

The soldier's body turned to dust, as did the top half of her head on the floor, leaving only the fragment.

The Harbinger picked it up and smiled.

CHAPTER 15

Vrath dropped Ballindor on the floor in front of Alina in her darkened room, noting the shocked expression on her face. The others followed the gargoyle in, carefully closing the door behind them.

Ballindor scrambled to his feet and quickly looked for an escape route. Too many people. Not enough windows. He was trapped. Settling down, he faced Alina and grimaced at the sight of her eyes.

"Had to have your muscle kidnap me," he spat. "Couldn't deal with our problems like adults?"

"Funny coming from you," she replied.

She tilted her head toward Vrath. "He looks very much not dead... well, you know what I mean..."

"We don't harm children," Severina grunted.

Alina laughed. "This little bastard is older than all of us. He's no child, but I get it. He looks the part and you are too delicate to appearances."

"We brought you his head, Alina," Vrath stated.

Alina rolled her eyes. "Letter of the law, I guess, if not the spirit."

"I believe you owe us an introduction to some particularly skilled magic users," Severina stated, glaring at the woman.

"Seek out the Cavalcade of Strays," Alina began. "The fortune teller knows much."

Vrath clenched his fists. "That's it? That's your information? Your *help*?"

"You want the right spell casters for such a task? She knows them all."

Vrath paused, containing his anger.

Alina tilted her head to the side again. "I realize this isn't exactly what you wanted, but I assure you the fortune teller will know. Now, if you will excuse me, my guards and I are going to paint the walls with this little shit."

Severina stepped forward. "That's not going to happen. Regardless of his true age, we are not murdering him. And neither are you."

"For fuck's sake, woman! He's dead. You're dead. I'm dead. We're all dead. Yes, it will hurt him like the dickens, but he'll just reform out in the fields tomorrow... perhaps a few memories lighter. He has to learn a lesson."

"It just feels wrong," Severina replied.

"You're telling me you didn't dust anyone to get to him?"

Alina felt the mood of the room shift and smirked. "That's what I thought. But, for argument's sake... would you rather I toss him in a cell? Would that be more benevolent? Now *that* would be true cruelty, true torture. Take some unsolicited advice: Stop approaching this world as if you are still alive. The rules of wherever you came from no longer apply."

Severina folded her arms, her expression furrowed in deep thought. She looked up at Alina, and something told her the curious halfling could tell.

"I don't like bullies... I don't like cruelty..."

"Then you *really* won't like this worm." Alina nudged Ballindor with her boot.

Severina continued, "If killing him isn't permanent..."

"It's not."

"Then make your point. Do it. Do it quick, without unnecessary suffering."

Alina arched an eyebrow. "Oh, I'm taking direction from you now?"

"Yes."

"I don't think you fully understand who I am, dear."

"Doesn't matter." Karas finally decided to join the conversation.

"Oh, I assure you it does," Alina countered.

"Nah," said Heliosa. "Trust us. If Severina comes for you, doesn't matter who you have in front of you."

"And you don't want to learn what I do to bullies," Severina said.

"I can't even put it in my songs. Too dark," Faustice added.

Alina leaned back and let out a chuckle. "Well, well, well... a new player has entered the game. Alright, Lady Stormbringer, we have an accord."

"Wait, you aren't *actually* going to let her kill me, right?" Ballindor pleaded, his voice dropping to a fearful lilt a true child might have.

Severina and the others turned their backs and were almost out the door, when Heliosa glanced behind her, spotting Ballindor in the shadows as Alina drew her finger across her neck.

"Ruined... My career is in shambles now."

Faustice paced around the small apartment, the anxiety practically dripping off him.

"Sorry helping your *comrades* whom you *died* with on the *battlefield* has become such an *inconvenience*," huffed Karas.

"What am I to do now? I can't show my face in public. The Nyxian Guard will be out for me. I mean, it truly looks like I was in on the whole thing. Hell, Ballindor's men are probably after me too." He ran a hand into his hair, tugging.

"After Alina and her people take over, I doubt Ballindor's men will be an issue," added Vrath. "But we may have inadvertently created a monster. She isn't much for compassion."

"Speaking of," began Karas. "Are we ready to leave and find the group of strays? The sooner we remove the monster inside Sevi, the better."

"Faustice, you might as well come with us. No use hiding here," offered Severina.

"Alas, stardom is a fleeting thing," he lamented.

CHAPTER 16

Vrath led them through the city for days, dodging and hiding their way toward their destination. Nox Valar's size was truly staggering.

"Are you sure about this?" asked Severina as they ventured closer to the center of the city.

"About as sure of this as I am about anything."

"That's not comforting."

At last, they arrived. Before them stood the temple to Quellon; Heliosa's faction. The structure was a stout tower, only three stories tall, painted white. Encircling the tower were three metal rings, each spinning in its own direction and speed. By all logic, the rings should collide and crash to the ground, yet—as luck would have it—they remained afloat and moving in sync. Perhaps it was the god of luck showing off.

Vrath turned to Heliosa. "Are you ready for this?"

She took a deep breath. "Do we have a choice?"

"No, but we do have luck," he mused as he opened the temple doors.

They entered the brightly lit foyer and moved into the main chamber that was alight with magical dancing orbs. Spaced equal distances apart were seven large chairs behind large desks, all against the wall of the circular room. Next to the entry doors, a large staircase led upward to the higher floors.

Seven robed figures sat behind each desk, dutifully working away at books, journals, experiments of all kinds, and potion making. Most of the clerics were human, but there was a dwarf and an orc among them.

The party approached the center, but no one acknowledged them. Heliosa stepped forward. This was her faction, after all. She opened her mouth to begin speaking, but the cleric seated in front of them held up his hand to stop her. He was an elderly-looking human, clean-shaven with a hawkish nose and deep brow.

"Heliosa, you have been absent from this temple for many days."

"Ran into some old friends."

He looked up at her with a wry grin. "How lucky."

"Yes. And we need means of leaving to seek the Cavalcade of Strays."

"As luck would have it, we have a caravan leaving soon for the Cavalcade."

"That's wonderful. May we—"

"As luck would have it, there is room for you and your entourage."

"Thank Quellon... do you need me to explain what—"

"And as luck would have it, we are far too busy to dive into the minutiae of whatever you have gotten yourself mixed up in. You are one of us, we will help... so long as you do not turn luck against the order."

"Lucky us," added Severina.

"When does the caravan depart?" asked Vrath.

"As luck would have it, in but a few minutes."

Karas leaned in close to Faustice, a smirk playing on his lips. "Maybe the god of luck can help with your career."

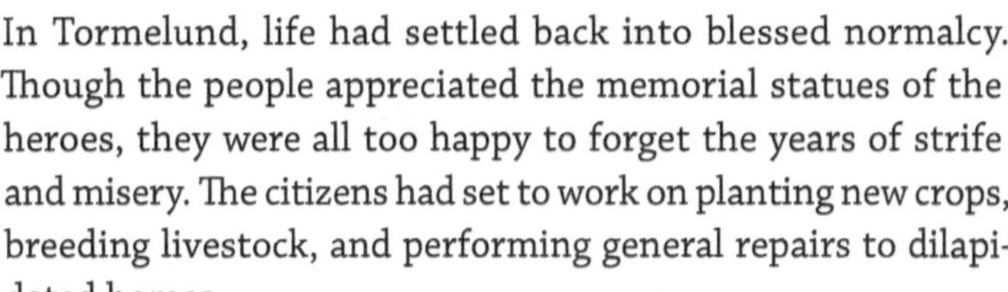

In Tormelund, life had settled back into blessed normalcy. Though the people appreciated the memorial statues of the heroes, they were all too happy to forget the years of strife and misery. The citizens had set to work on planting new crops, breeding livestock, and performing general repairs to dilapidated homes.

In the castle in Durren, Rennard worked diligently in his lab with his fellow mages, experimenting and devising ways to grow crops faster through arcane methods. They also focused on new means of protection of the realm; invisible alarms that never dissipated and never expired.

But every day, Rennard found himself staring at three jars on his desk. Each jar held something special in a liquid solution to preserve the contents. One jar held a finger, the second held an ear, and the third held an eyeball. The jars were labeled: SEVERINA, HELIOSA, and KARAS, respectively.

Every day, he told himself he would begin the work to resurrect his lost friends. He missed them terribly, but he also noticed a decline in King Ulren. What a gift it would be to bring them back. He dared not admit to himself the real reason he had not begun the process... deep down, at the very back of his mind, Rennard was terrified; terrified he might screw something up, causing some irreparable harm to their eternal souls.

Thoughts of Severina spurred Rennard to leave the castle and venture to Seafare to visit Elena. She was Severina's first friend in Tormelund after all, and unfortunately had grown weak and sad without Severina around to help out, and Rennard happily began visitations with the lovely woman shortly after the tragic battle.

He arrived in the peaceful seaside village, now virtually crime-free thanks to his dear friend. Walking his horse up the side street, he roped off the steed to a post in front of the Seagull's Shanty.

Inside, he found the usual customers eating, drinking, and socializing merrily. He spied Elena behind the bar, pouring ale from barrels into waiting tankards. She smiled as Rennard approached.

"There's the wizard himself," she said with a grin.

"How are you, Elena?" He took a seat at the bar.

"Can't complain. I'm gettin' by."

"Same here."

"What are we goin' to do ta change that?"

"We can start with one of those ales."

She smiled and poured one for her friend.

Later that night, Rennard sat in his study alone, nursing a bit of mild inebriation. He stared at the jars on the nearby shelf, at the contents within. The small remains of his dear friends. His heart ached at the thought of never seeing them again. The laughs they would not share. The struggles he'd face alone. The damn stubbornness of Severina.

Gazing over the books, scrolls, and potions laid out on the worktable, a fire rose within him. He was more determined than ever to follow through with the resurrections, beginning with Heliosa. He would not stop until he accomplished this near-impossible task.

As he stood to leave for the night, a window slammed open. A heavy gust of wind blew out several candles located in the deepest corner of the room. Rennard stumbled back, nearly falling over the chair at the sudden noise and shivering at the new chill. His gaze flicked to the window, where the strong gale no longer existed, then to where the unlit corner was, noting that all the others in the room were untouched.

Movement. Something stirred in the new dark. Rennard squinted, hesitantly taking a step toward the window. The shadows definitely moved.

A tall, armored being stepped from the blackness into the soft glow of the remaining candles. His appearance was obscured well, a deep hood keeping his face hidden, and the cloak of the cape flowing and pooling on the floor.

Rennard began to cast a protection spell when the man slipped a gloved and gauntleted hand from the cloak.

"There is no need for concern, Rennard Orbrun." Kanen spoke in a deep, commanding voice.

Rennard halted his magic, curiosity taking over. His last name had not been used in years, to the point that "the Wise" might of well have been it by default. "Who are you?"

"Who I am, and where I come from, is of no importance. All you need to know is that I come with a message of utmost importance," he stated, tone flat and untelling.

Unsettled, Rennard attempted to collect himself. In his decades as a purveyor of the magic arts, he'd seen his share of unnatural creatures and occurrences. But to have a being such as this simply appear in his private chambers was an exhilarating and terrifying experience.

He wanted to address this person properly, but the only words he could form were, "A message?"

Ignoring the wizard's sudden feeblemindedness, Kanen continued, "Do not resurrect your friends."

The mention of his lost friends snapped Rennard's mind into sharp focus. "Why not? What do you know of their fates?"

"We understand that you miss them. That many do. But trust this: bringing them would have dire consequences for your world as well as ours."

"But how so? I must know."

"There are machinations at play you know nothing about. If you care anything for the people of this land, heed our warning and end this endeavor. You will know when it is safe to attempt, that we promise."

The imposing man stepped back into the shadows, once more consumed by darkness, and silence fell. The chamber instantly felt lighter. Rennard exhaled, having not realized he'd been holding his breath.

The stranger never explained why. To make such a request with no enlightenment was insulting to some, but a challenge, a puzzle, to Rennard. He pondered the words, seeking some clue, but the man had chosen his speech carefully.

He found himself staring at the small jars of bodily remains once more, now pondering a different set of questions.

CHAPTER 17

The caravan of three carts made their way out of Nox Valar and into the Ashen Fields, opting to take the less traveled route through the wheat and away from the well-trodden dirt path. Powered by magic, the carts moved as though drawn by unseen horses, each loaded with supplies and five stowaways. Each of the drivers rode in silence.

Once the city grew small on the horizon, the companions ventured out of hiding and rode together in one cart atop soft bedding and cloth meant for the carnival.

"That wasn't so bad, was it?" asked Vrath.

"How did you know my temple would agree to lend us aid?" asked Heliosa.

"A lucky guess," he replied with a chuckle.

The others groaned.

After a relaxing silence, Faustice withdrew his golden flute from its case. "I'm happy to play some tunes to pass the time."

Everyone except Vrath was quick to politely decline.

"No. No. Don't strain yourself," Karas started, shaking a hand with a smile.

"That's quite alright. I'm enjoying the ambiant noise of the travel."

"You rest those fingers and lips of yours. You never know when we may need you to save our skin again," added Severina.

"Fine," he said with disappointment.

Feeling a bit guilty over shutting him down, Heliosa asked, "Faustice, how did you come by that magnificent flute? What made you want to become a bard?"

"Greta and I go back a long, long way," he began. The others looked at one another, surprised the flute had a name. "She was a gift from the most popular bard in my homeland. One does not choose to be a bard. The bard life chooses you."

"That is an awfully generous gift to bestow a stranger," noted Vrath.

"Well, by 'gift,' I mean he handed it to me as he was murdered."

They all perked up at the twist in the tale.

"Murdered?" asked Karas.

"He was ambushed on the road by people that didn't like his playing much." He shrugged slightly, flute case resting in his lap.

"So, they killed him over it?" asked an incredulous Severina.

"Yes... The group saw the bard in all his finery and saw an easy target. It was unpleasant." Silence fell over the group for a beat.

"Did they know you were there?" Vrath asked after a moment, an edge of concern present.

"They..." His brow creased in thought as Faustice weighed his next words. "They were the gang my parents ran with. I know that I come from an unsavory past, but I had no hand in any of it. My parents were criminals, they saw me as weak ... because I wanted to be just like him, the bard. Not them."

"I'm sorry, Faustice. That's no small feat," counseled Severina, a spike of guilt hitting her in the gut. "Going against the grain of what you've been taught your whole life, I mean. I'm sorry that you had to go through that."

"It's fine, nothing to be sorry about. You had no hand in it, *and* it brought Greta and I together, and she's taken care of me ever since. I ran away that night, never looking back. Just because my parents were thieves and murderers didn't mean I had to become one as well."

"Indeed. Apologies, Faustice," said Karas, offering a small smile that didn't quite reach his eyes. "Well done for breaking the mold they wanted you to fit in."

Heliosa gave a pat on his shoulder and a nod, not meeting Faustice's confused gaze at the apologies and drop in mood.

Wanting to replace guilt with camaraderie, Karas took up speaking next. "I've got no tale as exciting as Faustice here, but when I was a child in Tormelund, all my brother and I ever wanted was to be in the army. They were heroes to us. We didn't grow up in poverty or violence. We were fortunate to be raised by merchant parents living well in Durren."

He leaned back, touched the hilt of his sword, and continued, "The day we came of age, we joined the service. We were so full of inspiration and hope. Our parents worried because it was a time of war and the odds of us being sent to the fight were high, but we didn't care. What greater honor was there than to die for your people?"

His expression turned grim. "They trained us up and sent us right to the front lines. The war was brutal. My brother and I lost our innocence very quickly. Taking lives daily does that. Eventually, we turned the tide in our favor and it looked like victory was imminent. Our king even came to the scene to witness the final destruction of the enemy. This was before Ulren's time, mind. King Cypheron was the ruler back then. I still remember that terrible day."

He stared off into the iridescent sky, lost in memories. "The enemy had set a trap for us. They'd allowed us to think we had the upper hand, and we advanced too deep. We began to lose ground, fast. Our escape had been cut off. We were boxed in. The enemy saw our king atop his stallion on the hill and pressed hard to get through our soldiers to take him." Karas paused, shaking his head. "I was on the hill near the king. My brother was farther away, but I could still see him, the fighting growing thick around him. I was about to charge down to help him. Get him to safety. By my side... but the king's flank got exposed and I... I looked to my brother struggling, and the king under attack, and I had to choose."

Karas took a slow, deep, shuddering breath as a tear slapped his knee. "I chose to save the king that day. By the time I had secured his safety with the rest of the troops and turned back to my brother, it was too late. I chose duty over family. And I've *never* made peace with the decision."

They sat in silence, Heliosa pulling Karas into a hug, a sad frown on her face. Karas leaned into the hug, accepting the tenderness and comfort. Severina had drawn Wrath and was looking the ebony blade up and down. She made eye contact with Vrath.

"You said you were made to protect me, but you've never explained that. How exactly did I get so fortunate? I have no god of luck guiding my path," she asked, voice soft.

Vrath sat up straight, as if collecting himself. "I was hewn from Onyx and given purpose by the Arcane Artificer, Silas Callahan."

Severina's eyes widened a fraction, gaze flicking up. "That was my father's name."

Vrath nodded. "It was indeed."

"My father is *here*?! Here, in the Crossing? Why didn't you tell me sooner? Where is he?!"

"He hasn't been here for a long time. Remember, souls come here in case there is a chance they can be resurrected. They go to their afterlife if that doesn't happen within the allotted time, or if they've made their peace and don't *want* to be brought back to life. Your father made me so that I could look after you. On the day I was *born*, for lack of a better word, your father told me who you were and what my purpose was to be. At the end of that very same day, his soul moved on from this plane."

Severina brushed away the tear that had been welling in the corner of her eye. She reached out to grip the massive stone hand of the gargoyle.

"I'm glad you're here with me, Vrath."

The gargoyle smiled in return.

"You sure you don't want some music?" asked Faustice.

The group fell quiet, contemplating. "Go ahead, Faustice. Just keep it light and *not* entrancing." Vrath chuckled, and Faustice began a light, bouncy tune.

Rennard woke with a start and took quick stock of his room. Soft light from the moon outside the window cast a pleasant, yet eerie glow over the space. Something wasn't right.

He sat up and took several deep breaths. He had been dreaming of Heliosa and her return to mortal life. Ever since the strange being had visited him, he could scarcely think of anything else.

Despite the being's warnings, Rennard and his team pressed on with the resurrection research. Together, they had enhanced a simple ear and grew it to Heliosa's full body. They were nearing the time to cast the array of spells that would bring her soul back to this new body. Of course, he kept his ethereal visitor to himself, not wanting to unsettle his team. They needed purity of focus.

Now, sitting in bed, having awoken with a racing heart, Rennard sensed his current state was caused by something more than a mere dream. He swept the room from his bed, slow and methodical.

One corner of his room remained darker than the rest, with no moonlight on any surface of the area. Rennard took a deep breath and rose, donning the robe next to his bed before slowly moving to the desk farthest from the corner he knew the man would appear from.

"Show yourself," he whispered.

"I warned you," came the deep voice. "Do you care nothing for your fellow mortals?"

The large, imposing figure stepped into the moonlight from the unnaturally dark corner. He held his hands out to his sides in a gesture of frustration and disbelief.

Rennard steeled himself, not wanting to show fear or hesitation. "You'll have to forgive me. You came to me with a directive, but you presented no evidence of your extraordinary claims. Am I to believe a stranger without question?"

Hooded, Kanen let out a huff. "My initial withholding of detail was not without reason. The realm I come from is not meant to be known of in your world. Second, and more importantly, if I tell you the explicit reasons, you will tell your inner council. What is a deterrent for you may be motivation for one of them. Are you certain *everyone* within your inner circle can be trusted?"

"I trust them all implicitly!" Rennard retorted.

"So did every powerful soul whose blood ended up on the blade of a friend."

"You have to tell me something, Oh Messenger of the Great Beyond."

"Don't patronize me, Wizard... but if it will get you to halt the resurrection, I shall acquiesce this: A dangerous enemy you believe to be destroyed could come back to your world, should you resurrect Severina."

Rennard felt the blood leave his head, the words resonating deeply. "Scourge? You're telling me the god, Scourge, will return if I resurrect Severina? How does that make any sense?"

"She carries a shard of the god's soul within her. There are efforts underway to permanently remove and destroy it, but there have also been ... complications."

"What kind of complications?"

"That I can most definitely not talk about. We will handle our end. You, mortal, handle yours ... by doing absolutely nothing."

"How can I do nothing now? It sounds like my friend is in trouble."

"Listen to me, Rennard. If you attempt the resurrection, and I have to come back here a third time, I will make quite certain it does not happen."

A blade of pale white light glinted in Kanen's hand to illustrate the point. It vanished as quickly as it appeared.

"Do you understand?" he asked, watching from beneath the deep hood.

Rennard remained still, hands resting on the desk behind him as his mind raced. The threat was secondary to the impulsive idea that invaded the wizard's mind. Something so outrageous he almost dismissed it. Yet, in a bold move, he gave in to the unwelcome thought: If Kanen traveled in this unknown method, why couldn't he join him?

It was an enchanted item he had not used often, only when King Ulren was traveling a distance and he would need to call upon Rennard for magely assistance in the flesh, but he knew it well.

"I think I do. I think I do indeed," Rennard muttered, hand slipping into a desk drawer to grab the golden wired bracelet that was inlaid with small, rare, orbed gems.

Kanen took a step back, studying Rennard, and when he made no action, Kanen turned, heading back toward the shadow he seemingly exited from.

Rennard dove toward Kanen in that instant, grabbing the other man's wrist and slipping the bracelet on, squeezing tight to ensure the ends met.

Kanen's fist connected with Rennard's jaw shortly after, sending the man sprawling across the floor, winded and heaving to refill his lungs, blood running from the freshly burst lip.

"And *what* was that?" Kanen snapped, keeping his voice low so as to not risk alerting the guards. He checked his wrist over and spotted nothing out of the ordinary, but the accusatory gaze remained.

"I was..." Rennard paused, a wheezing cough shifting to a chuckle. "I was *going* to ask if you could deliver a message... Though it's quite out of the question now, I imagine." He winced, raising a hand to touch his lip, and hissed in pain.

Kanen took a single step closer and paused before turning away. "Remember the warning, Rennard *the Wise*. Do not make me return." He spat in disbelief, entering the shadows and vanishing.

Rennard stayed sat for a while, head tilted back as he patiently waited, steadying his racing heart. Once he deemed enough minutes had passed, he returned to his desk and brought out the twin bracelet to the hidden one Kanen wore.

"Time for a trip then, friend," he muttered, standing in the middle of his room before letting himself fall forward.

Weightlessness washed over him, and the nerves in his body fired up like pinpricks. He stumbled to regain his footing, head spinning from the sensation of suddenly standing, and noted the differing floor. He gazed at his surroundings and felt his heart skip.

Rennard found himself in a circular stone chamber, the windows revealing a purple vortex sky that cast a hue on everything. Desks and bookshelves lined the walls, each in varying degrees of disarray and dishevelment. Most of the desks stood empty, but some held occupants deep in their work.

He spotted his cloaked figure over to his right, speaking with a robed man. Rennard forced himself to take a step toward them despite still feeling disoriented.

The robed man, speaking to his mysterious visitor, spotted Rennard and did a double take. "What have you done?" he whispered, eyes wide in worry.

Kanen followed Drake's gaze and spotted the mortal wizard struggling to stand straight. "You foolish, *foolish* man!"

Rennard gave a wavering smile. "Take me to Severina."

Kanen moved swiftly, restraining Rennard's wrists behind his back to keep him from casting any magic, and looked toward Drake. "We need to send him back. *Now*," he demanded, fury making his voice waver.

"Indeed, we do, but this... May be beneficial to us," Drake pondered, moving over to the pair.

Kanen huffed, turning his gaze away to look at his wrist in an accusatory manner.

"Whatever you did to me, you will *undo* it so that this doesn't happen again, or you will return with one less arm," he stated.

Rennard held onto his courage, even against the restraint. "What is this place? Where is Severina? I just want answers."

The man in robes approached and gave Rennard a once over. "You're like a cat pulling a thread, aren't you? You won't stop until the whole tapestry unravels."

Rennard frowned deeply. "I will stop as soon as I know how I can help."

"You realize if you, a living mortal, were to die here, your soul would be completely extinguished. No afterlife. It is not safe for you."

Rennard paused, glancing toward the sky beyond the window as the words sank in. The weight of what they truly meant. "Where is here?"

The robed man sighed, waving a hand as he returned to his desk. "Consider this a reward for doing something that only a small number of living souls have accomplished: visiting the Sunless Crossing. It is an in-between for mortal realms and afterlives. Souls come here to wait for resurrection or to pass to their afterlife."

"Which one was it for my other friends?"

"I think I've shared enough." The robed man's eyes traced from Rennard to Kanen's annoyed body language. "I know Kanen can be a bit cryptic with his messages, so allow me to be blunt: Do not come back here. Do not attempt the resurrection. We will alert you when it is safe to do so. We do not want to kill you, but that is our last resort if you continue to threaten the realms for no good reason."

"Undo what you did to me before you leave," Kanen stated, releasing Rennard's hands and showing the wrist he had previously grabbed.

There was reluctance in the action, but Rennard brought his wrist closer, the bracelets wavering into view until solidifying. Removing it was quick and easy, and Rennard stole a glance up at Kanen.

The sunken features hidden beneath the hood were set in a tight-lipped glare, and once freed, he rubbed his wrist. His lips twitched as though wanting to say something before his head turned. "Back the way you came, mage. Enjoy this for what it was, a fleeting dream from me knocking you sideways." He mused flatly, hoping that Rennard would do as suggested.

Rennard sighed, looking between the pair and resigned to the decision. He was outnumbered, and the one called Kanen seemed able to hold his own in close quarters, something he easily admitted he could not. Pocketing the retrieved bracelet, Rennard covered his own with his palm and fell forward.

He felt the disorientation once again and stumbled, gripping the side of his bed as he pressed a palm to his temple in an attempt to halt the spinning.

Rennard inhaled deeply. He had failed to see his friend, but the experience was not without gain. He now knew Kanen's claims were true.

After what felt like an entire day of travel, the Cavalcade of Strays came into view in the distance. Bright hues of orange, white, and red illuminated a large area of the swaying grass. They could hear festive music, like something one might find at a rural carnival, drifting toward them.

As they drew near, they heard the jumbled rabble of a jovial crowd. Multiple wagons of different types and styles were about the grounds, each as colorful as the last. People were gathered in small groups, standing or sitting on large rugs, enjoying an assortment of food, drinks, and conversation.

The temple caravan parked and met with people from the Cavalcade. Severina and her friends left the clerics to their business, slipping away to explore the ongoings. The berth of grass was lined with all manner of entertainment and commerce. The members of the Cavalcade were dressed in a wide variety of clothing; no two people dressed exactly the same, but just as eclectic. Despite the remote location they had set up for the day, it appeared as if quite a few outsiders had come to visit.

Multiple stands had been set up, and foods that weren't familiar to the group were available for purchase, as were drinks that were all apparently self-made by the traveling group. Trinkets were on show for perusal, rooms within wagons were available for rent if needed, and small shows of feats were scattered about on small, pop-up stages.

At last, they came to a roofed wagon that was deep blue, hosting a sign for mystical arts available. Seers, psychics, and a fortune teller sat on stools talking to one another but facing the space to see oncoming customers. The conversation ceased once the group grew close enough, and a lean gargoyle who looked as though he was made from sapphire looked at the group, his clothing looking like multiple colorful sashes all sewn together in a type of robe.

"What can we do for you today?" he asked, his voice lighter than expected.

"We are looking for the fortune teller," Vrath said, looking between them all.

The gargoyle smiled, gently patting the knee of a green dragon-like woman dressed in a loose gown and wearing a patch over one eye. She stood, smoothing her skirt down as she moved to greet them, taking the steps into the wagon two at a time.

"Aren't you an eclectic collection of souls. Please, come inside," she greeted cheerfully as she opened the door, moving in and ushering them to follow.

They judged the size with skepticism, doubting that would all fit. Yet one by one, they entered—discovering the inside became far larger than the outside. They looked about in amazement. The walls were decorated with tapestries displaying art from several periods, some familiar and many not. The floor was littered with large pillows, incense burned near the center.

"I am Wren, reader of fortunes and interpreter of fates. What is it I can do for you?" She gestured to the pillows on the floor in invitation.

"How?" asked Karas, dumbfounded.

"Pocket dimension?" asked Vrath.

Wren pointed to the gargoyle. "We have a winner!"

"Amazing," added Heliosa.

Wren sat on the pillow at the head of a circle of pillows and motioned for the others to do the same.

"Now tell me, what is it that you seek?"

The Harbinger felt the fifth shard settle inside of him, taking root in his muscle and viscera. He could feel his god growing in power inside of him, and in turn, felt his own power growing. However, the efforts reaching this point were not without their cost. In this moment, he felt as if he could rip a mountain in half and take a three-day nap simultaneously. Very strong... very tired. He needed rest every time he added a shard; it took so much out of him. He needed time to gain a new equilibrium. Yet the voice of his god thundered in his mind.

There is a change in our timetable.

What's happened?

The time for discretion is over. You must acquire the other shards ... today.

My lord...

Severina is on the path toward destroying her shard. We must catch her.

Lead me to her.

She is outside the city. The other two are here. Get them and then we go after her. There is no time for rest.

The Harbinger took a deep breath and then forced himself to stand.

It will be done.

Wren inhaled deeply and exhaled slowly. They had laid out the entire tale for her and revealed what they needed. She kept her eyes closed and breathed deep again.

Finally, she opened her eyes. "This thing you ask, it is quite difficult."

"Alina advised that if anyone could help us, it's you," Vrath said, hopeful.

"She speaks the truth. I do know of three magic users capable of this endeavor. And you'll need all of them working together on this series of castings."

"Where can we find them?" asked Severina.

"As luck would have it, they are all attached to Legend's Meadow."

Heliosa smiled at the choice of words.

Vrath sighed loudly. "Legend's Meadow? Those outlaws?"

"That is where your casters will be."

Severina looked at Vrath. "What is it?"

"Legend's Meadow is a group that has been branded as outlaws by the Godless Monarchy. They fancy themselves heroes and have found a way to pop in and out of the Crossing. Those that are still living use this realm as a hideout from their enemies in the mortal world, much to the vexation of the Godless Monarchy."

Wren smiled. "They can be a lot of fun. Helpful, even."

"Fun? More like chaotic."

Karas grunted. "Why does it feel like we're getting the runaround? Go see this crime lord, but first kill this other crime lord. Now find this odd circus... *now* find a bunch of loonies..."

Wren held her hands out to the side. "While I understand that the Cavalcade is new, we are far more than a circus, as I'm sure you can tell by walking amongst our wagons... But I can only tell you what I can tell you."

Severina stood. "I get it, Karas. But, hopefully, this will be our last stop."

"Do you know where they are currently, Wren?" asked Vrath.

"Currently?" noted Heliosa. "Isn't it, you know, a *place*?"

"Those from Legend's Meadow you're searching for are not currently *in* the Meadow," Wren explained. "They're currently moving for their next trip. Last I heard, they were hanging out along the river on the clockwise side of the Lightless Chasm."

Vrath nodded.

Wren spoke softly. "Before you leave, I will tell you this. There is another like you, and even as we speak, he hunts you."

"*Like* me?" asked Severina.

"While you carry the whisper of a dead god, he carries the voice, clear and resolute."

"The Harbinger," she growled. "We need to go."

CHAPTER 18

The Harbinger led his motley company of followers through Nox Valar. They stuck to the back alleys, avoiding the main streets, as they worked their way toward the next shard.

They came to a door set in the middle of an alleyway and the Harbinger motioned for silence. He could sense the shard was nearby, a tugging as though all the shards wished to reconnect. He drew his sword and dagger and kicked the door in.

Standing at the ready in a small room, a Tormelund soldier held his sword straight out, pointing at the cult leader.

"Come, try to take it from me," he taunted. "I'll not go peacefully."

The Harbinger stepped inside, followed by eight of his strongest followers.

"We shall see," he replied calmly.

The soldier jolted and gasped, confusion spreading over his face. He looked down to see the Harbinger's dagger lodged in his chest. It was so impossibly fast that he hadn't even seen the man move. The soldier dropped his sword and fell backward, scrambling to put distance between them. The Harbinger stepped on the man's wrist and kneeled over him. With calm precision, he drew his dagger down and plunged his hand into the opening, removing the shard from the soldier's heart. He stood as the soldier's body crumbled to dust, turning his back, uncaring, and drove the shard deep into his own chest.

The Harbinger's body was wracked with spasms as the power surged through him. It hurt, but it was a beautiful pain. The force of the energy dropped him to a knee, breath shaking as he tried to compose himself. How had it come to this? Him housing his god with his body?

He remembered when he had a name, Axios. He had been raised in an orphanage, left on the front steps in the middle of summer with no one in sight, and nothing to indicate where he came from. In a home full of other discarded children, he always felt like he was the odd one out. They all arrived one day, already knowing their family's past and why they were there. But him? He did not earn the solace found in knowing one's family died in a heroic adventure. Whereas the other lost souls cried tears in between the comforting arms of the monks—his were always ones of abandonment. It didn't help his jealousy that they each came with great tales of dragons, gods, and magic, and all he knew was nothing more than the desert gardens and an oppressive sky of perpetual sun.

It took several years to build up the courage to explore outside the orphanage, sneaking out into the sand-filled streets of the local city. Crime was a word uttered on the lips of nearly everyone who lived within the walls. They were sinners and failures, each coming from discarded families—or sentenced to repent for their crimes against the arcane in the Forgotten Sands. Yet, down one back alley, tucked tightly away, was a small building welcoming anyone to hear the teachings. Always one for stories, he took to sneaking in and tucking away in a corner to avoid any of his brethren from discovering his whereabouts. He listened avidly as the elderly preacher spoke to the near-empty room about how his god made worlds clean and pure by devouring them. That in this devouring, what remained would be forged into something stronger than a dagger of pure diamond.

Axios returned frequently. He spent more time at the so-called church than the orphanage, finding the stories of worlds being cleansed and devoured just as fascinating as the ones he heard when younger, those of great deeds of dead adventures that left their children abandoned.

The intoxicating rhetoric soon filled his soul with purpose. He decided that it would be he who would help wash worlds clean. It would be he who would start this world over.

Working for the church was no easy task; he had to prove his worth to be able to receive the gifts of faith and the exchange was not a simple one. Forgotten reliquaries from desert ruins would yield a new flash of insight. Each item, a new reward. Again and again. As he continued, the challenges grew in difficulty as he grew in age. The "trials," as it was posed to him, were to ensure he was a true believer, one willing to help bring strength to the world once their god was ready to come and help it be reborn.

Through his dedication, he rose through the ranks quickly, gaining access to more and more of the scriptures. And in his faith he learned to commune with Thulsader, to hear his god's whispers on the music of a night breeze.

Soon after, Axios felt his god's growing disappointment with stolen trinkets buried in the corners of Tormelund's des-erts. Purity, Axios came to understand, could only be found by journeying into the terrain and wildlife of Tormelund, miles away from the desert. His adventure began, so Thulsader could see the land through him.

A new world to conquer. A new source of power.

If he were to become the mouthpiece to Thulsader, Axios realized he needed a new name. A title even. He would be the god's herald to usher in this new world order. What better title than Harbinger? A Harbinger that would usher in strength to a weak world, and in doing so would save the torment of abandonment or tears of weak children mewling over their so-called legends.

The Harbinger smiled as he thought back to his beginning. He failed to give Thulsader the victory over Tormelund, but he was still his god's champion, and together they would conquer this new realm. Thulsader's voice broke him from his reverie.

The second to last shard is inside the temple of the Keepers.

How will we get to it, my lord?

Trust me, faithful one.

He stood and marched toward the door with grim resolve. It was time to obtain the final shard in the city. Once absorbed, he would then hunt down and destroy Severina. With her fragment, he would be able to do the impossible: resurrect his god. The thought of the quest filled him with equal parts excitement and trepidation. He'd heard many tales about the Storm of Broken Worlds, and he genuinely feared venturing into that maelstrom. But to bring Thulsader back, it must be done.

Severina wished they had better transportation. Walking to wherever this group from Legend's Meadow was during such a time of urgency became an exercise in patience. Unfortunately, the Sunless Crossing had no animals existing within it, according to Vrath. Their afterlife remained elsewhere. And at the Cavalcade of Strays, no magic-infused carriages were available to take. All the housing and workspaces were of the members. Vrath had tried to negotiate for something called a shadow steed, but their party had nothing of interest to trade with the Strays that was worth even one. They did, however, manage to trade information about Alina and Ballindor's ongoings for a single "Fireblast in a Bottle."

As they plodded onward through the tall, swaying grass, they witnessed many travelers: Shepherds guiding new souls to Nox Valar, gargoyles flying above, and other souls wandering freely.

Severina, walking next to Vrath, noted two gargoyles in the sky some distance away.

"Do you miss it?" she asked.

Vrath followed her gaze and gave a soft hum, contemplating. "I do if I'm being honest. I miss it greatly. Flying is part of who we are and is as natural as breathing. But do I regret my decision? Not one for one second. I have no sadness over the choice I made, but I still mourn the loss... if that makes any sense."

"Your gift has saved my life more times than I can count. But if I had any say, I would surrender it back so you could be whole again."

"And that is why I am proud to have been able to give you aid."

"Don't be too generous with your praise. I've done things."

"We've all done things, Sevi. Every creature in existence has taken actions or made decisions they wish they could take back. That's just life. What matters is how we overcome our mistakes. How we learn and grow. Even here, after death, souls continue to learn."

"I would love nothing more than to have peace. To have time to figure out who I am. This shard stuck in me, the loss of

Menavaria, and the threat from the Harbinger just exhausts me. I wanted none of it. Yet here we are."

"We do not ask for the difficult things in life, but they are often what forces us into growth. When I was younger and was first charged with watching over you, I observed with horror as those bullies tried to attack you in the alley behind Domlin's shop."

"So long ago." Severina laughed, reflecting on the memory.

"They did not get the better of you. You dealt out punishment to each one. Deservedly so. But here's the thing. Given all the trauma and struggle you'd already experienced in life, you could have easily killed each of them. But you didn't. You gave them what they deserved, then let them live."

"Believe me, part of me wanted to end them."

"But you held back. You restrained yourself. It took a while, but even those idiots learned from your lesson. They grew to be respectable men and raised families of their own."

"They did seem different as we got older."

"Lessons come from the unlikeliest of places."

"Okay, Vrathington," she mused. "A heavy-handed metaphor, but I get what you're saying. Even though we are in a rough situation, there are lessons to be learned even now."

"Exactly."

Severina rolled her eyes. "You sound like my dad."

"Well, of course."

She paused for a moment, remembering Vrath's origins, and then kept walking.

"He was my father... but there's so much I never knew about him. I had no idea he was capable of creating something like you."

"He had to keep many of his arcane talents a secret in life."

"Of course, because the law in our country forbade the use of magic."

"He was quite powerful by my estimation."

Vrath took her hand gently in his. "And just know, my care for you is not only because I was made to. I've watched you almost your entire life. I know you. I know your heart. You are someone worth fighting for."

She smiled. "I would never doubt your sincerity, my friend."

CHAPTER 19

Karas had noticed Heliosa's silence over the past few days. As they journeyed to where the sought-after Legend's Meadow members were, she'd barely spoken a word. It wasn't like her. He'd known Heliosa for years and couldn't recall ever seeing her so melancholy and withdrawn.

He made sure to walk beside her after a break.

"Speak your mind," he said in a low voice. "It's just us."

"I don't know what you mean."

"Something is off with you."

"You... You wouldn't understand."

"Oh, so there is something."

"Sorry, General. I opt to pass."

"It's me, Heliosa."

She sighed. Clearly, there was no dissuading him.

"I worry that my good luck, and therefore *our* good luck, will run out. I lead a life devoid of strife. You all suffered tremendous trauma growing up and into adulthood. I have no such tale to tell. Since childhood, I've had a charmed life. I come from a long line of Quellon followers, and he has seen fit to bless us with luck."

"That's what's got you out of sorts? My dear, luck doesn't matter. It is action and consequence that determine the course of things."

"I knew you wouldn't understand." She sighed and shook her head. "Let me try again. I worry that my luck has been used up and that I will fall out of favor. Our group depends on this luck. It's gotten us this far."

"You are mistaken. Our strategy, perseverance, and heart have carried us. I admit your luck is uncanny and even alluring, but it is our choices that have brought us this far. And as far as you falling out of favor, I don't see how that is possible. As soon as you arrived in Nox Valar, you joined the Temple. Quellon must be pleased with this. And for all your years of service."

"I don't mean with Quellon, Karas... I mean with you all. If my luck suddenly stops, what reason is there for you all to keep me around?" she said, dejected, with eyes downcast.

Karas looked stunned for a moment at the reveal. His mouth was not able to form words straight away. Gently taking hold of her hand, the pair halted, where he cupped both her hands. "You truly believe we would leave you just because your good luck may flip to bad at some point? Dear girl, Quellon is the god of luck. Just because it has fallen in our favor doesn't mean that it always does. And you are still here, no?"

Heliosa gave a small, meek nod.

"Then that should speak volumes. We are friends with you because of who you are, *not* because luck falls in your favor more than it does others," Karas reaffirmed, gently squeezing her hands.

With a lighter spring to her step, the pair began walking again, taking their time to catch up with the unaware trio ahead.

"I will say... I hope he deems me a loyal enough servant that I'll remain in his favor for the struggle that is coming though."

"And we'll face them together, charmed with luck or not."

"Your optimism is infectious." She smiled, rolling her eyes.

"I learned it from you."

They continued walking in comfortable silence, still hand in hand.

The Harbinger approached the towering spire of falling sand alone, with his hands held out to the sides. He walked past the long line of waiting souls to the Nyxian Guard and the low-level Keeper monk stationed near the temple entrance.

The gargoyle held out his hand, the white marble looking brighter than the bone of his armor.

"No line jumping. You will have your turn in due time."

"I believe your master has been looking for me," the Harbinger replied. He opened his robe to reveal a bare torso with the jagged tips of blue shards jutting out from his skin.

The low-level monk's hand froze mid-writing as she saw the shards. "Keeper Drake needs to see this. Now," she stated, hurrying inside.

The Harbinger smiled.

Moments later, the Harbinger found himself standing in a sizable semi-circle chamber. He noted the window was closed; a lock latch was newly installed based on the shine it held. An elderly human man shuffled in with more monks and guards in tow.

"Axios, I believe?" he asked.

The Harbinger winced at the use of his birth name, but forced a smile.

"Yes, sir. I apologize for the inconvenience. I should have come to you sooner, but I was scared. Please, can you help me?"

"Yes, of course. We have been working toward a solution for this problem."

"Oh, I am not the first soul you've seen embedded with the shards of a god's soul?"

"No, unfortunately. There are others. And every one of them is in great danger. We have another here. A dwarven woman."

Drake gestured to a monk of draconic ancestry, who turned to leave.

"I'll have her brought here. You can hear from her all the good we've striven toward and how well we've treated her."

As the exiting monk left, another rushed in.

"Master Drake! There's something of a riot at the front temple. People squabbling over places in line. It's getting violent."

The Harbinger's head snapped to the new monk, concern etched on his features.

Drake gestured for the Nyxian Guards in the room to go help settle things down. "Worry not, Axios. The guards will handle it swiftly. I assure you, you are safe here."

Two minutes after they had left, the draconic monk returned with a stout dwarven woman. Her pants had a hole cut in the front of the left thigh to make room for the blue crystalline shard poking out from her leg. The second her eyes met the Harbinger, her mouth fell open in shock and terror.

"That's him!" she yelled, instantly on alert. "That's the servant of this vile *thing* that's in my head!"

Two monks dove in an attempt to grab him, a third rushing out of the room for reinforcements.

The Harbinger's face stretched into a wicked grin, his eyes flaring with blue light. With speed greater than eyes could follow, he turned toward one monk and put his fist straight through their chest and out their back, nonchalantly. He pulled his fist free, shaking the ashing blood off before turning to the other. It took just as little effort as he grabbed their head and snapped their neck, head tilting as he watched the body begin to turn to ash. Satisfied, he stopped in front of the dwarven woman. One hand gripped her throat, holding her aloft, the other grasped the end of the shard in her thigh.

"This belongs to me, I believe," he stated, ignoring the feeble kicks, punches, and scratches she was dishing out.

He ripped the shard out of her thigh unceremoniously, her choked screams of anguish filling the room as she was hurled at Keeper Drake, who had barely moved since the start of the blindingly fast attack. Mid-air, her body became dust, landing scattered on the floor before a stunned Drake.

"You... You murdered her! For what?" he yelled furiously.

"For the power. To bring my god back. What else is there?" the Harbinger admitted, still grinning as he stabbed the new shard into his own thigh, wincing as the electric pain flashed through him. It was short-lived. The sound of approaching footsteps snapped him to action.

Power surged through him as he turned to look at the one window. He swirled his hands around each other and a blue orb of light began to grow between the palms. It reached the size of a grapefruit before he hurled it at the window. Drake dove out of the way to ensure he wouldn't be hit even by a stray window piece. The ball of energy blew the glass from the stone frame, and without hesitation, the Harbinger ran and leaped through the opening with inhuman grace.

He landed with ease and bounded down the street, ducking around a corner and into an alley where a few acolytes were waiting with a disguise of new clothes. They hurriedly changed the Harbinger and continued down the alley, splitting off into smaller groups, all playing the part of friends on the way to get more coins. Shouts of alarm behind them made them pause, looking back, then skyward as others in the street began pointing. A squadron of Nyxian Guards flew above toward the Keepers of Eternal Sands, paying the citizens no mind, unaware of the killings and escape that had just hap-pened seconds earlier.

When they had gone another few blocks, one of the aco-lytes in the Harbinger's group broke the silence.

"Your mission was a success, Master?"

"Indeed," the Harbinger replied.

"Three of our own were arrested in the diversion riot. What should we do about them?"

Nothing. They have served their purpose.

The Harbinger shook his head. "Soon, we will be the lords of this realm. Then we can free our kin from their cells and laud them as the heroes they are. For now, we have to focus on finishing the task."

Correct. Now we must leave the city, find the girl, and claim the last shard. We must hurry, faithful one.

The Harbinger grimaced at the voice thundering in his mind, head pounding in pain. He was so strong and yet felt so tired, and somewhere deep down, something gnawed at him that left him ... unsettled.

Severina doubled over, stopping among the tall blades of grass. The jolt felt like electricity coursing through her and centering on her chest—the shard. The same creeping dread she'd felt at the temple of the Keepers flooded her mind. Her mind was being assaulted with feelings of panic and fear.

"Are you alright?" asked Vrath, the others stopping to check on her.

"Something is wrong ... with the shard. Maybe it... it *knows* we're getting closer to its destruction? My mind... It doesn't feel like it's fully my own... Like there's a worm buried deep in there."

Realization dawned on her. She looked at her friends with a horrified stare. "It's *him*. He's in my head … this whole time… He's been trying to influence me."

"Him who?" Faustice asked, only half paying attention.

"Scourge!" Severina answered.

The feelings intensified, wracking her with pain as they swirled and formed, scratching around her brain as though things were being engraved. And then words… She could hear words forming, alien at first but familiar. The noises from the fight… And then, clarity.

Hello, Severina, Scourge's voice purred, amusement accompanied by a smirk evident from the tone alone.

I suppose the time for pulling your strings in secret is over. However, if you are to address me, do so correctly. I am the great despoiler, consumer of worlds, purifier of the weak. My name is Thulsader.

CHAPTER 20

The Harbinger stood amid the tall grass and golden wheat of the Ashen Fields and surveyed his assembling army. They had been forced to disperse into smaller teams to leave the city without raising suspicion. A man dripping with divine power, bearing seven crystalline shards embedded in his flesh, and leading a cadre of over fifty souls, was not exactly inconspicuous. What made him smile was not the familiar faces in the crowd, but the new ones. His flock had been busy spreading the good word of Thulsader and about one-third of this congregation were souls picked up in Nox Valar. Offering power to the powerless is a tried-and-true way of circumventing moral codes.

Some of his acolytes had been solely focused on this, growing their numbers. Others had a different task, and the Harbinger beckoned those individuals over. They approached, each with large bundles slung over their backs.

"How did you fare, my kin?" the Harbinger asked.

One, a tall, broad human with a heavy brow, responded, "For a city of all dead folk, they sure gots plenty o' killing tools around."

They dropped their bundles and unfurled them to reveal dozens and dozens of weapons. There were longswords, hand axes, daggers, and spears.

"Excellent," replied the Harbinger. "Now, hand them out among the ranks. Be quick about it. We must get on the move."

Once the company of cultists had been armed, the Harbinger addressed them.

"My flock, our triumph is imminent. We must hunt down the non-believers who hold our god hostage. Then we will accomplish a truly legendary task. We will resurrect a GOD!"

The acolytes let out a resounding battle cry.

"Our quarry has a head start on us, but we have the favor of our lord, Thulsader. Let me show you the boon he grants."

The Harbinger's eyes glowed blue as he crouched down, digging his fingers into the dirt. All around him, the grass and wheat began to rot and fester. The pestilence spread, causing the soil to take on a sickly green tint, the dying vegetation curling inward on itself, beginning to clump together. The ground started undulating and quivering as distinct mounds of fetid soil and rotted vegetation bulged upward. The mounds sprouted legs and pulled themselves free from the ground, and moments later, the followers of Thulsader were looking at an entire herd of four-legged creatures with no heads made entirely of putrid dirt and rotted plants. There was one for every acolyte.

The Harbinger was the first to climb atop one of the grotesque abominations.

"Mount your steeds, true believers! We ride to victory!"

The invisible dwarf in their midst had to fight to hold back his retching at the sight and smell. He watched helplessly as the unholy cavalry took off into the fields, faster than he could follow on foot. Enough was enough. Alina needed to know about this.

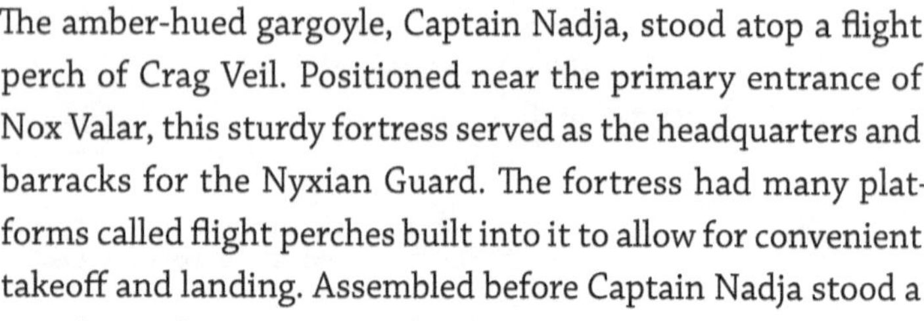

The amber-hued gargoyle, Captain Nadja, stood atop a flight perch of Crag Veil. Positioned near the primary entrance of Nox Valar, this sturdy fortress served as the headquarters and barracks for the Nyxian Guard. The fortress had many platforms called flight perches built into it to allow for convenient takeoff and landing. Assembled before Captain Nadja stood a squadron of sixteen gargoyles clad in matte white armor.

"We've received word from an unknown source that a large assemblage of souls is traveling the fields riding atop some fell abominations," Nadja declared. "We believe they are led by a fanatic carrying shards of a god's soul, and they bear the Sunless Crossing ill intent. Our mission is to track them down and assess the threat, potentially engaging with deadly force."

The Nyxian Guards thumped their chests in unison and then took to the skies.

Vrath pointed to a soft yellow glow in the distance.

"There is our destination," he declared.

"Oh, you think so?" quipped Heliosa. "The only light we can see for miles in any direction that *isn't* Nox Valar is where we need to go?"

"Ignore her." Severina placed a hand on Vrath's arm. "She's just cranky. She hasn't walked this much in... well..."

"Ever," Karas finished. "I'm trying to remember any instance where Heliosa ever traveled more than a city block without the aid of a horse or carriage."

"Keep it up, Old Man, and the next time you're in need of a little divine healing, I may just be too tired." Despite the words, there was a teasing tone and a smile present.

Karas chuckled at the jape.

"But honestly," Faustice chimed in with a hint of whine to his timber. "This place is so big... and no horses? Poor planning. We should have bartered or even just taken one of those large wagons; a mere band of circus performers against the Legendary Faustice and his entourage? No contest."

Vrath shook his head. "Don't let their whimsical exterior fool you... the Strays are no circus and they know how to handle themselves in a fight. There's a reason they thrive out in the fields where most souls wouldn't last."

Severina picked up her pace. They'd almost made it. She hoped these sorcerers would be able to perform the extraction, not to mention the shard's destruction afterward. And then there was the issue of the other shards and the Harbinger. Having this many unknown variables made her nervous.

"We'll be there in less than a day," concluded Vrath.

"How can we tell?" quipped Karas. "Out here, there are no timepieces to mark its passage."

"Spend enough time here, you start to feel it," Vrath said, shrugging.

CHAPTER 21

Those from Legend's Meadow had carved out a life in the Sunless Crossing that didn't conform to the rules of the Godless Monarchy and the laws of Nox Valar. The community stood as a beacon of righteous rebellion. A symbol of freedom and individuality. A shining star of heroic antics in a sea of dullards and boredom. At least, that's how the residents viewed themselves.

They made a mockery of the realm's regulations by traveling back and forth to the living world at will. Using arcane powers, some via artifact, others through innate ability, they performed specific tasks, usually for the betterment of themselves. Occasionally, they found alignment with the goals of the Nox Valar representatives and would work with them secretly. Officially, Legend's Meadow was the home of outlaws. And they enjoyed that mystique.

Structurally, the journeyed group's camp acted more like a hamlet. Tents lined the outer ring in a massive oval. The center bustled with a few select merchants and potential clients looking to pay for a hero's services, such as delivering messages to living loved ones, retrieving valuable artifacts from the living world to be used in the afterlife, and sometimes even revenge.

Into this thriving marketplace stormed Vrath, Severina, Karas, Heliosa, and Faustice. They wasted no time in beginning to approach everyone they could, asking for the sorcerers with the names provided by Wren.

Karas noticed a dwarven woman clad in chain mail, a mace at her side, and a floppy oversized hat atop her head. She sat on a stump whittling a stick, deliberately *not* watching them go from person to person asking for the sorcerers.

Karas approached her and said, "Pardon me, but do you know where we might find Virion, Chorlen, and Aronos?"

She looked up at him with innocent eyes. "Who are those people? What do you need them for?"

Karas peered back at her in appraisal. There was more going on behind her eyes than the woman was letting on.

"We hear they are great masters of the arcane arts," Karas replied. "Perhaps even the best in the Crossing. We have a particular problem that only the most skilled magic users can solve."

She smiled. "Sounds like you need a hero!"

"Indeed, we do," Karas called the others over and pointed out Severina. "You see, my friend here has the fractured shard of a god's soul stuck in her chest. We need to remove it, without destroying her. Then we need to obliterate the shard to ensure the god never returns."

The woman nodded. "That is indeed a task worthy of a true hero... a *Legend* even. What were those names again?"

"Virion, Chorlen, and Aronos," Severina answered.

The dwarf woman stood, removed her hat, and gave a little bow. "Aronos Hillmantle at your service. I'd apologize for probing a bit before telling you who I am, but I'm not sorry, so I won't."

"You'll help us then?" Vrath asked.

Aronos stepped closer to Severina, ignoring Vrath. "You really have a piece of a god's soul in there?" She pointed at her chest.

Severina nodded.

"Not just any god," Heliosa added. "An absolute monster that cannot be allowed to be reborn. The fate of our world... possibly even this realm... depends on it."

"You don't need to keep selling me, dear. I'm already on board." Aronos put her thumb and index finger in her mouth and let out a loud, melodic whistle. In response, two individuals broke free from a small huddle in the next tent over. One was a tall, slender elf who looked gaunt, his clothing loose, fashioned on him with belts, and a deep hood sewn to his tunic, pulled deep to obscure his face The other was a stocky lilac tiefling with horns that went backward, almost spiraling.

Aronos waved her hand at the slender elven figure. "I give you Virion, the Flame."

The person bowed deeply with a flourish.

"And Chorlen, the Chaotic."

The tiefling smiled and bowed as well, much more simply than his counterpart.

"What's the story, Aro?" Chorlen asked.

"The story is, we're about to go down in Legend's Meadow history."

We are being hunted.

What? By who?

Those flying stone creatures.

They could be after Severina.

Perhaps, but they will catch up to us before her. We do not have time to waste battling them.

What do we do?

Bring the company to a halt. Order everyone to lie flat against their steeds and to trust their God!

The Harbinger held a fist up, signaling the stop. The rotten abominations slowed and halted. The acolytes all obeyed their leader and pressed their chests to the body of these monstrosities. They found themselves being pulled into the bodies of the creatures, enveloped in the dirt and tangled grass. And then the four-legged horrors sank and melded into the ground, mingling their fetid grasses with the healthy swaying grass around them.

They lay like that, silent and unmoving. He counted his breaths, making the most of the ability to stop and rest, his eyes closed as he awaited further instruction. For the better part of an hour, there was nothing. No movement or sound to indicate anything was happening. Just when he thought to ask his god, he swore he felt shadows swoop overhead despite the darkness of the soil.

We can continue. The sky rocks have moved on.

We'll still have to face them, my lord.

Yes, but we can now take them by surprise. Perhaps they will even be locked in confrontation with our enemy. We can take both groups out in one fell swoop.

You are truly magnificent, my lord.

Severina finished explaining her story to the trio of mages. Each had a different reaction: Aronos smiled brightly, Virion's jaw dropped, and Chorlen furrowed his brow.

"Well, this is a new flavor of madness," noted Virion.

"But you said it could be done," Karas said to Aronos.

Chorlen interjected, "It can, but the risks are extreme, to say the least."

"Not only to the shard carrier, but to all of us," added Virion.

"But think of the accolades," countered Aronos with a smile. "We call ourselves Legends... Lads, what's more legendary than assisting in the destruction of an evil god?"

The trio stared pensively at each other as if having an unspoken discussion.

Severina and her party fidgeted and paced impatiently, near frantic.

The three nodded to each other, turned toward Severina, and announced, "We'll do it!"

The moment the words left their lips, something large and heavy thundered into the ground between them. The force of the impact kicked up ash, sending them all staggering backward, hacking and coughing. When the ash cleared, they saw a towering amber-colored gargoyle clad in the matte white plate armor of the Nyxian Guard.

"Prongs! Everyone scatter!" Aronos shouted as the rest of the Nyxian squadron landed in the encampment. Severina's heart sank as she watched her last hope disappear in three puffs of arcane smoke. Around them, the denizens of Legend's Meadow who did not possess teleportation abilities scrambled to pack up precious belongings and flee.

Faustice noticed some of the Nyxian Guards watching where each one scattered, as though wanting to apprehend them for crimes not evident to the group. However, the presumed leader kept her gaze fixated on Severina.

"Severina Stormbringer, I am Captain Nadja of the Nyxian Guard..."

Severina cut her off, her despair at the vanishing mages replaced with fury at the gargoyle. "You just scared away my chance at solving this problem. If you so much as make one move toward forcing me back to the city, I will end you. That is not a threat, it's a goddamn promise."

The group shifted their stances slightly, getting ready for a fight in case it came. Vrath balled his hands into fists while Karas grabbed the hilt of his sword. Heliosa rubbed her holy talisman, and Faustice twirled his flute through his fingers.

Captain Nadja held her hands out in a show of peace. "You did not get off on the best footing with those at the Keepers, and in the Trove, I understand that. But for the moment, we have a more dire matter to address. We had been tracking a horde of those fanatics from your world. They were heading in this direction, but we lost them. For all we know, they could b—"

A company of mounted abominations burst into the clearing and charged forward, their battle cry deafening and the accompanying stench of rotted vegetation revolting. The Nyxian Guards leaped into action, forming a line and soaring forward to meet the assault. With a sickening clash, the two sides met. Soil abominations were reduced to crumbling mounds while Thulsader acolytes were cut down. However, the initial bout was not completely one-sided. The Harbinger single-handedly dispatched one gargoyle, melting their stone skin with a touch. Two more shattered and broke under a slew of attacks from a dozen assailants.

Severina felt a tug on her arm.

"Let's go!" said Faustice. "This is our chance to slip away. We can try to find those mages again."

"Strategically, it's not the worst move," added Karas.

"Sure is lucky they're so busy fighting each other," Heliosa chimed in.

"For gargoyles, death is final, but if those fanatics get their hands on you, it'll all be over," Vrath said, sounding conflicted.

Severina looked at her friends, looked at the stretch of field they could disappear into, and then at the fighting.

"We can't," she said, still watching the fighting. "The Nyxian Guards, they aren't bad... they're just trying to protect their world... we can't leave them."

When she turned back to her friends, she saw they already had weapons and magical implements ready in their hands.

Karas shrugged. "Like we didn't know you were going to say that."

Behind them, Severina saw some of the heroes from Legend's Meadow rushing forward to the fight rather than fleeing.

Severina drew Wrath and led the charge with a roar. She and Vrath formed a front line for their little squad, hacking and punching their way through acolytes and soil abominations.

Heliosa called upon Quellon to gain protective enchantments for her friends. She then pointed her palms at groups of Nyxian Guards, bathing them in white light.

Karas stuck by Heliosa's side, keeping her safe from assailants. She noted her protector and gave him a smile that said *just like old times*.

Vrath kept close to Severina, guarding her flanks.

Faustice held Greta up to his lips and played a tune meant to assault the senses of their enemies. To his targets, it sounded like explosions were thundering within their ears. The worst affected doubled over, clutching at their heads in agony, allowing a nearby team of gargoyles to make quick work of the distracted fanatics.

A soil abomination pounced on a Legend's Meadow hero, a reptilian man wielding a spear. The abomination let him pierce the spear clear through the center of the creature's torso, ignoring whatever damage this may have caused, and continued to burrow downward, pushing him into the ground itself. He let out a final cry before the creature buried him alive, using the weight of its body to hold him underground.

The hero's green-scaled hand grasped upward, barely staying above ground, thrashing for a few seconds before going still. Seconds later, it dissolved to nothing.

Emboldened, the nearby acolytes struck harder and faster, cracking and destroying a blue marble gargoyle.

Severina sprinted to lend aid, using Wrath's otherworldly sharpness to shred through follower after follower. She paused as her vision grew hazy with all the ash floating around her. Vrath halted by her side, his head swiveling for threats.

The acolytes had the numbers, but the Nyxian Guards, heroes, and Severina's friends had skill and training. Despite a few losses, momentum was solidly on their side.

Having watched from the sidelines, the Harbinger decided to enter the fight, strolling through the battle haze as an eerie beacon of blue light holding his sword and dagger at the ready. An elven woman with twin blades lunged at him, but the Harbinger swung his blades with such speed that the woman became dust before she even realized she'd been cut.

Vrath instinctively put himself in front of Severina. The Harbinger didn't notice her and kept his sights on the gargoyles ahead. The heroes and Guards saw him coming and took up positions of attack.

As he approached, the Harbinger tensed up and loosed a roar full of rage and hate before levitating above the battle. He bellowed again, a low rumbling tone, causing the heroes below him to begin retching in violent convulsions. One by one, they collapsed, dropping their weapons, helpless against the affliction. Their mouths showed signs of rot and gangrene, and a black ooze leaked from within. They died in anguish and pain, turning to dust one by one. A few gargoyles of the Nyxian Guard stumbled back, spitting, wiping, or coughing out what seemed like molten stone or gem. Unsteady, they were pushed to the back to recover, each continuing to expel the molten version they were hewn from until they collapsed, going still.

As the Harbinger returned to the ground, he appeared drained, tired from the assault. A small team of nearby Nyxian Guards moved in on him, hoping to take advantage. As they neared, the Harbinger tensed once again, his eyes glowing that eerie blue as he gave his attackers a sinister grin.

The glow from his eyes intensified, seeming to take physical form, and as each of the gargoyles entered the cone of light, they cracked and shattered, tumbling lifelessly to the ground. The Harbinger looked down with pity as a few small rocks that used to be Nyxian Guards rolled to a stop against his boots.

"No!" Vrath yelled, pain and grief drowning his voice.

Looking around, the Harbinger smiled at the new odds. So few of his enemies remained.

Severina exchanged a look with her comrades. They nodded in acknowledgment. Severina and Karas charged in unison, weapons at the ready. Faustice played a tune targeting the Harbinger, forcing the cult leader to clutch at his ears in pain while Heliosa blessed her charging friends with divine protection, clutching her holy talisman.

As they closed in, the Harbinger focused his blue glare at Faustice. Greta's sound wavered and became garbled as a thick, black, mucus-like liquid bubbled out the holes before she cracked and fell apart in the bard's hands. Faustice choked, grabbing his throat as the very same black mucus dribbled from his lips, the skin around his mouth turning a raw red with green veins. Heliosa raced to his side and desperately began praying and casting, calling on Quellon for aid.

Karas and Severina lunged forward, bringing their weapons down with powerful swings. The Harbinger parried both attacks with his sword and dagger, smiling and twisting his blades to go on the offense.

He outmaneuvered Karas and drove the dagger at his ribs, but the blade refused to connect; Heliosa's protection spell keeping the older warrior safe.

The Harbinger took a long step back, reassessing his foes.

Severina and Karas spread out to flank their enemy and closed in quickly, Faustice's screams spurring them into action. They had to end this bastard *now* to save their friend.

They lunged at the Harbinger, but he was ready. Instead of bringing his weapons to bear, he gave a brief, powerful shout that pushed Karas off his feet. The force of the spell sent him hurtling a dozen feet backward, where he hit the ground hard. As Severina came in, the Harbinger turned his fiery blue eyes to her, and she felt Wrath's hilt become scalding hot in her hands, the length of the blade dancing with blue spider webbing lines. Sensations of panic bombarded Severina's mind, coming from the mental link she and Wrath shared. Her sword was afraid. With a brilliant blue flash, Wrath's black blade cracked and shattered in her hands.

Behind her, Vrath cried out in anguish, a hand reaching back to where his wing had been.

Rage took hold and Severina attempted to cast a fireball, hoping to knock him back a few paces. Nothing happened, as though her reserves were spluttering and empty, but a nagging feeling attempted to draw her elsewhere. Dismissing it, she took the bottle of fireblast off her belt and threw it at the Harbinger with all her strength, unwilling to get close while adjusting her grip on her sword.

The Harbinger underestimated the strength of whatever was in the bottle, and was thrown back as an explosion of blue-purple fire erupted from the shattering bottle. He rolled a few feet away, dazed and disoriented momentarily.

Severina held fast to Wrath's hilt, fighting back tears from pain, looking over to where her friends were. Karas was nearly recovered, standing and shaking his head. Vrath remained hunched over, gripping at his back and grunting in pain. Heliosa kept one hand on Faustice's back, the other squeezing her talisman as she continued her prayers to ease his pain.

The Harbinger rose from the ground with grim determination, smoke wafting off his body and clothes. Patches of his skin were charred black, and the holes in his shirt and pants glowed with the dying embers of the fire.

Finish her off. Take the shard and make me whole.

Yes, my lord.

The few remaining acolytes coalesced around their leader.

The Harbinger charged at the distracted Severina. She spun round in time to see blue eyes and a badly damaged body with crystalline shards protruding pounce on her. She fell back with the Harbinger atop as they collided, her sword hand stomped on and her sword hilt kicked away. He thrust his dagger toward her chest, but Heliosa's protection spell deflected the strike.

Severina held her free hand out and tried to summon the magic again, knowing an arcane energy burst should do the trick. Again, nothing happened.

The Harbinger went to plunge the blade into her again, a faint blue misting around the dagger.

Severina roared with a primal fury, snatching the magic from its hiding place deep in the recesses of her mind.

A jagged bolt of lightning, pure black, erupted from her palm, striking the Harbinger in the chest. The attack sent him hurtling backward, and he skidded along the ground, muscles spasming from the spell.

Severina scrambled to her feet to see several acolytes charging her from both the right and left flank. Vrath and Karas, both recovered enough to throw themselves back into the fray, crashed into the assailants on the left with sword and fists.

Severina held her hand up to the enemies on her right. Again, she unleashed a burst of jagged black lightning that scorched through the attackers, leaving nothing but ash. She turned her palm toward herself, marveling at this ability. In life, she'd never done anything like that.

Vrath broke off from the fight and ran to Severina's side, shaking her from her reverie. Severina looked up at him, and tears instantly filled her eyes as she hugged him tightly.

"The sword! I'm so sorry," she sobbed.

"It wasn't your fault, Sevi. I'm fine."

Karas finished the last of the acolytes, their zeal and numbers no match for his years of experience. He then rushed to Heliosa's side, checking on the pair in case she needed help with Faustice.

The Harbinger stirred slightly and let out a grunt.

Severina's face became a mask of pure anger as lightning pooled around her hands before bursting in his direction. He screamed as the black lightning enveloped him, making his muscles tighten and spasm, leaving him floored.

Not taking any chances, Karas thrust his sword into the prone Harbinger's chest, pinning him to the ground.

"Why isn't he dust?" Karas asked, frustrated.

The shards within the Harbinger's body began to glow again, causing Karas to jump back. The Harbinger appeared unconscious, but his limp body still levitated up into the air.

"Get away!" called Vrath.

The light intensified, building to some inevitable end. Everyone quickly dove for cover amongst the wheat, covering their heads.

The light exploded with no sound or warning.

Vrath felt a chunk of his arm get cut out of him as the light grazed his bicep. Then the light vanished, along with the Harbinger.

CHAPTER 22

Heliosa begged Quellon for intervention as Faustice fought. She had channeled what magic she could into healing and cures, but this divine rot was too powerful for her to excise.

Faustice's frantic breathing slowed as his eyes began to roll back. His spasming muscles stilled and went rigid and Heliosa let out a pained wail and hugged her friend.

The others approached, slow and uneasy.

"Is he … dead?" Severina asked.

"He'd be a pile of ash if that were the case," Vrath noted.

Heliosa looked down with tear-filled eyes and noticed that Faustice was still breathing in a weak, raspy cadence.

"He's in some coma-like trance," she realized, relief flooding her and forcing a sad but happy laugh from her lips. She bore a surface crack that ran from the right side of her forehead down her right cheek to her jaw. It looked remarkably like a scar.

Severina looked around amid the ash piles and saw a few more people in the same catatonic state as Faustice.

Captain Nadja landed nearby with a thud.

"Don't get too excited about that," she warned. "A dead soul in the Crossing, when dusted, will simply reform out in the fields on the next day. After multiple deaths, the souls do begin to unravel; losing memories, losing faculties... but *this*..." She gestured at Faustice. "This may be worse than death."

"Way to lighten the mood," Karas grunted.

Nadja turned her whole body to face him, her expression grim. "I'm not trying to lighten the mood. This is very bad. I have been here in Crossing and part of the Nyxian Guard for over ten thousand days. I have never suffered losses like today. Look around. My entire squadron is dead save for myself and one badly wounded corporal." She pointed at a gray granite gargoyle reclining on the ground, missing his left arm.

"The city..." Heliosa countered. "The city is bursting with clerics. We can find help for those afflicted."

Nadja nodded. "We can try." She shot a glance at Severina and added, "But that would mean you actually *accepting* our help."

They took some time to rest and take stock of the damage.

Seated and leaning back against a broken carriage from the Legends, Vrath did his best not to move his wounded arm. The blast had sliced off nearly half of his right bicep. The wound stung deeply. Severina sat with him, gently leaning against his undamaged shoulder.

"I'm so sorry," she whispered.

Vrath didn't reveal that his back still ached from the destruction of the sword. The blade forged from his wing had still maintained a metaphysical connection to his core, and its destruction burned.

"There is nothing for you to be sorry for," he replied, tone soft and dour.

Karas had an arm around Heliosa's shoulders.

"It's not your fault," he soothed. "It was Scourge that did this to him."

"Quellon didn't lend aid; didn't intercede at all," she whispered. "Has he forsaken me? Have I offended him in some way?"

"If he didn't lend aid, I'd have been skewered on the Harbinger's blade. Your god has been more helpful than any other in this endeavor. It may be too much to expect him to simply solve all our problems."

"But why? Why would he protect you but not save Faustice?"

"We cannot pretend to understand the machinations of the Universe. All we can do is care for those we love and live the best lives we can."

Severina gazed longingly at the worn leather straps that were wrapped around the pure onyx that had been the hilt of her mighty weapon. It was as if she'd lost a friend and counselor at once. She dropped it on the ground and sighed.

She needed a distraction and stood as Vrath rested, looking over the destruction wrought by Scourge, and felt disheartened. A voice thundered in her head, bitter and terrible.

This is all your fault. All this suffering.

Scourge?!

My name is Thulsader!

Get out of my head!

I would be happy to. Just return the shard to its brethren, so I may claim my new empire here.

Absolutely not.

Then you and everyone you care about will die in agony... again... and again... and again!

Shut up! Shut up!

"Shut up!" Severina screamed aloud, grabbing at the sides of her head. The others all jumped and looked at her with worried expressions.

"It's Scourge... or I guess ... *Thulsader*," she explained. "He's in my head. I think he's been here the whole time. He's been spying... trying to influence me... he wants the Sunless Crossing."

"The Crossing is a nexus between countless mortal worlds," Vrath said. "If he gains control of this realm..."

"He'll spread his filth over world after world," Karas finished, horrified at the idea.

"Maybe someone should have let our mages do their jobs in the first place," Captain Nadja huffed.

"Your people weren't exactly the most warm and reassuring," Heliosa countered softly.

"Let's not do this right now," Severina said. "We can throw blame around all day while the world doesn't die. I made the choices that got us here. Whether or not this asshole inside my mind was influencing me is irrelevant, but we have to get this shard out and destroyed."

"Do we even have time to get back to Nox Valar? Who knows where the Harbinger has gone or what his next move will be."

"Hold on, let... let me try something..." Severina closed her eyes and sat down cross-legged in the dirt. She slowed her breathing to a controlled rhythm. The others watched her intently. At one point, Severina's head twisted, her expression strained into a pained grimace. She gritted her teeth and snapped herself out of the meditation. She panted and wiped away a trickle of sweat from her brow.

She looked up at her friends with bloodshot eyes. "I thought maybe I could open myself up to the connection with Scour—er, Thulsader... and maybe glean some kind of feeling as to where the other shards are... he did not like that." To

Heliosa, she added, "Got any minor healing spells at the ready? My head feels like it's been used as an orcish war drum."

Heliosa placed a gentle hand on Severina's forehead, channeling divine salve into her.

"Did you learn anything?" Karas asked.

Severina nodded and pointed toward the dark horizon. "The other shards are in there."

"The storm…" Vrath asked, a deep frown on his face.

"What is that place?" Heliosa asked.

"The Storm of Broken Worlds," Captain Nadja replied. "It encircles the entire realm, and everyone knows that entering it is dangerous. Too long in there can turn you to ash. What most people don't know is it is a graveyard … for dead gods."

"The kind of place someone looking to resurrect a god would go," Karas noted.

"Doesn't make sense though," Heliosa countered. "I thought he needed the shard in Sevi. If not, why attack us at all? Why not just go straight for the storm? Wasn't the whole point that he needed a bit more of the god's essence?"

Severina jumped up to her feet, eyes wild with terror.

"Menavaria! Shards struck her."

"Who's—" Captain Nadja started, quickly being cut off.

"Severina's god," Vrath cut in, terrible realization spreading. "She died."

"Then she has a temple somewhere in there," Nadja replied.

"Shit," Severina cursed. "Even if I wanted to go with you… we don't have time to go all the way back to Nox Valar."

"You want to go after him," Vrath stated.

"You can't," said Karas. "What if that's what he wants? For Severina to bring her shard right to him. We have to get it out of her." He shook his head, resolute in the decision.

"We can help with that," said a new voice.

They all whirled around to see the two mages, Virion and Chorlen. Virion had his hands hidden within his sleeves, head lowered deeper than before. Chorlen seemed to be cradling something in his hands.

"You!" barked Severina. "You left us! You said you'd help, and you left!"

"Self-preservation instincts are a bit of a requisite out here," Chorlen replied. "Especially for those of us still alive."

"Cowards," Severina spat.

"Sevi!" Heliosa said. "At least these two came back…"

"Aronos came back," Virion said, a waver in their voice. "In fact, she turned around and came back almost immediately once those creatures appeared."

"She wanted to help you," Chorlen said, his voice cracking.

"Where is she?" Karas asked.

Chorlen opened his hands, revealing a small pile of black ash.

"Oh…" Severina paused. "I… I'm sorry." Guilt at her jabs overcame her.

"But she'll just come back, right?" asked Heliosa, hopeful.

"No." Nadja shook her head, tone gentle. "No, she was alive… *alive,* alive. And when a living soul dies here, the Crossing consumes them. No more soul. No afterlife. They are truly, wholly gone." She shot a glare at the two mages. "Which is why we don't want those of you who are alive coming here in the first place!"

Chorlen hung his head, averting his gaze. Virion, notably, seemed unbothered by the comment personally, but placed a hand on Chorlen's arm in support.

"We'll help any way we can, regardless," Virion said.

The wheels of Karas's tactical mind began turning. "Okay, okay, we can figure this out. We head into the storm. We stop the lunatic. These two get the shard out. Everything is saved."

"The extraction ritual called for three," Severina replied in a defeated tone.

"I'll be their third then."

They all turned to Heliosa.

"This ritual could destroy you," Virion warned. "Have you ever worked with magic at this level?"

"No," said Heliosa. "But I'm not worried... all I need is a little luck, right?" she said, a hopeful but worried edge to her voice that she tried to hide with a smile.

CHAPTER 23

The Harbinger's mind drifted aimlessly through an ethereal sea.

I failed you, my master.

As long as this form survives, you have not failed.

But the last shard—

It matters not. During your battle, being closer to that great storm, I felt the presence of another fragment.

Where is this other?

Inside a god.

The Harbinger regained consciousness and sat up with great pain and effort, the sword he had been impaled with to the side, as though it had been pushed out and fell. Much of his skin was charred the color of coal and his pant legs hung in tatters, his shirt was missing large patches. He forced himself up onto his bare feet and surveyed his surroundings. To his left, he saw the vast fields of the Sunless Crossing. Immediately to his right, the Storm of Broken Worlds awaited. The chaotic maelstrom filled him with dread, but he knew he must persevere. The black storm clouds spat ominous lightning more frequently than it had seemed from a distance, and the howling winds whipped about, ash and pebbles flashing in and out of

view. It stretched upward like a wall of dark, roiling terror. The Harbinger gritted his teeth and stepped into the storm.

Heliosa clapped her hands together. "So, uh, where are we doing this thing?"

"This *thing*?" Virion replied, "By *thing* you mean the incredibly difficult and dangerous ritual that, if we err in the slightest, will annihilate us all and likely set off a cataclysm? That *thing*?"

Heliosa pointed and winked. "That's the one."

Vrath folded his arms and said, "The Quarry is not far. We can't go inside, and they'd never allow us to perform the ritual there. But the fields around it are open and kept clear."

"But we will need to stop within and warn them," noted Nadja.

Vrath nodded.

"What is the Quarry?" Karas asked.

Nadja replied, "You've undoubtedly noticed how common our kind are here. And are aware that the Arbiter is always a gargoyle?" She waited until they nodded. "Well, in a realm that we protect for the souls that journey through it, that doesn't mean we don't also crave something that is wholly and completely for us. The Quarry is the birthplace of gargoyles. A place where only gargoyles are allowed to tread. No souls, dead or alive, may enter."

"Fun name," said Heliosa. "Cheeky."

"Yes, our kind is known for our wit," Nadja said without any hint of irony.

"Then let's get a move on," Severina urged.

"What about Faustice?" Heliosa asked.

Captain Nadja gestured to the one surviving Guard from her squadron, the one who'd lost an arm.

"The corporal here will fly back to Nox Valar and retrieve reinforcements. They'll send someone to tend to these afflicted souls, as well as mobilize a larger force to back us up with any potential battles on the horizon."

Without waiting for Severina or anyone else to respond to Nadja's statement, the corporal nodded and took to the sky.

The rest gathered up their things and set out for the Quarry. They walked on, moving slowly due to their injuries. Nadja only grumbled once about how annoying it was to have to walk rather than fly.

Karas fell in beside Severina. "I saw what you did during the fight, that black lightning. You've never done that before. I mean, I've seen you wield lightning, but it always seemed more ... natural."

"I know," Severina replied. "I'm as confused as you are. I didn't know black lightning was even a thing."

"Could it be..." Karas gingerly gestured to the general area of Severina where the shard was lodged.

"I don't think so," she replied. "If anything, I feel like Scourge has been trying to hinder my abilities."

"Did we hear you say earlier that your god is dead?"

Severina and Karas were startled at the sound of Virion's voice. They hadn't noticed the mages eavesdropping on their conversation.

"Yeah?" Severina answered.

Virion and Chorlen looked around, specifically checking to see if Captain Nadja was in earshot.

"We've heard rumors..." Virion started.

"Barely rumors. More like whispers, really," Chorlen clarified.

Virion nudged the man. "Anyway, the *whispers* say there is a faction within the House of the Sovereign... warriors and magic users who have ties to gods that have since died. Yet somehow, they managed to retain a modicum of the power gifted by their gods."

"But the power changes," Virion continued. "It becomes ... unique."

"They call them the Godless." Chorlen shot a furtive glance at Nadja, and despite her seeming lack of awareness about the conversation, added, "Again, just a rumor, of course."

As they plodded on, Severina found herself staring at the Storm of Broken Worlds on the horizon. Somewhere in there, the Harbinger was moving closer to his goal, closer toward resurrecting Thulsader. She would not let it happen. For a brief moment, she felt a swell of hope. He did not have her shard still. And without it, perhaps he could not succeed.

Oh, it is going to happen, child.

Get out of my head, filth.

Soon, child, soon. I will have my own body again and will no longer need to hitch rides on pathetic worms like yourself.

Not without the shard in me, you won't. Your soul gem won't be complete. I hold the advantage.

The arrogance of mortals always amuses me. Whoever said I needed ALL my shards?

What?

Silly girl. I don't need ALL the shards. Do you think my soul gem broke perfectly into eight neat and tidy pieces? No, no, no... there are splinters of me scattered all across your world and this one. I just need enough of my gem. A substantial portion of my soul combined with a mortal soul's sacrifice. I'll be back, good as new.

I know you need my shard. Why else would your lapdog have attacked us?

I thought I needed your shard. And then I sensed another substantial fragment. One much easier to claim.

Severina's face dropped.

Leave Menavaria alone! You vile stain of existence!

You left me no choice. You could have just surrendered your fragment to me and I'd not need to disrupt the grave of the deity you let down.

You could still have my shard. Leave her alone and I'll hand mine over.

So Amusing. Goodbye, Severina.

He went silent. She tried to bring him back.

Sco—Thulsader. Come back. Let's make a deal. Come back! Please!

There was no response. Severina let out a scream of frustration, causing the others to stop and look at her. Raising her head, she looked back at them.

"We have to hurry. They are heading to the grave of my god right now."

Not long after, the Quarry become visible on the horizon. A large stretch of huge boulders packed together forming a wall.

"I'll fly ahead and inform them of our plight," declared Nadja.

"Sounds good," agreed Vrath. "See you there."

The gargoyle took to the air and flew toward the mass of stone.

Severina noticed an emotional weight on Vrath. "What's wrong? I mean, besides the obvious *everything* going on around us."

"I haven't come here in a long time." Vrath gestured to his back. "There are some here who don't approve of this."

"You sacrificed your flight to help me, to *protect* me... I'd have thought that'd be seen as a noble act?"

"To most gargoyles, it is. To others, well, they put a strong emphasis on the distinction that we watch over mortal souls, but we are not subservient to them. That faction believes what I did crosses the line, makes us look lesser."

"Elitist gargoyles..." Severina mused sarcastically. "How wonderful."

CHAPTER 24

adja waited for the others outside the entrance, which was an arrangement of massive boulders that rose twenty feet high. The entryway itself was blocked by two broad, hulking gargoyles standing shoulder to shoulder.

She pointed to an open field nearby.

"We can conduct the ritual over there. They are also willing to send out aerial scouts to make sure we are not surprised by any incoming hostiles. I know we're all tired and would like rest, but we'll have to do it out here. None of you may enter." Her eyes fell on Vrath. "And there were even some who wanted to deny you access should you wish to enter."

"I'm not surprised," said Vrath.

"However, those dissenters are not the majority," Nadja added.

Vrath turned to Severina, took her hand, and said, "I won't be long."

"You're leaving us?"

"I promise to return soon." He gestured to his wound. "Just need to be patched up."

Severina sighed. Hope and confidence were hard to come by these days, and Vrath leaving her side did not help.

She forced a smile and said, "Hurry back."

Vrath headed for the entryway, and after a brief greeting, the two gargoyles in the path shifted to allow him passage.

Severina watched him go until he disappeared around a bend and then hurried after the others toward the chosen ceremony site.

Rennard sat alone in his workshop. Before him, in the warm candle glow, sat two vials of liquid—one green, one blue. He stared at them with trepidation in his heart and mind.

Before surrendering all thoughts and goals of resurrecting his friends, he had to know the whole story. He had to be sure she was indeed going to be well. And he had to know if Kanen spoke the truth about her role in this plot he'd laid out. Would bringing her back actually endanger all of Tormelund as well as the afterlife realm?

These potions would hopefully show him all he needed. The risk involved gave him pause. With this action, he truly put everything on the line.

He sighed deeply, staring at the green and blue vials.

The door to his chambers opened with a low creak, and in slipped a cloaked figure. Rennard looked up and said, "Thank you for agreeing to this, your majesty."

The figure pulled back their hood to reveal the weathered face of King Ulren himself.

"I ask again, Rennard, why me? Why not employ one of the many skilled mages under your purview?"

"Because you are the only one that I know, beyond any shred of doubt, I can trust."

Rennard pointed at the items on the table. "Once I am ... gone, you will need to watch over my body and eventually pour the blue potion down my throat. Please give me at least a few hours, three or four. You can wait longer. I'm willing to take the risk, but the potion's efficacy will begin to wane after five or six hours. After twelve, it won't work at all."

"And you'll stay dead," Ulren finished.

"Which I would like to avoid."

Rennard picked up the green vial and steeled himself. He removed the stopper and glanced at the king, raising the potion in a mock cheers.

"To your *health*, your majesty."

"That feels highly—" King Ulren's words caught in his mouth as Rennard swallowed the poison.

Rennard felt a burning sensation surge through his chest as the vile liquid flowed down into his stomach. A searing agony like fire in his veins raced through every fiber of him and he fell from his chair to his hands and knees. The pain was far greater than he had anticipated. His muscles twitched and spasmed, vision blurring. Every part of him screamed in pain. His eyes narrowed on the remaining vial atop the desk.

The blue potion. He had to grasp it; had to ingest it. Now. Immediately.

However, he found himself unable to act on those urges. He had no feeling or control of his limbs, and he slumped, King Ulren catching him and gently lowering him to the floor.

Vrath walked the long pathway down into the massive pit. The reactions from the gargoyles he passed ranged from polite nods, to indifference, to blatant glares. He returned the polite nods, ignored the indifference, and met every glare with unblinking eye contact and a neutral expression.

The floor of the Quarry served as something of a community square, a nexus. Four Gargoyle statues that had been there for eons were situated in the center, each facing outward in a different direction. When a gargoyle decides their time is done, they can give themselves over to eternal rest. Most in the Sunless Crossing take up positions around the walls of the great mesa supporting Nox Valar. But these four had been awarded a special honor.

Vrath continued past the homages and entered a network of cave openings. Each cave represented a home, community center, or work lab. More gargoyles milled about, performing their daily tasks, chatting with friends, and gathering stones for research or construction.

"The wretch returns," whispered a nearby gargoyle, intentionally just loud enough for him to hear. The words stung, but he was used to it.

At last, he came to a familiar cave with artistic carvings etched along the opening.

"Lorin the Jade," he called into the cave. "You have a visitor."

Five individuals approached him from behind. Their supposed leader growled, "You are not welcome here."

Vrath turned to face the hate. "I am a gargoyle, and I am welcome here."

Their leader pointed toward Vrath's back. "You gave up being a gargoyle the day you did *that* to yourself."

The five stepped forward, trying to intimidate Vrath, but he didn't budge.

"I'm here for Lorin. Not you."

An ancient gargoyle made of stunning jade and wearing necklaces laden with gems emerged from the cave and addressed the beings at his doorstep. "I'll not have my client harassed. Kindly depart."

The leader snarled, "You dare side with him?"

Lorin smirked. "What are you going to do about it?"

The hostiles traded nervous glances. After a few tense moments, they backed away, their faces etched with mixtures of anger and embarrassment.

"Sorry about that," said Vrath.

"It is *I* who should apologize to *you*, Vrath. Please, come inside."

They entered the comfortable dwelling and Lorin motioned for Vrath to sit as he did the same.

"I never imagined I'd see you again," said the jade gargoyle.

"I wouldn't have come if this were not a matter of the most dire stakes. A crisis that threatens the entire Crossing is at hand, and I'm seeking help from you once more."

"This certainly sounds grave. Continue."

After Vrath laid out the situation and explained what he had come here to do, Lorin leaned back in silent contemplation.

"What do you think?" Vrath asked.

"I think you came to the one person who can do this for you."

"So, you'll help?"

"I didn't say that. This is a difficult and controversial thing you are asking."

"You understand the urgency of this situation. We have to try."

After a long pause, Lorin slowly rose. "Very well. Come with me."

He led Vrath deeper into the cave, eventually to a workstation littered with tools, potions, scrolls, and a large forge.

"You're certain about this?"

"It must be done."

"Kneel, Vrath the Onyx."

Vrath took a deep breath and did as asked. Lorin picked up a large, curved sword and placed a small topaz stone from his necklace against the flat side of the blade.

Lorin moved the stone slowly up and down the sword and quickly a low hum began to rise. He repeated the movement twice more and the blade suddenly filled with a brilliant golden amber hue. He turned to the waiting gargoyle.

"Prepare yourself."

Vrath tensed his body and closed his eyes.

Lorin touched the blade to where Vrath's remaining wing connected with his back and began cutting. Each stroke of the blade burned like molten stone, delivering agonizing pain. Vrath grunted and grit his teeth, bearing the torture.

And Lorin kept going. Once started, there was no stopping the process. No turning back. He mourned the loss of his friend but admired his courage and dedication to the mortal. The glowing sword worked its way down the line, painfully severing his wing.

At last, Lorin cut through the last few inches, allowing the wing to drop free and heavy to the floor. Vrath collapsed and found he could barely move. Every breath and movement caused excruciating pain. He fought to stay conscious but lost and drifted into blissful nothing.

Vrath awoke to the sound of Lorin's hammer and chisel. He sat up, noting the lack of pain from his chest, and realized that, while he slept, Lorin had patched up his chest, the onyx a slightly cleaner shade than the rest of him. He looked up from his mended chest to see the older gargoyle hunched over the length of black stone that had once been his wing. He muttered incantations as he worked, filling the air with the static energy of raw magic.

Finally, when Vrath found the strength to stand, he watched as he approached, Lorin continuing the hypnotic ritual of hammering on the wing and uttering the mystical words.

"I'm making some modifications, given what you told me about the previous weapon," said Lorin, without looking up.

Vrath felt the spell permeate not only the room but also his own body. He breathed the magic in and felt it against his stone skin.

As the shape of the wing gave way to a weapon, the ache of loss set in, and Vrath fought against his despair and pushed his sadness back. This cause was too important for selfish mourning. If they were to have a chance against this foe, they would need every advantage possible.

At last, Lorin held the nearly carved sword in the air. The craftsmanship was unmatched. He checked the balance—perfect. He checked for bows in the blade—none to be found. Satisfied, he placed the sword into the coals of the forge.

Uttering more incantations, the coals burned brighter and hotter. When ready, he pulled the blade out and placed it once more on the bench.

"Deep breath, Vrath," advised Lorin as he held a small onyx stone over the blade. Vrath held tight to the bench, drawing in a slow, deep breath.

Ancient incantations dripped from Lorin's mouth, causing the onyx stone to emit a deep black aura that transferred from the stone to the sword and made it vibrate with a low hum. Lorin looked at Vrath and uttered the final set of words. Vrath felt something, an energy or life force or power, pull free from his person and enter the sword, causing the vibrations to cease.

Vrath staggered back, drained and exhausted, and looked upon his friend's handiwork. The sword was magnificent, gleaming onyx with an aura of power. The blade teemed with life.

CHAPTER 25

What Rennard first noticed was the burning pain in his chest had dissipated, replaced by a warmth that enveloped him and left him feeling comfortable. The warmth melted away, and he opened his eyes, being greeted by fields of golden wheat surrounding him.

"Okay, not exactly what I expected."

As he climbed to his feet, Rennard was surprised at how … corporeal he felt. The stiffness in his joints and ache in his back had gone, but otherwise, this felt very similar to being alive. It was then that Rennard noticed a large figure approaching. Rennard felt fear grip him as he realized this creature was a towering Minotaur woman.

Rennard's fear melted into confusion as the Minotaur gave him a huge, warm smile.

"Greetings, friend! My name is Posie. I'm here to help you!"

"Uh, hi?"

"Hi! Oh gosh, you look confused. Don't fret. I can explain. See, this place is the Sunless Crossing. Unfortunately, you—"

"I died," Rennard cut her off. "I died, and I came here because I am destined for resurrection."

"Yes... How did you... Have you been here before?" she asked, seeming relieved.

Rennard gave a so-so hand gesture. "I need to find someone... scary guy named Kanen."

"Does he ... wear a cloak, have pale gray skin, and a really big hood he hides beneath?"

"You know him?"

"Nope." Posie pointed over Rennard's shoulder.

Rennard turned to see Kanen galloping toward him astride what appeared to be a large horse made of pure shadow. They came to a sharp halt a few feet away, kicking ash up into the air.

Rennard stared up at the figure glowering down at him.

"You're a foolish bastard, Rennard."

"I know," Rennard replied.

Kanen kept his eyes on Rennard. "You can go, Shepherd. I'll handle this one."

"Oh, well... That..." Posie stumbled, unsure of what to do in the scenario.

Kanen sighed, and in a tired tone, reaffirmed his request. "I speak with the authority of the House of the Sovereign. You are pardoned of guiding this soul."

Posie relaxed and gave a soft sigh. "As you say." She hurried away, sparing a parting glance at Rennard. "Good luck!"

Rennard held his hands out to his side as he spoke to Kanen. "Look, before you smite me or whatever, I'm here. Let me help my friends."

Kanen stared down at the wizard for a few long moments, and Rennard spotted that his eyes were impossibly dark but filled with tiny speckles of white and blue and red.

"Dammit, you are a pain," he sighed and held his gauntleted hand down. Rennard took it, and Kanen hoisted him up onto the shadow steed behind him.

"You know where they are?"

"I think I do," Kanen replied. "An injured Nyxian guard returned to the city with troubling news."

"A what?"

"I guess I'll explain on the way. Hold on tight, wizard."

The shadow steed took off at a shockingly fast pace, and Rennard barely managed to hang on as they tore across the Ashen Fields.

The Storm of Broken Worlds lived up to its name. The Harbinger stumbled through it, nearly blind by the constant pelting on the wind and the flashes of lightning, some that were too close for comfort. The moving shadows didn't help any, following and harassing him to no end. Always staying in his peripheral, he could never get a good look at them.

He felt they were curious about him, this stranger in their midst, and perhaps sizing him up. No outwardly hostile actions had befallen him though, and that gave him some comfort. The tension, however, drove him mad.

As he walked deeper into the Storm, he began to see structures come into view. Some were giant stone monoliths reaching several stories tall, others were small and decrepit, worn down by the ever-punishing wind. He approached one and discovered markings and symbols carved into the frame of a massive stone door.

What is this?

A place for dead gods.

These temples are all graves?

Best not to stay in one place too long. I do not know what the shadows are, nor their motives. We have a task that cannot be delayed.

The Harbinger was all too happy to keep moving. The sooner they finished, the sooner they could depart. He kept moving through the unrelenting storm, the ash burning his eyes and infiltrating his ears. The hood conjured from dirt and wheat through the use of Thulsader's powers offered some protection against these elements, but it whipped at him relentlessly.

Soon he came across another structure, this one lower to the ground and longer. Several beings gathered about, working on the stone and the area around it, and it seemed as if they were tending the temple. They were humanoid in shape and movement, and he debated approaching them.

In his hesitation, one turned and spotted him. Five in all, the figures came toward him, each in a heavy woolen cloak with deep hoods and veiled faces.

The sword that had been beside him when waking up accompanied him now, his own sword and dagger lost in the prior fight. The Harbinger drew the blade as the figures approached, but they made no move to draw weapons of their own, stopping about a dozen feet or so away from him.

In a low, almost hiss of a voice, one spoke. "You are a fool to be here. Especially with no proper protections."

"I have no choice."

"You always have a choice," another figure said, and the others nodded, eyeing him over before taking their leave.

One lingered, looking between the group and the Harbinger. "Watch out for the Bleeding Wights, friend," they said, hurrying after the group.

"The what?" he shouted.

They didn't respond or look back, continuing through the storm at a slow but steady pace, as though unimpeded by the violent weather.

"Well, shit," he uttered under his breath and moved along, now even more paranoid.

With the onyx sword in one hand and a leather sheath housing another sword slung over his shoulder, Vrath waved farewell to Lorin and made his way back up the path toward the Quarry entrance. All eyes went to him, this wingless gargoyle. His eyes met looks of disdain, shock, and sorrow that bordered on apologetic.

The five bullies from earlier caught sight of Vrath as he walked swiftly away. They could not believe their eyes. This traitor had taken the insult a step further. Instead of harassing him, however, they let him proceed. The sooner he was gone from their midst, the better.

Vrath reached the slope upward and paused. He turned to have one last look at the place that had once felt like home. He suspected he'd not be returning.

Walking upward, the entry stone formation came into view, as did the guards and Nadja. No one saw him yet, their attention directed outward. He breathed in deeply, nervous for everyone's reaction.

Soon Severina came into view. She hadn't seen him yet, pacing back and forth with a dour expression on her face.

Severina couldn't stop her pacing. She grew more worried each moment Vrath didn't reappear. She hoped he hadn't gone through with what she feared he intended.

Coming up the road, she spotted a hulking black onyx being approaching. He had no wings... And as he drew closer, she could tell it was Vrath. Her strength left her as her fears were revealed to be true and she fell to her knees, unable to halt her sobbing.

Karas went to her side to console her, one hand rubbing her back in confusion. Raising his head, he saw Vrath nearing them and realized why she had begun crying as she did.

Nadja turned around and sighed at the sight of him. The two guards beside her appeared stoic, revealing no emotions.

Vrath went straight to Severina and went to one knee to be close. "Severina, please do not cry or mourn for me. It had to be this way, and I have no regrets."

"You shouldn't have done it. You shouldn't have."

"It is the only way that we stand a chance of surviving."

"I don't deserve this."

"Yes, you do."

"I loved Wrath, and I love you, friend, but it's too much."

"I did it because I love you and to show you I'll always be by your side. You will never be alone again."

Still near the ground, their faces close, Vrath gently held the new sword up for her. Her tears came in heavier sobs as she looked upon the beautiful blade in his hands. Smoother than the previous sword, the gleaming blade held mystical runes etched upon it. The sword also seemed longer, with a thicker hilt.

Vrath and Severina stood together, her eyes locked on the sword held up in his hands. Everyone else kept their distance, looking from afar, but one opinion rang true amongst them: the sword was beautiful.

He presented it to her ceremoniously, holding the sword out to her with both hands. Severina wiped her tears from her eyes and cheeks and took a deep breath. With a trembling hand, she took up the sword and gave it a few test swings. She noticed immediately that it felt lighter than the previous one, even though it was longer, and it felt like a natural extension when in her hand. Something tugged at her chest and she felt the gentle connection form between herself and this sentient artifact. The feeling washed over her, filling her with warmth.

What shall I call you? she thought.

Anything but 'Wrath the second.' The sword spoke in her mind.

You speak. You can talk to me.

When I have something important to say.

We are going to get along just fine, Wrathy.

No. Not that either.

Aw, come on.

Nope.

The others noticed a strangely long silence from Severina.

"Introductions," explained Vrath. The others nodded, understanding.

Nadja came to Vrath's side. "I admit I wasn't sure if you'd go through with it."

"Do you think less of me for it?"

She leaned back to examine his mutilated back. "Well, you are a bit odd-looking, but there is a symmetry to you now. That whole one-wing thing was not a good look."

"Thank you for your fashion critique." He smiled, chuckling.

Vrath looked over at the two guards, who had witnessed the scene play out. Instead of judgment from them, they nodded respectfully at their wingless brethren.

Remembering the sword on his back, he removed it and offered it to Karas. "Your other one vanished with... Well, and the one he had broken, so I got you a new one."

Karas drew the sword, the metal black and glossy, but different from Severina's and less impressive. "Oh, we're playing favorites, are we?" he asked in jest. "Thank you though, Vrath. I appreciate this." He bowed his head slightly, taking to getting a feel for the new sword.

Severina at last rejoined them and immediately threw her arms around her gargoyle guardian. "I promise to do my best to be worthy of such a gift. I cannot begin to know what you have endured to grant me these miracles. I will do whatever I can to make you never regret for one second doing this incredible act. I can never repay you."

"You can repay me by destroying this menace once and for all. And, of course, avoiding the permanent destruction of your soul."

"Never that," she said and kissed his cheek.

Karas paused his practice and admired the blade close up with Nadja as Severina held it out for them.

"I've never seen such a thing of beauty," said Karas.

"I concur," added Nadja. "What are the glyphs inscribed on it?"

"The maker made some improvements," informed Vrath.

"Oh? Such as?" Severina asked.

"He didn't say. I suppose you'll just have to discover them as you wield it."

"I'm not usually a fan of surprises, but in this case, I'll make an exception."

She stepped back and practiced with the new sword, swinging and thrusting to get a feel for it.

Enjoy the new toy while you can. This gift will not save you.

Is that fear I detect?

Come for me then, child. Let us see who will know fear by the end.

Count on it, vile wretch.

Heliosa came out of her trance, opening her eyes to see Karas, Nadja, a wingless Vrath, and a sword-bearing Severina return to the clearing. Nearby, Chorlen and Virion sat in meditation.

"I feel like I missed something." She nodded at Severina's blade. "Looks amazing, by the way."

"Thanks," Severina replied.

Heliosa clapped her hands, snapping Chorlen and Virion back into consciousness.

"Are we ready to pull this shard out or what?" she asked in a chipper tone.

Severina removed her armor and carefully set it aside before opening her shirt a fraction and laying down in the space set up for her once ready. The mages gathered around her. Heliosa sat at Severina's head, while Chorlen and Virion took positions on either side of her torso.

Heliosa breathed in deeply, then gently exhaled.

"Are you sure you're up to taking the lead on this?" Virion asked.

She nodded. "I know Quellon will guide me in his own odd way."

"You mean you're going to *rely* on *luck*," Chorlen said.

Heliosa smirked. "If you want to call it that..." Her smirk dropped, and she added, "Remember, once we form the arcane chain, we cannot break it."

The Cleric of Quellon gently touched her fingertips to Severina's temples and began a low murmur of chants in the sacred dialect of old. Severina closed her eyes, trusting in her friend to see her through. Heliosa moved her hands from Severina's temples and held them out for Chorlen and Virion to grasp. The two mages each grabbed one of her hands and then reached across Severina's torso to grab each other's free hand, forming an unbroken chain of magic. Having picked up the cadence, they joined Heliosa in the chant. All their eyes glowed with white light.

Severina felt an excruciating pain surge through her chest, as if the shard was pressing up from the inside. She screamed and tensed on the slab, her body contorting. Karas and Vrath gripped her arms and held her down by her shoulders and legs, ensuring that no part of them was within the triangle the mages formed. The magic users chanted louder and faster, each word making Severina writhe in agony.

A bulge began to rise beneath the flesh of her chest, and the onlookers bit back their reactions. Heliosa, Chorlen, and Virion chanted louder and faster.

The flesh in the center of Severina's chest split down the middle, revealing slick, bulbous meat. Streaks of blue could be seen beneath the layers of sinew. The mass of flesh and crystal rose higher as she cried out a blood-curdling shriek, revealing veiny strands and tendrils holding the crystal to Severina's body. The slick object tried to pull free, but the sinewy strands held it fast.

The thundering sound of something fast approaching drew the attention of those not engaged in the ritual, but no alarm was heard, the chant maintaining its increasing pace as the shard fought back.

At first, it resisted being pulled. And then it began to pulse with a dark blue glow. Short arcs of lightning began to burst off the shard.

Thulsader's voice thundered in Severina's head, ***STOP!***

The arcs of lightning intensified in power and frequency. Heliosa felt one singe the side of her head, but she remained steadfast. So close. She was close to freeing the shard.

Another burst, more powerful than any before it, erupted from the flesh-encased shard. It struck Virion between the eyes, snapping the man's head back sharply. He fell backward, his limp hands pulling free from Heliosa and Chorlen, and his body was ash before it hit the ground.

A low, painful moan escaped Chorlen's mouth and Heliosa squeezed Chorlen's hand tighter, continuing her chant. She felt a new hand clasp hers tight, and a robed arm shot across Severina's torso, grabbing Chorlen's still outstretched hand, reforming the arcane chain. Tears streamed from Heliosa's glowing eyes, the chant continuing, unending.

"Finish it, Heliosa! Finish it!" bellowed Rennard's voice.

The grotesque object pulled farther from Severina's body, showing a dark cavity beneath. Still thrashing, tears were flowing freely as the pain became too much for her. "Stop! Please stop!"

The strands of sinew slipped off the shard one by one. Severina convulsed violently, her whole body spasmed and shook as the last of the flesh fell away, back into her chest cavity. Severina went limp, her chest still open, the shard still hovering above her.

Heliosa wanted to turn her attention to Severina, to heal the gaping wound in her chest. But the shard still fought, forcibly pulling her focus toward it. All three magic-users felt stuck in the moment, transfixed, paralyzed even. Beneath them, Severina's breathing grew shallow and ragged.

A hand of black onyx reached in and plucked the shard out of the air. As it was removed from the arcane chain formed by their arms, Rennard, Chorlen, and Heliosa felt control come back to them. They let go of each other, slumping and panting from the draining event.

All Heliosa wanted was to collapse into a puddle of unconsciousness, but her friend still needed her. She refocused, placing her hands at Severina's temples. Rennard put his hands over hers, sharing his magical reserves with the near-spent and exhausted Heliosa as she screamed a desperate prayer to Quellon.

The cavity in Severina's chest began to close, knitting itself back together. In seconds, her wound had healed, and her breathing returned to normal. Heliosa sighed with relief and slumped backward.

The shock of Virion's death, the surprise of Rennard's arrival, the fear for Severina... all of it was secondary in everyone's mind as they turned to Vrath, who still clutched the shard.

Severina's eyes fluttered.

"What now?" the gargoyle asked.

"Crush it!" said Karas. "Destroy it!"

Severina began to shake her head back and forth.

Vrath looked to Nadja, who gave her fellow gargoyle a nod. He placed the shard between his massive stone palms and began to squeeze.

"NO!" Severina cried out.

Everyone froze and looked down at her.

"Don't," she managed to say.

They all stopped and looked at her, expectantly.

Between labored breaths, Severina explained, "It … won't work. Just make … more shards."

"Well, what do we do?" Nadja asked.

"I have … an idea." Severina laid back down. "But maybe a short nap first?"

CHAPTER 26

The Harbinger stumbled through ash and dirt, barely holding onto consciousness. He had traveled for what felt like days, spurred on by Thulsader's voice in his head. He dared not disobey his god, but in his heart, he began to doubt this errand.

Then there were the shadows. They stalked him at every step, but never allowed themselves to be seen fully. They always remained in the haze of the storm.

As he wandered, his mind drifted in and out of consciousness and clarity. Unable to continue, he stopped walking. The storm was maddening, the howling and constant battering of the wind and what it carried, the barrage of lightning and thunder, and the vast emptiness. His mind could no longer cope.

Collect yourself and keep moving.

I have nothing left.

You are close now. I feel the fragment. It's not far.

Strange that I do not.

You are a mortal.

I cannot go farther. I must rest...

You will continue!

The Harbinger collapsed to his knees, no longer caring what Thulsader wanted. He was too fatigued, the fuel from the motivation and passion empty.

Rise.

The Harbinger gave the god no response.

You dare ignore me?

Silence.

Get up, now.

Thulsader had not anticipated this turn of events. His rage at the disobedience was tempered, however, by the acceptance that he may have overestimated the capabilities of the feeble mortals.

The shadows returned, coming into view as they circled the Harbinger, surrounding him like predators. The Harbinger's barely conscious mind began to understand his predicament. The thinnest urge for survival sparked within him, and he forced himself to stand, wavering.

One of the shadows came in closer than ever before, loping by him, then disappearing once more into the storm. The Harbinger caught a glimpse of the being at last. The creature was humanoid in form and coated in a dark, slick fluid. Another passed closer and he realized the fluid was blood. Bleeding wights. The grave tenders had warned him of these beings, and now he was stalked and surrounded by them.

All this time, why had they never attacked? Waiting for him to wear down, become easy prey? Fueled by the need to survive, the Harbinger found the strength to draw his new sword.

I knew you had more fight in you.

Ignoring his master, the Harbinger readied himself for battle.

And on they came. The first bleeding wight charged in from the side, just out of his line of sight. It swept past, raking a vicious claw across his shoulder. The wound delivered an unusual sting, burning within him.

Another rushed at him, but the Harbinger was ready. He dodged low and swung his blade high, slicing the creature's chest. As his sword cut deep, blood splattered from the slick surface and landed on his charred cheek and neck. He felt an immediate burn at the contact points. Their coating was toxic.

The wounded beast stumbled out of range, but more shadows came in closer. It seemed the time for assessment of the prey was over and the kill was at hand. The Harbinger quickly wiped the burning blood from his skin using scraps of his pant leg that he tore free, careful not to touch it with his fingers.

As the bleeding wights came closer and allowed themselves to be seen, he noted just over half a dozen of the creatures. They were grotesque, having no skin to hide the rotting muscles, blood-stained bones, and viscera. The blood-like substance that covered them constantly flowed, dripping off their long, clawed hands. Their humanoid-like faces allowed none to distinguish what they may have once been, yet their hollow sockets perceived what was present.

The Harbinger readied himself as the wights circled him. "Come on then," he taunted. "Do your worst."

Three of the wights charged in from different angles. He thrust his blade through the belly of the first, but the other two pounced on him from behind, bringing him down. They rapidly clawed and thrashed at him, his cloak offering little resistance and his burned clothing easily shredding.

With his burned back now exposed, the wights began raking their claws across his tender flesh. He screamed and struggled, but could not throw them off. He felt the searing of their blood coating into the fresh wounds, draining the fight from him.

Thulsader would not have his plans thwarted by these lowly creatures. His vessel was giving out, and he was still needed for the plan. He activated the embedded shards, carefully weaving his power between them, making the Harbinger's eyes light up a brilliant blue once again.

The shards exploded in an unseen force that tossed the assailants aside and knocked down the others in the circle around the Harbinger. As the shards remained glowing, the Harbinger gripped his sword tighter, not willing to release his only weapon, regaining his strength.

The bleeding wights recovered and cautiously moved around their target, as though waiting for whatever guard had been put up to be dropped again.

Thulsader pushed his power out again, ignoring as his Harbinger heaved and strained from the power being forced through him and the toll it was taking. In moments, the wights fell to the ashy ground, writhing in pain as rot and pestilence grew and spread over their blood-coated bodies. Lowered to the ground, the Harbinger bent over with his hands on his knees, choking in air before watching as putrid diseases ravaged the bodies and destroyed each wight.

By the time the brutal decay ran its course, only gore and bones remained.

He spent no more time looking at the masses as they slowly began to ash, sheathing the sword to his hip. Though still exhausted, being in the open would serve no benefit, especially when he spotted more figures shuffling around in the storm, some drawing closer to the commotion.

We can use these creatures.

Not if they destroy me first.

You will have to reach the shard first, then. Run.

I can't...

RUN!

The Harbinger felt his legs being tugged as if he were a marionette controlled by invisible strings. Despite the maddening aches, the blisters, and the skin peeling off his bare feet, the Harbinger ran deeper into the storm.

Vrath, Karas, Heliosa, Nadja, Chorlen, Rennard, and Kanen all stood over Heliosa and Severina. All of them wore versions of a contemplative frown.

"I thought all we had to do was remove this shard from the playing field, and Scourge would be defeated?" Confusion saturated Karas's voice.

Severina shook her head. "He just needs *enough* of his soul, apparently. The Harbinger is close with what he already has..."

"But he still needs yours, no?" Vrath said, holding up the wrapped wad of cloth containing the now extracted shard.

"No..." She shook her head. "Menavaria. If they find her grave, they will have all the shards they need."

"Shit," cursed Heliosa.

Severina looked at Kanen. "You know a lot about the Storm of Broken Worlds?"

The Pale Horseman folded his arms. "I know a thing or two."

"Do the tombs of gods often possess their signature vestiges? For example, if a god were known for her battle hammer... would that hammer be in the tomb?"

Kanen took a breath. "It is often that a god's tomb will contain their, as you put it, signature vestiges. Especially if they are as well known as the god themselves, or other combining factors," he stated.

"Menavaria's hammer," Karas said in realization. "You want to use her hammer to destroy the shards."

"That's right," answered Severina.

"Absolutely not," said Captain Nadja and Kanen in unison. They traded glances, and Kenen gestured for her to continue.

"There is no way we can allow you to venture into the Storm of Broken Worlds," she stated, wings tucking in tighter. "We don't have the equipment, an idea of where the tomb is, and no one experienced enough to lead."

Severina countered, "Menavaria was also killed by the explosion of Thulsader's soul gem. He let it slip in my mind that the shards in her are all he needs to return. The Harbinger is heading there right now."

"Then he's doomed," Kanen stated. "A lone mortal soul stands no chance in the storm. He is hopefully lost, disoriented, and either taking shelter in a different tomb hoping someone rescues him, or he is already dead."

"He's not alone though," Karas stated, annoyance growing as he continued. "He carries part of a god with him. You haven't seen what he's capable of."

"Damn," cursed Nadja. "Dammit all to every hell there is... they're right. We can't sit back and simply hope he fails when his god is actively aiding him. I've seen what havoc just a modicum of this foul god's power can wreak."

Kanen huffed in frustration. "And how do you all plan we catch this soul? I have one shadow steed and we have two gargoyles, only one of which can fly."

Nadja turned her head toward the Quarry. "I have a thought on that. It would be a long shot, but a potential avenue for us to progress."

CHAPTER 27

Captain Nadja and Vrath stood before a crowd of gargoyles in the center of the Quarry. The onlookers frowned and murmured after hearing her request.

"We need at least five, but we'll take all the help we can get."

"To fly mortal souls into the Storm? Preposterous," spat one in the crowd.

"And the betrayer? You're mad," yelled another.

Vrath stepped forward. "Whoever said that is welcome to come forward and say it right to my face ... unless you are afraid of a wingless gargoyle?"

More murmurs rippled through the crowd, but no one stepped forward.

Nadja put her arm on Vrath's shoulder and said, "Any one of you would have done the same thing in his place."

Some nodded or made sounds of agreement, while the more skeptical or hostile balked at her.

"His maker forever linked him to a living mortal. In a realm he could not journey to, and you all know this. But what you may not realize is this woman, his charge, lived a life of danger and violence. He couldn't protect her from here in the Crossing.

What else was there to do? What else could he have done? I say he did the right thing."

She was met with silence. No one knew quite how to feel.

"And now she is here, fighting to save many. Vrath still protects her, as any gargoyle worth their stone would do. Time is of the essence and every moment we waste, the chances of this destructive being brought back rises."

Vrath added to the plea. "The threat we are fighting could destroy not only the Crossing, but every other realm in existence. This thing, this god, has designs to corrupt and decay everything we know and love. You may despise some of us or have no concern over the struggles of mortals, but they are risking everything to try and save this realm."

The murmurs and conversation held a much softer tone this time around.

Lorin stepped forward. "I will help you. This is a great, noble, and honorable task."

More hushed whispers.

A female gargoyle made of garnet stepped forward and raised her hand. "I'll fly them. I'll help."

To Vrath's shock, she was one of the five bullies who harassed him earlier. The crowd went silent for a moment, the air thick with tension. The leader of the group started to protest, but she whirled on him and shouted, "Shut your mouth, coward."

Then a topaz male entered the circle. "I'm in as well."

More hands went into the air.

When it was all said and done, more than two dozen gargoyles had volunteered.

Vrath seemed hesitant to believe this was real.

He gazed at all the faces looking back at him. All hostility had vanished, and he fought back tears of joy.

Severina stared in awe at the hulking platoon of gargoyles that marched up the Quarry path to meet them. It was overwhelming, and they were grateful to have them on their side.

"How will we find this god's tomb?" the garnet gargoyle asked.

Kanen gestured at Severina. "The Godless will guide us."

"Excuse me?" she replied.

"Once we enter the storm, your senses are going to be under assault. You need to try and blot it all out. Focus and you should be able to feel the way toward the crypt of your god."

Nadja stepped over to Severina. "If you'll have me, I'll carry you and lead the way."

Severina nodded.

Lorin shouted to the others, "Well, grab a mortal and let's get this done!"

"Wait," said Karas, looking at Chorlen. "You're still alive... you shouldn't go into the Storm. What if you die there? You've already lost Aronos and Virion."

Chorlen gave a sad smile and a shrug. "Aronos is dead and gone forever. I either join her in nothingness or become a Legend and rub it in Virion's face when he returns come the new day. This choice is mine to make. I've made it."

Rennard patted him on the back as he passed, laughing. "Careful with all that courage, friend. You're making the rest of us behind-the-front-lines mages look bad."

Moments later, a fleet of gargoyles took to the sky, soaring straight for the Storm of Broken Worlds. Each of the mortals was held tight to a gargoyle's chest, save for Kanen who insisted on riding his shadow steed. Lorin carried Vrath and he would never be able to explain the euphoria he felt being in the air once again.

Severina pointed them in the proper direction and onward they sped.

CHAPTER 28

The Harbinger left bloody footprints that slowly became ash with every step. The skin on the bottoms of his feet had been ravaged by the harsh landscape. The burning in his lungs and chest was pure agony. And yet still he ran, wights following him by some distance.

At last, the tomb of Menavaria appeared to him: a flat-topped pyramid with steep, angled walls. Menavaria's symbol, two closed eyes and a third open eye set within the head of a battle hammer, was etched above the stone slab door.

The Harbinger hurled his body at the door, cracked nails grasping for the iron ring. He pulled, his bony arms straining.

The door didn't budge.

The Bleeding Wights drew near.

HELP ME!

Without a response, the shards within him glowed, and he felt an unnatural strength rise. With a scraping groan, the door opened just enough for him to squeeze through. The Harbinger ducked inside just as the tip of a wight's claw brushed harmlessly through the cloak.

He sprinted down the catacomb hallway, not bothering to close the door. The wights were a bit larger than him and would have to work to force themselves through the narrow opening.

Deeper into the tomb, the Harbinger ran. He passed rows of gleaming suits of armor, not bothering to notice his sickly emaciated reflection, the guttural snarls of a few wights echoing off the walls after him.

Finally, the Harbinger reached the centermost area of the temple of Menavaria. Tapestries of different monumental moments lined the walls, including the shattering of Thulsader's soul stone. His stomach churned at the sight and he approached the stone coffin which rested central to the room, the god's likeness engraved on the lid. He pushed it, straining some even with the help from the empowering shards, letting it fall unceremoniously to the floor.

There was no body. The orb of foresight rested on a soft gray cushion to the left, and the battle hammer to the right. But there, sitting as though they had been discarded, were the three blue crystal fragments. From the positions, one would have struck her stomach, one her shoulder, and one her thigh.

The Harbinger heard the scratching steps of wights drawing near. One by one he plucked the shards up, not bothering to question why there was no body, and jammed the shards into his feeble body. As he picked the third one up, four wights burst into the chamber and rushed him. He searched frantically over his skin-and-bones body for a place to add this fragment, and upon finding little space unoccupied, he stabbed it through his left palm.

The Harbinger then spun toward the wights and held out his shard-pierced hand, squeezing his eyes shut and turning his head, fear prickling his senses. A burst of blue light danced behind his eyelids, and inching his eyes open, he saw that the wights had skidded to a stop mere feet in front of him.

Blue lights began to swirl and coalesce, forming orbs in their eye sockets.

A sigh of relief escaped him, a smile brushing his lips again. The desire for rest remained, but he felt reinvigorated by the new surge of power from the three new shards. He strode past the wights, and they made no hostile moves, falling into step behind him.

The Harbinger found more of the abominations waiting outside the tomb, small clusters of them wandering. He let the power of his god wash over them all and, as if responding to unspoken commands, the forming army of bleeding wights turned in unison to face outward. He turned and climbed Menavaria's tomb, taking a seat halfway up the pyramid, and looked over his new soldiers, then out into the darkness of the storm.

"I know you're coming Severina..." he mused with a chuckle and closed his eyes.

The force of gargoyles rocketed across the sky, giving some of the residents of the Sunless Crossing quite a show. Their flight path took them over the campsite that some of Legend's Meadow had set up and over the Cavalcade of Strays.

Severina sensed that their destination lay deep within the Storm. Seeing the wall of tumultuous clouds ahead, she did not relish the idea of traveling into that sinister place. But Menavaria waited, and Severina had a chance to set things right, to atone for what she'd done to her goddess.

Just before reaching the endless wall of shadows, the gargoyles descended and landed.

"What's happening?" Severina asked Nadja. "Why have we stopped?"

"We travel on foot from here on." Nadja removed one of her forearm bracers and clutched it tight while muttering an incantation. She then stuck a long, sturdy stick in the ground and tied the bracer to it. She looked back at the others and explained, "Reinforcements from Nox Valar should be nearby. They'll be able to track me with this bracer."

"Walking will take too long," Severina implored. "We may be too late as it is."

"It is too dangerous to fly in that," she said, pointing to the chaotic, lightning-filled sky. "We move quickly and direct, assisted by protection spells and ones to enhance our speed."

It didn't take long for the gargoyles skilled in such arts to begin imparting the gifts amongst the group, but those that did apologized and bowed, fatigued and needing to rest. The group was thankful for the help regardless and took to running, Severina toward the front, following the tugging sensation in her chest. As they ran, Severina caught sight of black shadowy things darting past and following on their periphery.

On they ran, fast and smooth, through the wind and ash and lightning. Severina hoped they wouldn't be too late. She looked over to Heliosa, still carried by a gargoyle, and hoped she'd awaken by the time she was needed.

❧

Why are we still here?

I have a score to settle.

I have given you power. I have given you an army. Leave this wretched place and make for my tomb. We are so close to victory and you would throw it away for a girl?

Respectfully, my lord. Severina is coming for us. We know she is coming here. It is better to face her here than to have them come upon us while traveling.

Don't preach tactics to me, child! I want to live again! I am tired of feeling like a mere shadow of myself...

You're tired? My lord, I have given you everything. Will you not grant me my vengeance over one who has vexed us so?

You have suffered much. And because of that, I will grant you this mercy. But should you question me again ... your time as my favored will swiftly end.

Understood, my lord.

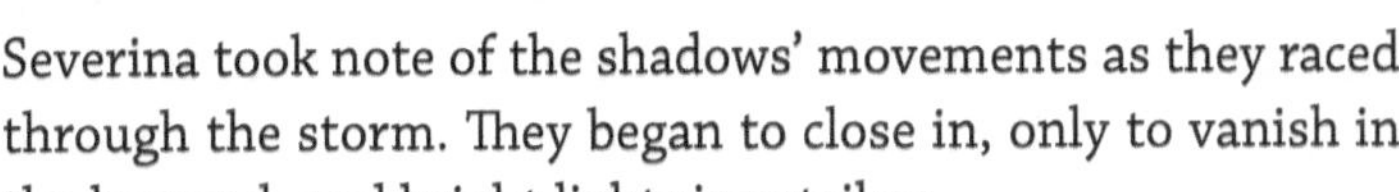

Severina took note of the shadows' movements as they raced through the storm. They began to close in, only to vanish in the hazy ash and bright lightning strikes.

"What are they?" she yelled to Vrath running to her right.

"Bleeding wights. We think they were living once, but we don't rightly know," he yelled back.

Nearby, she spotted a few gargoyles swatting the shadows aside as they came in too close. Then two shadows rushed in, revealing their sickening bloody bodies and deadly claws.

A few times, one of the creatures tried to swipe or lunge, but they were either batted away or bowled over. The speed of these great stone creatures was incredible. Severina felt a swell rise in her chest, and she knew they were close.

She saw the silhouette of the flat-topped pyramid appear in the distance and waved her arm above her head in signal to the rest of the group. As they got closer, Severina felt a pit grow in her stomach. Something was amiss. *Tainted.*

As the base of the tomb came into clearer view, the blue glow from hundreds of bleeding wight eyes pierced the darkness of the storm. Severina saw the waiting horde, and then the Harbinger sitting halfway up the pyramid. He looked dead. His broken, emaciated body was riddled with shards, including one through his left hand, and he was slouched, sitting on the side of the temple of her god. The Harbinger stood, however, as the group came to a stop some distance away, and with his non-pierced hand, drew Karas's sword and pointed. The horde of wights began to march forward.

Severina gave a quick scan of their menagerie: herself, Vrath, Rennard, Kanen, Captain Nadja, Lorin, and about two dozen gargoyles, with Karas looking annoyed about his sword being in the wrong hands and Heliosa confused and being caught up on what had happened.

Severina pointed her new sword toward the oncoming abominations and shouted over the winds of the storm. "I am going in there. I can't, in good conscience, ask *any* of you to follow me into what will very likely be a painful death—"

"Oh, shut it," Karas cut her off, drawing his weapon. "As if we weren't all coming with you, regardless. I have a sword to retrieve, anyway."

Severina stared back at him, mouth agape. Rennard and Chorlen readied their spell components, with Heliosa doing the same after being caught up, and atop his shadow steed, Kanen conjured a reaper blade. Many of the gargoyles had brought weapons, which they now brandished. Vrath simply cracked his knuckles and said, "Sound the charge, Commander."

CHAPTER 29

The front line of gargoyles crashed through the wights like stampeding bulls, reducing some to pulp in an instant. Atop his shadowy steed, Kanen sliced through them as though he were simply gutting a fish. Severina and Karas hacked at clawed limbs left and right, and the spell casters incinerated the abominations with bursts of fire and arcane energy.

One to one, the wights were no match for Severina and her war band, but the Harbinger had yet to join the fight himself, and the abominations had the numbers. In seconds, over two dozen wights had been felled, but despite this, the horde managed to fold in around the heroic war band. From atop his mount, Kanen could see that more wights were being pulled into the fray. No doubt they had been drawn here by whatever power the sickly figure atop the pyramid was wielding. He saw a gargoyle, the topaz one, fall under a host of wights who clawed and tore at his stone body until he was just rubble, but he had taken more than a few down with him.

Kanen sliced through the throng of creatures, destroying another half dozen to get closer to Severina. She dispatched one herself and looked up at him.

"We need to deal some serious damage now! We can't stay like this, or we'll soon be overrun. Their leader keeps pulling in new wights!"

Severina looked toward the Harbinger and then down at the open door to Menavaria's tomb. "I have to get in there and retrieve Menavaria's hammer. With it, we can destroy the shards permanently!"

Kanen held a hand out and went to pull her up behind him.

Vrath bounded over, bellowing, "Where she goes, I go!" smacking wraiths out of the way as he went.

"You lovesick puppy," Kanen muttered, sighing in annoyance and swinging from his horse. "If you're so adamant about being by her side, then take this and *do not lose it*. I want it returned to me." Kanen pulled a small black opal from his pouch as the steed behind him vanished, handing it to Severina.

Severina took the opal, and Kanen raced off, dispatching oncoming wights before they got too close with fluidity and ease. With their backs covered, she rubbed the opal, and another horse made of shadow appeared, although it looked different from Kanen's, larger and sturdier. Vrath helped her up, climbing on behind her before they took off toward the tomb.

They barreled over any wights in their path, breaking out from the battle and sprinting across the open ground toward the door. Higher up the pyramid, the Harbinger saw them coming and looked down at them, energy collecting around his shard-pierced hand. Before he could unleash whatever attack he had planned, she pointed her hand out, firing an arc of black lightning. The Harbinger leaped into the air, barely avoiding the assault, before crashing hard into the ground.

The Harbinger coughed and pushed himself up from the ground just in time to see Severina and her wingless gargoyle pet dart into the tomb.

Get up, you fool and go after them!

Why? We have the advantage!

The hammer, you idiot! They're going for Menavaria's hammer!

The Harbinger scrambled to his feet and took off after them into the crypt.

Heliosa cried out as she watched the claws of a wight push through Karas's chest and out his back. Blood streamed from his mouth, his eyes found hers, and then he was dust. With another scream, Heliosa unleashed a beam of pure radiant energy that vaporized the wight along with five others nearby. She dropped to her knees. The spell, the fight, the loss, all took their toll. Things seemed to slow down around her. She saw Rennard and Chorlen throw fireball after fireball. She saw one of the quarry gargoyles get taken down. They had destroyed so many of these monsters, and yet there were still so many left.

"My Lord Quello-Quell…" she prayed quietly, using the nickname for her god. The elder clerics of her faith always hated that, and no one had any idea how Quellon felt, but to her, it felt natural. "I know I may have been leaning on you a lot lately for good luck, and I promise that once all this is done, there will be no more pushing it. The luck can fall both ways without my complaint. What I'm saying is, if it's not too much to ask, can I get one last little bit of luck?"

A bleeding wight broke off from the horde and made for Heliosa, toxic blood and fluid dripping from its bony claws. Heliosa squeezed her hands around her talisman, eyes pressing tighter, bracing for the hit. There was a heavy thud before her.

She hesitantly inched an eye open, a mass of matte white armor with flashing of dark gray slate peeking into sight, broad wings and a thrashing tail before her. There was nothing but a splatter wight beneath the gargoyle's feet, slowly turning to dust. Heliosa looked around and saw more hulking forms in white armor crashing into the wights with weapons or wings, removing them from the fight. Twenty, no, *thirty* powerful warriors clad in matte white armor, wearing helms shaped like animal skulls and wielding weapons of inky black metal. A one-armed gargoyle, the same from the fight at Legend's Meadow, seemed to be leading them.

Heliosa smiled, tears pricking her eyes. "Thank you, Quell."

Inside the tomb, Severina and Vrath walked into the central room of the temple, the gem shoved deep into Severina's pocket. There was hesitance in her steps as they came upon Menavaria's coffin, and she winced, fighting back rage-filled tears at the sight of the desecration and disrespect. Vrath stood by her side as she gazed at the coffin of the deity who had meant so much to her in life.

She heard the Harbinger enter before he even said anything. Severina whirled around and charged at him, letting out a guttural roar. Their blades clanged off one another, Severina attacking with savage ferocity and the Harbinger parried and deflected, shifting to an offensive stance once she stumbled back.

Now going on the attack, the Harbinger, with his speed and reflexes enhanced by Thulsader, was able to land multiple painful slashes in quick succession against Severina, who struggled to block but a few. His last strike caught her across the leg, forcing her down to a knee.

The Harbinger reared back for another powerful strike, swinging down with a wide grin of maniacal satisfaction. A mass of gleaming steel appeared in his sword's path. The Harbinger's blade shattered against the hammer of Menavaria, now held in the outstretched hand of Vrath. The ringing from the breaking metal echoed off the tomb walls.

The Harbinger staggered backward, his arm shaking with reverberations as he dropped the broken hilt. Vrath pulled Severina up to her feet and together they squared off against the decrepit, shard-riddled, corpse-like man.

Run

No! I can defeat them!

I command you to run!

A pair of Bleeding Wights stumbled from the tunnel behind the Harbinger. Severina and Vrath steeled themselves, preparing to face down the Harbinger and these two abominations. To their surprise, the wights each grabbed one of the Harbinger's arms and then took off, sprinting back down the hall, the man shouting in protest as they dragged him away.

Vrath took steps to follow them but noticed Severina was not alongside him. When he turned, he saw her standing over Menavaria's coffin. "Severina?"

She gave no response, head bowed and hands gripping the edge of the sarcophagus so tight her knuckles had become white.

He looked back down the hall the Harbinger and wraiths left through, studying it before carefully moving some of her hair. "Sevi—"

Severina's eyes had rolled back in her head, showing blank white.

Vrath took a step back, cursing the timing and taking guard at the entrance of the room.

Severina's consciousness traveled through an empty void. The last thing she remembered was contemplating an attempted resurrection of her god. They had a crystal with power in it, so why shouldn't they use it in a way that would be beneficial? Some unknown force had pulled her mind into this place... this abyss of nothingness, before she could voice the idea. The solitude of the void stirred memories, painful reflections. She found her mind and spirit drifting into her darker past.

Why had life chosen to take her parents from her at such a young age? Why was she shunned for mis-stepping once with magic against someone who deserved it? Weeks after proposing, why had the man she believed she loved share his bed with someone else? When she stood on trial, why had she been left with no one but her parents to speak on her behalf? If Winter would have reacted the same, was sympathetic, and yet the shackles of the realm held her steadfast in one direction... But why did it have to be like that? The questions burrowed into her, weighing her down in the vast, pale nothingness.

It would be nice ... to stay like this a while, Severina thought, curling in on herself, finding respite in the idea that here, there was no way to be disappointed. To lose others who loved her, that she loved.

Something that was barely a whisper brushed by. Then again, louder, taking form until it was a voice, reaching out through the nothingness as a small tendril of golden, dancing light. Heliosa's voice, soft and welcoming and warm, beckoned her.

"Severina, you are safe. You are among those who love you. Hear me. Hear my voice. You can do this."

Hearing an objective voice, one other than her own, pushed her thoughts aside. Memories of Tormelund pushed their way to the surface, thoughts of her friends and the aide that she was able to give with what she had been shunned for using and enjoying.

Elena, Karas, Heliosa, Rennard, and Ulren meant everything to her. Even Faustice had grown on her. In life, she had grown to trust them, to love them, and if she trusted them, they must have spoken true when they expressed their friendship. When they showed joy at being in her presence. She simply could not dismiss their viewpoint.

Even as the despair fought for a stronger foothold, she found herself able to accept her past. The love of her friends and how they saw her aided in her healing. She understood now that she was all of it. Her good deeds and her bad. Her mistakes and her triumphs. These things made her the person she was now. Each of these elements, even the uglier ones, was a vital part of her.

The void now seemed smaller, pulling back and receding. Her metaphysical, spiritual path became clear. She was loved for who she was. A security welled up in her and washed over her soul. And then intuition delivered the prize.

She felt rather than saw the presence of Menavaria. Dormant and unaware, her goddess floated in the ether, invisible to mortal eyes. Severina approached, sensing a coldness, a silence from the soul.

Unsure how to proceed, Severina trusted her intuition. "Menavaria," she called. No response. Severina reached out, gently touching her god's hand and focusing, calling to Menavaria's being. She had to trust her gut and give herself to what instinct demanded.

Feeling her soul intermingling with Menavaria's more and more, she tried again. "Menavaria. Please come to me. Wake up."

A subtle disturbance in the soul emerged. A minute awareness sparked and Severina knew she was no longer alone in the void.

"Menavaria," she called out again.

"Who disturbs my rest?" asked Menavaria in a not unkind tone.

"It is Severina Stormbringer, your champion. It is time for you to awaken. You are needed."

She was met with silence. Severina could almost feel a sensation of despair emanating from her god's essence.

Severina had not expected this reception. She assumed the goddess of Instinct and War would return hungry for a chance at retribution.

"Do you not know where you are or what happened to you?"

"I know, child. I know. I died."

"There's more. Your body rests in the Sunless Crossing."

"As it should."

"But the god you destroyed survived. Thulsader is his proper name, we've come to discover. He means to destroy all of existence. Every realm. Every world. We need your help."

"Is that what you want? You wish me to be remade? To take up my hammer and wage righteous war across the cosmos?" She sounded tired... exhausted.

Shock stabbed Severina. She couldn't believe what she was hearing. How could her proud, powerful goddess fall into such a state? "You are the goddess of Instinct and War. We need both right now."

"No one has ever *needed* war, child." There was a hint of disappointment.

"Please..."

"Why are you so desperate for my return? You don't need me, Severina."

"Because," Severina felt tears well up, "you died because of me. If I had not begged for your help..."

"If I had not come, would Scourge have been defeated on that battlefield?"

"No."

"And he would have spread his corrosion and decay across the living world."

"Yes."

"My death was in no way your fault. Am I some puppet for your use at your discretion? No. I am a goddess. I made my choice to aid you and help save that world." The exhaustion in the god's voice was almost painful.

"We have gone through so much to get here. We have fought against impossible odds."

"And you made it here. And so again I say, you do not need me, Severina Stormbringer. I'd offer my forgiveness, but you do not need it. I release you from any guilt or debt you may feel you owe me. Now go. Let me rest and do what you were meant to do."

Severina's body gasped as her consciousness returned. She stumbled and almost fell, but powerful hands steadied her. She panted, orienting herself before looking around to see Vrath and Heliosa.

"Sevi, are you okay?" Heliosa asked, her words heavy with concern.

Severina nodded and replied, "The battle..."

"Is almost over," Heliosa finished. "Some who battled alongside us have been lost, but... we're winning."

"The Harbinger?"

"Gone," Vrath answered.

"Then we haven't won yet," Severina said through gritted teeth. She pushed herself up and shook the sleep from her limbs.

"Wait," Heliosa called after her. "Menavaria! Should we try..." The question trailed off, asked only in thought to comfort a grieving friend.

"We should return the lid and let her rest. It would be right." Severina shook her head, offering a thankful smile to Heliosa.

She moved with Vrath and Heliosa to return the lid to the sarcophagus, and once done, she moved toward the exit, calling over her shoulder, "Vrath, bring that hammer. We have some shards to destroy."

The two wights bounded across the harsh landscape with the Harbinger in their arms. They had pulled him through the waning battle, narrowly avoiding multiple strikes from Nyxian Guards. Now that they were a good distance from their enemies, he struggled to free himself.

"Release me!" he yelled at the wights. They gave no indication that they heard his demand.

They obey you only when I allow it.

I wish to walk on my own.

No time. We have to be as quick as possible. My grasp is slipping.

Give me my dignity.

Dignity? You are on the cusp of becoming the most powerful mortal soul in the cosmos. Show a little gratitude, whelp, and enjoy the ride.

Severina emerged from the tomb, scanning the horizon for the Harbinger. All around she saw fetid globs of flesh and piles of ash that had been wights and scattered rubble that had been gargoyles. She saw Nadja barking orders to teams of armored Nyxian Guards as they worked to corner and destroy the remaining wights. She saw Chorlen, still alive but bearing a nasty slash down the left side of his face resting against the wall of the tomb. Rennard and Kanen saw her and rushed up. Severina saw much of Rennard's robes had been scorched away and his right arm and leg bore nasty burns. Kanen looked positively untouched.

"Karas," Rennard said. "He didn't..."

"He'll be back," Kanen said. "His soul will return to the fields before long."

"The Harbinger. Where is he?" Severina asked, looking between each person.

Rennard pointed and said, "That wa—" The words caught in his throat, as he saw his hand growing more translucent by the second. He looked down at himself. His body was becoming incorporeal.

"Rennard, what's happening to you?" Heliosa asked, eyes wide with worry.

"He's being resurrected," Kanen answered for him.

"No!" Rennard lamented. "There's still so much..."

The wizard disappeared right before their eyes.

Kanen looked from where the wizard had been standing back to Severina to see she was already atop his shadow steed again, Vrath behind her.

"I'm gonna need to borrow this a little longer," she said to the pale horseman.

Kanen shrugged. "How are you going to track them?"

Severina retrieved the leather-wrapped shard of Thulsader they'd extracted from her. "You know what a divining rod is?"

CHAPTER 30

The wights dropped the Harbinger in front of a simple stone temple with no decorations, but much like Menavaria's, it was not yet suffering erosion. Unlike Menavaria's, however, it seemed as though no visitors had yet stepped foot within based on how undisturbed and still the area felt. A simple stone door about ten feet tall sealed the square structure.

Command the wights to the door.

The Harbinger grew weary of having control only when allowed. He had given everything to Thulsader, had been devoted since he was young, and yet he felt shackled, unable to act freely unless his god allowed it. After all he'd done, he deserved at least a little respect.

The Harbinger sighed and gestured to the door and the wights silently plodded forward and pulled the door open, the heavy stone dragging across the floor and leaving scratches.

Enter and let our time of triumph commence!

Without a word, the Harbinger entered the crypt of Thulsader.

Severina and Vrath tore across the barren terrain atop the mighty horse of shadow. The wind whipped at them like razors and lightning struck, narrowly missing them more than once. Every so often Severina adjusted their course.

"How do you know where to go?!" Vrath hollered just behind her ear.

"Back when I had the shard in me," she called back. "The few times I was close to the bastard, I felt this odd sensation! This almost vibrating pull! I never said anything because I was afraid of what it might have meant! I thought maybe I was drawn to the Harbinger!"

Silence hung in the air.

"I mean, like the allure of power! Like part of me deep down wanted to align with them to gain their power! Part of me has always wanted power... and that scares me!"

Vrath took a moment, then squeezed her arm and replied, "Bad people don't concern themselves worrying about whether they are good or not!"

Severina smiled. "This chat would've probably felt much more sentimental if we didn't have to have it shouting over the wind!"

The Harbinger was surprised at what he found in the heart of Thulsader's tomb. It was a dank cavern with a pitch-black hole in the center. Four stone tablets were on the floor, lying as though discarded, written in a tongue that the Harbinger knew he never learned, but understood, each one talking about a world that his god had devoured. There was no sarcophagus or depiction of Thulsader however, and thinking back on the physical shape of tentacles, muscular arms, and a faceless head, perhaps that was for the best.

Now he carried so much doubt. His frustration with his treatment made him question the truth in what Thulsader had promised him. Would he follow through with any of it?

It is time to return my soul shards, oh most treasured child.

Where?

You know where.

The Harbinger looked down at the dark pit and paused. He didn't want this. He didn't want to give up this new power to a Supreme Being who cared only for himself.

Have you gone deaf? Do what I said.

No.

What?

I'll be keeping the shards for myself.

You dare defy me?

The shards began to glow, and the Harbinger felt his limbs being pulled, working against his will.

No!

You forget who's in charge here.

The Harbinger dug deep within himself to find the means to resist and fight back against Thulsader's power.

I'm through with this. I will be used no longer.

I will use you until I see fit to dispose of you, mortal.

The Harbinger felt his strength grow, his inner fire igniting. Perhaps he could regain control of his body. Maybe he could control the god's soul.

This is my body. I control it.

You are nothing more than my vessel.

Just release me then! I'll give you the shards! Let me go!

The shards flared as the Harbinger's body began to contort against his will, his arms, legs, and back bending in horrid impossible positions. The Harbinger shrieked and screamed violently, the will to resist evaporated as his focus shifted to desiring a way for the pain to stop.

The Harbinger's bones began to snap, his body no longer contorting. The wights entered the chamber and grabbed him, raising him as though he were an offering.

"No! No! Please, no!" he cried.

Foolish. You served me well, for a time. But your usefulness has come to an end. Be grateful that you are having a hand in my rebirth.

The Harbinger continued to scream, unable to thrash about and free himself.

You have collected so many parts of me. So much of my power. And you have grown with it... And now, I shall grow from that... But you are no longer devout, and for that... You will take my place in death, and I will take yours in life.

The Harbinger let out one last begging wail.

Be thankful. You will forever be a part of me.

The wights tossed the screaming Harbinger down into the black abyss.

CHAPTER 31

Severina gripped the shard tighter, focusing on the subtle vibrations that shifted depending on which direction it was held out in. Through the flashes of lightning, she saw a nondescript structure drawing near. It was a nondescript cube of unadorned gray stone, the doors slightly ajar. The shard went still.

She turned her head slightly, eyes trained on the building, "I think that might be—"

The stone structure exploded in a spray of rubble and debris, and towering above the lightning-scorched ground, stood the remade form of Thulsader. Faceless head atop a dark stalk of flesh with two arms and one long tentacle, all supported by a revolting bouquet of smaller tentacles beneath him. He was smaller than he had been the last time, Severina was sure of it, but that made him no less intimidating or imposing.

"That seems to be the place!" Vrath shouted.

"We go on foot!" she yelled back, waiting till Vrath gave a confirmation tap to her shoulder before dismissing the shadow steed mid-stride. They both landed on their feet, braced for the sudden stop of momentum and running with it a short distance before stopping. Severina drew her new sword with one hand and formed a ball of crackling black lightning in the other, while Vrath hefted Menavaria's hammer with both hands, adjusting his grip. Time to kill a god.

Thulsader reveled in the many sensations he now experienced. Despite the lack of facial features, he could smell charred residue from the lightning strikes, hear the constant cracks of thunder, and feel the stone beneath his tentacles. He could see ... the two pathetic insects, Severina and Vrath, approaching him with confidence and determination. This was pure ecstasy, being whole, being alive once more, and whilst he wasn't as large as before, he was most certainly just as dangerous.

Existing as little more than a voice inside a few measly mortal minds had been such torture. Unable to influence the world as much as he wanted and having to rely on them to do his bidding whilst he sat and watched, it was disgusting... Once he took over, he had to get better followers, *stronger* followers.

He tilted his head to the side as the would-be heroes came forward. This was going to be fun.

"Okay," Severina said to Vrath, keeping her eyes locked on the looming behemoth. "Speed is key. We've got to be fast. Never stop moving. We need to cut him open, get to the gem inside, then you smash it with the hammer."

"Easy breezy," Vrath replied.

Severina shot him a raised eyebrow.

"Something your dad used to say."

She smiled and then said, "Go!"

They split apart, each one running at a wide angle as if to come at the god from opposite sides. Thulsader bellowed and lashed out with his longer tentacle, the strike aimed at

Vrath. Severina unleashed an arc of black lightning, striking Thulsader in the side. The god arched back, screaming in agony from some unseen mouth. Relief washed over Severina as she realized he could indeed be hurt by her different magic.

The relief was short-lived, however, as Thulsader turned toward her and slammed his two humanoid fists into the ground. She backtracked, managing to avoid the titanic fists directly, but the force of the strike caused the ground around her to crack and shake. One piece of earth dipped lower than she expected and her foot caught the edge, sending her sprawling.

Thulsader reached for her with his hands as one would reach to squash a gnat, but before he could, he emitted another guttural howl of pain, hands retreating as he turned his attention elsewhere. Severina looked past him as she hurried to her feet, spotting Vrath pulling the hammer away from one of the god's many lower tentacles, which was now a mess of pulped flesh. The god reacted swiftly, lashing out with his long tentacle-arm and snatched up Vrath before he could get out of the way, lifting him high.

Severina cried out, reaching her empty hand forward to summon another burst of lightning. She couldn't lose Vrath. She would rather sacrifice herself than let him die for her. The lightning came, but this time it was different, more intense... brighter. Severina felt pain inside of her as if her attack was siphoning energy away from her soul. It worked. The lightning not only harmed Thulsader, but burned a hole right through his slick, leathery hide. The deity bellowed in agony, dropping Vrath as a hand moved to clutch the gaping wound.

Sudden fatigue made Severina slouch, her mind stuttering on what her next action should be, but she forced herself up and charged. She hacked and slashed at the writhing mass of lower tentacles, trying to get closer to the god's body. While there seemed to be many more tentacles in this iteration than before, each being hacked at before they could touch her, she noticed that those that did come into contact with her didn't burn like they did before. A small blessing.

Thulsader's attention shifted to Vrath and sent his fist flying toward the onyx being, but the gargoyle swung with the hammer hard enough that he stumbled a fraction, successfully batting away the attack. Expecting the first attack to be parried, Thulsader's arm-tentacle came right behind the fist, swatting him off his feet. The onyx gargoyle hurled through the air, slamming against a boulder with enough force that parts of him chipped free, leaving him dazed and unresponsive.

Severina, unaware of the attack Vrath sustained, continued cleaving through the lower tentacles. His attention no longer split, the remaining tentacles restrained Severina with ease despite her slashing and thrashing.

A deep hissing voice filled the air. ***It is over, mortal. You are too late.***

As the giant hand of Thulsader moved toward the tangled Severina, she fought back against the creeping despair. *It cannot end like this. Not after everything…*

The hand snatched her from the tentacles, held her aloft, and began to squeeze before pausing, a hiss of annoyance echoing free. Severina looked around, frantic and unable to break herself free from the suffocating grip.

In the distance, the Nyxian Guards and the surviving Quarry gargoyles, flew high through the storm led by a single gargoyle, each dodging lightning strikes, heading straight for the towering pillar of pestilence. As they drew closer, Severina didn't recognize the new, soft brown colored gargoyle who was dressed in leather, giving hand signals and barking directions.

Thulsader raised his free hand, stretching it out in front toward the oncoming fleet, jets of noxious fluid rocketing across the sky. All but two of the gargoyles managed to swerve out of the way, and those struck melted into misshapen rock and armor heaps as they plummeted.

This did not slow the assault, however, and the first wave slammed into Thulsader using swords, axes, mauls, and hammers. The god reared back with an angry roar, his free hand and tentacle attempting to swat the airborne foes away.

A gargoyle carrying something swooped overhead and released what he was carrying. Soon enough, Kanen had run down the length of the arm and sliced at the hand's fingers. The hand released and waved about, dropping the two some distance away, where they landed with rolls, springing to their feet and moving away.

"Vrath?" Her eyes were wide as she scanned the area.

"He's going to be seen to!" Kanen reassured. "What do you need?"

"We need to cut into the core of his body, find the reforged soul gem, and then smash it with Menavaria's hammer." She pointed. "Last time, his soul gem was right in the center of the chest area. I need to get up there."

"I can help. Give me my shadow steed back."

Severina quickly handed over the small black opal, staying alert for any oncoming attack, but Thulsader's attention was greatly focused on the gargoyles who circled about him, hitting and retreating before he could strike back.

Kanen rubbed the opal between his hands and cupped them, blowing a breath inside. With a swipe, the steed summoned, and he quickly mounted it, pulling Severina with him.

"How is this going to get us—" Severina clung to him as the horse began to gallop, not just forward, but upward, as if stepping on invisible stones, climbing higher and higher.

Severina watched three gargoyles hold one of Thulsader's hands out, each grasping a finger, while two more hacked at the wrist with their blades. The god cried out as the massive hand was severed and dropped. As it fell, the hand exploded in a ball of sizzling acid, splattering down, luckily hitting none full force, only with splatters on armor.

Severina heard the hissing voice again. This time it seemed as if it were only in her head.

Every inch of me is death, child. It's time you finally learned that. I think I'll explode my entire form… send a tidal wave of my lovely essence flowing toward those fields. I can always regrow.

Severina gripped Kanen's shoulder and yelled, "Get me up there, now!"

Vrath came to, seeing the worried expressions of Heliosa and Lorin staring at him.

"Are you okay?" Heliosa asked.

"Fine," he growled and got to his feet, accepting a hand from Lorin. Surveying the surrounding chaos, he swelled with pride at the damage already done and spotted Severina with Kanen galloping upward. "How did you find us?" he asked, picking the hammer up and looking for a way to get to where he knew Severina would be heading.

"We began following you both once we had regrouped and sent those too injured back to recover with an ask for reinforcements. And well… It's hard to miss a thing like that, even in the storm," Lorin answered.

"Thank the realm… But I have to get up there." Vrath pointed, clutching the hammer. "I'd give my life for some wings right now."

"No need for that." Lorin shook their head. "Your continued friendship is enough."

Kanen brought the steed in close, intending to simply make a strafing run, hacking and slashing and getting out of the way for another pass. Without warning, Severina leaped off the back of his mount, driving her sword deep into the flesh of the god, giving her something to hold on to.

"Oh, for goodness—" he hissed, quickly shifting tactics from the lack of communication.

Spotting the tentacle sweeping toward Severina, the blade in his hand morphed, stretching into a spear. He turned his mount downward and raced toward it, spear outstretched, and drove the spear through the tentacle, using the momentum to help break the thick skin that offered resistance. Thulsader's body shuddered in pain, and Kanen continued galloping downward until he reached the ground, where he pinned the tentacle down with his spear.

Holding onto her sword with both hands, Severina summoned the power from within, willing her life essence to empower the spell. She felt herself get weaker, more tired, her grip on the sword growing slack before she forced her hands to tighten, feet bearing against the body more to keep her position. A tremendous force pulsated in her hands, urging for release, thrashing against her hold. She released it, channeling the power through her sword. A blast of black light danced through her onyx sword before lightning tore through the skin, muscle, and sinew of the god, creating a wide, deep cavity that revealed the reforged soul gem, held in place by various tendons and ligaments.

Thulsader roared in pain, shuffling backward in a wobbly fashion, flailing his slashed hand and his stump to swat away the assault and cover his exposed soul gem. His skewered tentacle continued to writhe in an attempt to break free, wrenching against the spear and other weapons that had been thrust into it to keep it immobilized. Available gargoyles and mages shifted their attention to the unrestrained limbs, releasing a flurry of blows to halt their paths and keep them occupied, buying time for the death-dealing blow to land.

Severina scrambled into the opening, nearly free-falling at the new additional liquid that splashed free. With new purchase, she swung her head back, realizing the one flaw in her plan was not having the hammer with her. "Vrath!" she screamed in desperation, her head swinging around as she gripped her sword with a hand, the other pressing against the wall of the grand wound for stability, feet slipping and repositioning in an attempt to stay where she was.

And then there he was, being carried by Lorin toward her location. Severina breathed a sigh of relief, waving a hand.

The hand that had once grabbed Severina batted the gargoyles away, sending them careening through the air. Severina watched, screaming for them to move as it swept toward her friend, snatching Vrath and Lorin from the sky.

They vanished from her sight and her heart sank. Her feet struggled to find purchase for a moment, slipping on the viscera of the god, eyes watching blow after blow hit the closed fist... It shook back and forth as though attempting to disorient those inside, but damage was being done... And when the top finger loosened just enough for Vrath to break partially free, he took it, throwing the hammer high toward Thulsader's body, his yell for Severina being cut short.

With no time to sheath her sword, Severina stabbed it into the flesh of the god and reached outside the wound to catch the careening hammer, almost slipping out of the body as the weight attempted to pull her to the earth. Her heels dug in, teeth gritted and she used her sword to counter the momentum, it dragging through the flesh some, making the god thrash more, flinging the captured gargoyles aside into the distance, the hand moving to the wound to wrench the invader out.

She wasted no time sprinting to the gem, skidding on the slick and uneven ground as she swung the hammer with every ounce of remaining strength. Severina skidded to an abrupt halt as the hammer connected to the soul gem, and everything seemed to pause. There was a deafening sound, as if thousands of windows all shattered in unison.

Thrown back and out of the hole in Thulsader's body, Severina fell, weightless, mind going blank as she watched the towering figure begin the bloat.

She hit the ground. There was no pain or exhaustion, only darkness.

CHAPTER 32

That day in the Storm of Broken Worlds was the second time Severina died. The feeling of warmth that enveloped her was calming, and she enjoyed the moment of peace and rest as she floated in a formless state. When she opened her eyes next, she was staring at the now familiar purple, swirling vortex, golden wheat surrounding her, and the friendly face of Torvil staring at her.

Thirty-three years and seven months later, Severina sat in her home. Justice, the name she'd given her sword, was now safely displayed above the fireplace. She could tell he loved being the center of attention, so what better spot for him when she was at home?

An easel rested in one corner, a painting half complete, and on the walls, many paintings already hung, each with various subjects, tones, and themes. Her skill level had visibly improved over the years, and many of the paintings were of her beloved Menavaria. Some imagery portrayed the goddess as she appeared, while others maintained the fantasy she had held of her while in the living world: the strong woman with a hammer in one hand and an owl on the other arm.

"Too bad you don't have an owl," she said aloud to no one. "I think an owl would be fantastic."

"Why an owl?" said Kanen as he walked right in to sit down across from her, not waiting for an invitation.

"Instinct and War... owl and hammer. Seems obvious to me."

"Far too literal. When you get to be several millennia old, you want to keep more of an air of mystery."

"How is everyone?"

"In the living world? Old Rennard is annoyingly curious as ever. Poking around in matters that don't concern him, but otherwise well. Ulren is hanging in there, though I wonder how many more years he's got it in him to rule."

"Are you sure we can't communicate directly?"

"Against the rules. Besides, it's not healthy for you or for the living to fixate on each other so much."

"I get it, but still. I wish there were a way to at least let them know I'm fine."

"Are you?"

Severina paused, looking around her home. "Honestly? Yes. I don't think I've been this happy. Ever."

"Perhaps, then, they already know this," Kanen said with a smirk and a shrug, crossing his arms.

Relief made her shoulders sag, a small smile forming. "Thanks, Kanen."

"Don't thank me yet. I've got another summons for you. They want to meet up at the Requiem."

Severina looked up at Justice and gave an exaggerated sigh. "Duty calls."

A short while later, Severina walked the streets of Nox Valar. She stopped for a moment by a large crowd currently enjoying the musical stylings of the city's most popular bard. Up on stage, Faustice danced about, playing on a new flute that was just as gaudy as the last. She smiled, still grateful to this day that the healers had been able to save him, and then continued.

She moved deeper into the heart of the city, entering the Road to Eternity, passing by dozens of temples dedicated to major deities. As she approached the temple of Quellon, she gave a small head bow, a mix of feelings assaulting her.

Heliosa's resurrection attempt came first... Who better to have assisting in bringing the others back than a skilled cleric whose god was that of luck? But the temple of Quellon felt like home to her now, and whilst she missed Rennard and Ulrin, she didn't want to return to the living realm and forget the greatness she contributed to and all those she had bonded with... So she remained at the temple, rising in rank slowly and communing with her god frequently.

Karas had carved a small, calm life for himself, wanting nothing more to do with fighting and adventure, putting it down to his old age and that his retirement was ready for him after a second time dying. An opportunity for resurrection knocked, and he left it unanswered, reassuring Severina that, like Heliosa, he was ready and happy with what he had contributed in life and had little more to give. He passed on to his afterlife not too long after, bidding the pair goodbye.

Heliosa followed years after, finding peace with her friend's passing and wishing Severina all the luck that she would find an afterlife one day when she was ready. There was a sad joy in watching her friend leave, but Severina respected her decision and watched as Heliosa entered her temple one last time, Karas's gifted handkerchief tied around her wrist.

Severina left the Road to Eternity with a heavy sigh and headed along the path that led to the Onyx Requiem, the castle of the Sovereign and Arbiter, rulers of the Sunless Crossing. She found a few familiar faces waiting for her, just inside the outer gate. There was Vrath, early to the meeting as usual and as always, bearing the hammer of Menavaria on his back. There was also the gargoyle Nadja, no longer a captain, now bearing the rank of marshal. And then there was Keeper Drake de Leone.

The ancient monk nodded and greeted her with, "Mistress Stormbringer."

"You know I hate it when you do that."

"Well, you know I hate it when you cause a near-cataclysmic ruckus."

"That was so long ago!"

"Not to me, it wasn't. Time is relative, my dear."

"Ahem," said Marshal Nadja. "Can we get started?"

"Yes, of course," replied Drake as he unfurled a scroll. "Our Shepherds have noticed some peculiar happenings. A handful of new arrivals all seem to know one another and are extremely interested in the Storm of Broken Worlds." He looked up at Severina and Vrath. "And apparently they all worshiped a god known as the World Eater."

Vrath sighed,. "*Another* cult of fanatics looking to resurrect him? That's the second one this year."

"Yes, well," Drake gestured at Severina, "you know the mortals and their flair for the dramatic."

"Don't lump me in with them," she balked. "I'd love to just relax for a long while, like a few decades."

"Oh, please," groaned Vrath. "You'd be so bored."

"Yeah," added Nadja. "You love this."

"Hey, I can't help it if I'm simply the best there is when it comes to saving the world. It's a curse, really," she joked, a smirk on her lips.

Vrath groaned, rolling his eyes, and Nadja laughed.

A short while later, Severina and Vrath stood in the Ashen Fields, the city of Nox Valar looming far above them atop the great mesa. They each pulled out small black opals and rubbed them, summoning a pair of shadow steeds and climbing onto their mounts.

"Ready for another adventure, Vrathington?" She looked over at her wingless friend.

"As I'll ever be." He shrugged, taking off in a gallop toward the Storm of Broken Worlds, Severina hot on his trail.

EPILOGUE

In the living world of Tormelund, an aged Rennard sat at the foot of the statue of Severina. The elements had aged the statue some, but it still stood in the courtyard. As the generations passed, fewer and fewer visitors came to pay respects.

He stopped by nearly every day, visiting the monuments to pay respects to Karas, Heliosa, and Severina, but her statue called to him most, as though life lingered in it despite the failed resurrection. Three out of three left a stinging sensation that had taken time to heal.

"I miss her too," Ulren said after a long silence, sitting a short distance from Rennard, still looking as strong and virile as he did the day the trio left.

"I try to take solace in knowing she's doing great things where she's at."

"How you sound so sure I don't know... But I'd prefer it if she could be doing those great things *here*," Ulren countered. "That last dragon attack was a close call."

"We handled it though. These young mages may be entitled, but they have potential."

They fell into a comfortable silence, watching the clouds lazily drift by.

"Will you ever share how you know that she persists?" Ulren asked without warning, standing and stretching.

"Call it a … midnight gut feeling." Rennard laughed, forcing himself up with a grunt as a knee groaned at the action, following his king.

"You and all your secrets, wizard," Ulren chuckled, shaking his head. "Given what you know, would you follow through with a resurrection if you had the means?"

"Funny you should ask."

"Oh?"

"I have come into possession of a book. It speaks of a different belief system on afterlives. Ideas I never dreamed possible."

"And how did you come by this strange tome?"

"As luck would have it, the thing just dropped from a high shelf recently. I don't even know how it got into my lab in the first place."

"So what's it all about?" asked Ulren.

"Well… how do you feel about reincarnation?"

THE END

BOOK CLUB QUESTIONS

1. *To Slay A God* is a classic fantasy tale of high adventure. What aspects of the story did the author get right? And what areas fell a bit short?

2. One of the core relationships is between Severina and Vrath. How would you describe it?

3. What characters, items, or situations from the book would you like to see in a future TTRPG campaign from Storytellers Forge?

4. If you adapted the book into a movie, who would you cast in some key roles?

5. If you could ask the author one question, what would it be?

6. What is your take on the authority figures of Nox Valar portrayed in the story, such as Captain Nadja, Keeper Drake, and their colleagues? In a TTRPG game, what would their alignments be?

7. What do you believe to be the main takeaway of the book?

8. How relevant or relatable are the themes to your own life or society today?

9. In the end, what was your opinion of the Harbinger?

10. What was your favorite scene in *To Slay A God*?

AUTHOR BIO

Brian Fitzpatrick is the author of the bestselling science fiction trilogy, *MECHCRAFT*, and the co-screenwriter for the upcoming science fiction film, *THE SIMIAN TRIALS*.

Fitzpatrick's writing journey began at the age of seven after accidentally watching the horror classic *Night of the Living Dead*. After a week of sleepless nights, his mother encouraged him to write stories of his own. Fitzpatrick put pen to paper and has been creating tales of wonder and terror ever since.

Fitzpatrick grew up on Spielberg, Carpenter, Lucas, R.A. Salvatore, King, Rice, Koontz, and Barker.

Science fiction, fantasy, and horror are in his DNA.

He plans to continue working with Storytellers Forge, as well as his own screenplays and novels.

Fitzpatrick's current project is the next tale in his *MECHCRAFT* series, *THE TRAGEDY OF SASHA*.

When not writing, he enjoys spending time with his family, watching movies and TV shows, reading, and cooking. And if you want to win him over, use coffee.

www.ingramcontent.com/pod-product-compliance
Lightning Source LLC
Chambersburg PA
CBHW032348310726
48973CB00007B/1913